FERAL ICE

PARANORMAL FANTASY

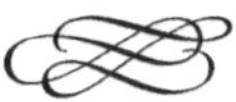

ANN GIMPEL

CONTENTS

FERAL ICE

ICE DRAGONS SERIES, BOOK ONE

Paranormal Fantasy

By
Ann Gimpel

Tumble off reality's edge into myth, magic, ice, and dragons

**Scientists don't believe in dragons.
Dragons never think much about humans at all.
Maybe it's time for their worlds to collide amidst the
dangerous beauty of Antarctica.**

Doctor and biochemist, Erin signed up for six months aboard an Antarctic research ship to escape her stifling surgery practice. Jerked from her cozy cabin, she's dumped in an ice cave by men who assume she's dead.

Konstantin and Katya, twins and dragon shifters, have lived miles beneath the polar ice cap for hundreds of years. Other dragons left, but they stuck it out. When several humans—all but two of them dead—end up not far from their lair, the opportunity is too good to pass up.

If the lore is to be believed, humans can become dragon shifters. Delighted by a simple solution to their enforced isolation, the dragons lure the humans to their home. Surely, they'll be thrilled by the prospect of becoming magical.

Or not.

Too bad no one shared the script with the humans. Science be damned, they're horrorstruck in the face of fire-breathing dragons. All they want is to escape, but home is thousands of miles away.

Ice Dragons is a trilogy, so a long tale split into three books that need to be read in order. I was fascinated by Antarctica long before I visited there, and my two trips were so incredible, I still stumble over words to describe the awe I felt at the vista of ice-crusted ocean, hardy mosses and lichens, and the proliferation of wildlife. Tame critters who are as likely to peck at you or sit on your lap as they are to put on an amazing show—as if you weren't even there.

A story about ice dragons has been percolating for a few years now. It was time to breathe life into it.

"They're closing in on us. Bastards." Konstantin trotted restlessly from one end of a grand hall inlaid with crystals and rich veins of gold and uranium to the other. His dragon wanted out, but he couldn't risk flying. Not today.

Not yesterday or last month or last annum, either. The once mostly empty seas at the southern end of Earth teemed with stupid ships. Once they'd limited themselves to remote whaling stations. Not anymore. The whaling stations had mostly fallen into ruins, and ships sailed everywhere. Even during the long winters where Sol never showed his face to brighten perpetually dark skies.

"We have always been here. We were here before humans' distant ancestors crawled out of the sea," Katya said, her tone soothing. It should have calmed him, but it had the opposite effect.

"You're exaggerating. We haven't been here nearly that long."

She shrugged. "Time means nothing to us."

Fire slithered from his mouth and nostrils. "I say we kill them. That will slow them down."

Katya, his twin sister, hooked a hand beneath his arm and swung him to face her. "I don't wish my next annums to be naught but bloodshed. If we start murdering humans, thousands of them will converge on our tiny retreat. They will find us and lay waste to everything we hold dear."

"They can't kill us," he growled.

"No, but they can make our lives miserable."

"So? We'd leave."

"Finding a place to settle has always posed huge problems," she retorted. "It's how we ended up here, or have you forgotten?"

More fire, this batch mixed with ash, spewed from his mouth. He averted his head, and flames bounced harmlessly off the stone walls.

Katya tightened her grip on his arm. Of a height with him, copper tresses shot with golden highlights fell to her waist. Like all dragon shifters, her eyes were a swirl of gold with deep-green centers. Neither of them bothered with clothing unless they went outside, and sometimes even then they relied on magic rather than fabric to do the trick. Their underground lair was warm. Beyond their home, a labyrinth of sapphire-blue lakes extended for many kilometers.

Konstantin swallowed smoke and fire. No point getting even more riled up than he was. He offered his sister a half-hearted smile. "What we have here is scarcely a retreat. Not anymore."

"Pfft. The rest of our kin were cowards. They left."

He pushed his shoulders straighter until bones cracked. "Let us hope they found safe harbor."

"We never received a single message—from any of them." Katya bowed her head for a moment, closing her eyes and murmuring a prayer to Y Ddraigh Goch, one of many dragon gods, and the deity closest to their people. When she opened her eyes, she sank to a crouch on a floor inlaid with green-veined tumbled marble.

"Sit, Brother."

He knelt, facing her. Before she could say anything, he asked, "Do you believe we should leave too?"

Her high forehead creased in worry. "I have tried to scry our future, but the mirror clouds. The harder I push, the worse it gets."

It was the first he'd heard about this, and it worried him. "How long have you sought knowledge? And why did you not tell me?"

She screwed her face into a grimace. "I'm telling you now."

"Yes, but how long?"

Katya shrugged. "Months. Annums. Centuries. So long I no longer expect answers from my glass."

"What does your dragon say?"

She looked away from his direct stare, long dark lashes curling over her high cheekbones.

"Well?" he prodded.

"She who dwells within no longer speaks to me." A single tear formed in the corner of one of Katya's eyes. It took its time falling, but when it hit the ground a gemstone formed.

Konstantin gentled his voice. "Do you know why?"

Katya did look at him then, her eyes liquid with tears, and nodded. "She wishes to fly. After the hundredth time I explained why we couldn't, she retreated, and I haven't heard from her since."

"How long ago?" he prodded.

She shrugged. "Why does it matter? I'm not even certain I can still shift."

Konstantin marshaled his thoughts. Pain for his beloved sister mingled with fury at her dragon. The beast had always been highhanded, but it wasn't as if any of his kin had a choice. They were born with their dual natures, the dragon taking ascendency shortly after birth to establish its form. Depending on the dragon, maintaining the upper hand was sometimes very difficult.

But he'd never heard of a dragon simply checking out. They forced shifts. Lay waste to countrysides. Mowed through entire herds of livestock. What they didn't do was vanish.

He weighed his words carefully. "If you're uncertain about shifting, leaving isn't an option. Not until you're stronger."

"Oh, Kon." She placed a hand on his thigh. "Escaping was never an option. How many times can we run away? We abandoned our home world because it was on the cusp of exploding into our Sol, leaving shards to sink beneath the sea."

"Yes, but there are many worlds," he began before he caught himself. Dragon shifters from Mu had dispersed a short time before their world became known as a lost planet. Hundreds of them had set out to find new homes millennia ago. Their group of fifty had discovered a lush warren of caves and tunnels beneath an ice sheet coating the southernmost part of Earth.

They'd worked hard, carving out a place for themselves. Buildings like the one rising around him were the result. Once they'd been full of dragons. Squabbling dragons. Happy dragons. Determined dragons.

He and Katya were all that remained.

Lakes, fields, and plentiful food stocks had nourished his kin for a long time. The lakes and fields remained. Seals, penguins, and fish provided rich variety, but the crops— grown from seeds they'd transported from Mu—withered on the bush or vine or stalk. No one could figure out why, and it was the reason the other shifters had left. They sought lands with a more temperate climate—and a growing season. The perpetual dark that lasted half the year had been quite a disincentive as well.

Never mind their subterranean burrow had to be illuminated by an ongoing infusion of magic, or it would have been pitch dark all the time.

He and Katya had bid farewell to their kinsmen and opted to remain, living on what they could capture from the sea with a combination of magic and physical means. It wasn't ideal, but it was enough to sustain them. He'd expected to hear something from the other dragon shifters, but enough annums had come and gone, he assumed they'd left Earth for another world.

"I see only two choices," he said at length.

Katya just sat, shoulders slumped, and didn't say a word.

"It isn't like you to give up." He squeezed the hand she hadn't moved from his thigh.

More gemstones clattered to the floor, joining the one glittering up at him. "What are the choices?"

"We will have to leave here someday. Humans are killing Earth. If we left a bit sooner, it wouldn't make much difference."

"But—"

He shook his head. "We have to encourage your dragon, make certain she is willing to fly. We won't be leaving soon, but we shall plan for a journey."

"And the second choice?"

He pushed smoke through his mouth, grateful his sister wasn't too despondent to ask questions. "It is intertwined with the first." Fire joined the smoke; he waved both aside. "We grow our ranks."

Her eyes widened, and she jerked her hand away from his leg. "I am not mating with you, Brother. Such is forbidden to—"

"I was not suggesting such a thing."

"What, then?"

"Humans. If they share blood with us, we can create dragon shifters."

Katya shook her head. "That's a myth. You have no idea if it's even possible."

"How could I?" He agreed with her. "Our world was nothing but dragon shifters, yet the legends grew from something."

"Have you conferred with your dragon?" She narrowed her eyes. "I assume he's still speaking with you."

"He is, and I have. He is honest and says he doesn't know, but he encouraged me to try."

"So instead of killing humans, we lure them to our side? Do we tell them what we are ahead of time?"

"Yes. We have to. Otherwise, the transformation will have no hope of success. A human must welcome the seeds of change or the new dragon will not come. Once they've embraced becoming like us, then we will mate and swell our ranks in more mundane ways."

"You've made many assumptions that may not bear out." Katya angled her head to one side, listening.

He did the same and sat straighter. Humans were closer than they'd ever been to their lair. Perhaps Y Ddraigh Goch had heard their desperation and was offering a gift.

Or maybe it was simple coincidence. He jerked his chin upward and raised his eyebrows into question marks.

"The disturbance we sense above began days ago. It's ebbed and flowed, but I've been tracking it. First there were many, and a lot of dead, but two living remain." She scrunched her face into a worried expression. "No. Wait. One is leaving. Or trying to."

Konstantin zeroed in on what Katya sensed. A small blast

of magic cut off the human's escape. He fashioned more magic into layers of thicker air to cushion her fall. If he killed her, he'd be back to square one.

Breath whistled from Katya's half-open mouth, accompanied by smoke and ash. "Now what?"

"Now, we watch. I am curious to see how resourceful this human woman is."

Katya laughed. "I do love you, Brother mine. Always focused on the future. So if the woman is dumb as a pointed stick—?"

"I shall return her to the cavern from whence she began," he replied a bit stiffly.

"Fair enough." Katya paused a moment as power flashed from her upraised hands. "Hmm. The one remaining above is male, but he is wounded. I can fix his injury."

"Do it," Konstantin urged. "And then we shall see."

CHAPTER 1

Consciousness returned in a rush. I clapped my hands over my ears, but it barely made a dent in the incessant noise battering me. Water crashed over rocks. Far from soothing, the noise pushed me toward madness. I was screaming too. The ungodly racket blasting from my throat didn't help anything. I could do something about that part, so I shut up. My fingers were cold. So cold, maybe I hadn't felt them in a long time. Did I even still have fingers? In the world I remembered—the one apparently lost to me —extremities withered and died from frostbite.

I know these things. I was a surgeon back in a distant universe. Dr. Erin Ryan. I muffled a snort that sounded more like a groan. At least I remembered my name. It was a start.

Images of blackened fingers and toes flashed through my mind. Right along with men clipping off dead appendages with scissors, a bloodless proposition because bodies had a way of jettisoning their losses.

I let go of my head, took my gloves off, and stuffed my hands into my pants right on top of my stomach. Maybe if they weren't too far gone, I could save them.

For what?

The bitterness in that question pounded a whole lot home. Like how desperate my situation was. Maybe letting myself fade from the tips of my body inward wasn't a bad thing. Dying from cold wasn't painful. There were worse ways to go. Lots of them.

Exquisite agony shot through two fingers as blood returned to them, coaxed by the heat of my belly. Soon the other fingers joined the party, screaming in protest. They'd liked being dead. Saved them a whole lot of trouble.

I rolled to my knees, awkward without using my hands for balance. From there, I forced myself to my feet. They were just as numb as my fingers had been, but I hadn't noticed them when I was crumpled in a heap on the ground.

I hurried up and dragged my heavy, insulated overmitts back on. No point in allowing the subzero temperature of my prison to cancel the good work my stomach had begun.

Where the fuck was I? I blinked against the cave's dimness, willing my eyes to bring me more details.

It didn't work, so I reached for the headlamp built into the hood of my suit. Clumsy with gloves, I finally located the switch. Nothing. It must have died hours ago. Or was it days? How long had I been here, anyway? I paced in a circle, trading the pins and needles return of sensation in my hands for similar misery in my feet.

"I am not ready to lie down and die. Not yet."

I spoke out loud to steady myself. The words echoed off the walls of the cave that might well become my tomb, if I didn't get moving and hunt for a way out. Stumbling to a ribbon of half-frozen water splashing down one wall—the same cascade that had forced me awake and maybe saved my life—I angled my head to drink. The liquid had a funny, metallic taste, but Antarctica was full of mineral wealth. Untapped riches. Icy chunks mixed with the water made my teeth hurt. I wrapped my arms around myself and started pacing again, trying to remember what had happened. How the hell I ended up here.

The harder I pushed my sluggish brain to spit out something, anything, the more mulish it became. Bits and pieces of memories battered me like flashes of time-lapse photography, and got me nowhere.

Before waking up here, I'd been part of a metallurgical research expedition. We'd been based on a ship, the *Darya*, but we'd spent time at many of the research stations dotting the Palmer Peninsula. Scientists liked to compare notes. It was a cheap and dirty way to replicate findings, without actually doing the work.

I'd signed on with the expedition as a lark. It might have been stupid of me to walk away from a lucrative surgical practice, but I was burned out dealing with insurance companies and batshit crazy practice partners. At the time I left, I told myself I was taking a break, nothing permanent.

The looks I got—like I was the worst kind of fool—annoyed me. What business was it of anyone's if I chose to take advantage of my master's degree in biochemistry? I figured some of them were jealous because I had the freedom to walk away. No husband. No kids. No more student loans. No mortgage. Free as the proverbial bird.

Because they were jealous—and resentful—they'd labelled me selfish, immature, self-indulgent. I'd laughed it off and left anyway.

My job was assessing the effects of Antarctica's severe climate on human bodies. That part of things had gone well; evaluating physiological changes was right up my alley. What wasn't so fine were rival firms, all wanting to tap Antarctica's stores of mineral wealth. The Antarctic Treaty forbade mining rich veins of gold, silver, cobalt, copper, chromium, and uranium, but there wasn't much of a police force in Antarctica. In my months at the southern end of the world, I'd discovered the conglomerate I worked for was almost the only honest one. They stopped at mapping Antarctica's mineral wealth. Other less scrupulous groups came behind us, drilling the sites we'd recorded.

Illegally, I should add. Antarctica is controlled by twelve countries, the original signers of the Treaty back in 1959. Drilling and mining are off the table. Not allowed under any circumstances.

When my bosses complained, reported the scavengers to the Antarctic Treaty System, retribution was swift in a place with zero law enforcement. Men boarded our vessel, forcing us into several Zodiac rafts. I'd resisted. All my struggling did was earn me a blow across the back of my head from the butt end of an automatic rifle. And that's where my memories jump off a cliff into the abyss.

I reached up, intent on assessing the lump behind my head, but taking off my gloves again and unzipping my insulated suit enough to push the hood back were huge deterrents. Warmth is my friend. Warmth will keep me alive. If I sustained a concussion, it wasn't incompatible with life. Probably because I was focused on it, my head throbbed, but not much I could do about a subdural hematoma.

And it probably wasn't as serious as something like that since I was up and wandering around.

Maybe this place, the one I'd been chucked into like so much trash, was one of the many ice grottos dotting the Palmer Peninsula. I considered it, but too many things didn't fit. For one, it's too warm in here, and the running water suggests otherwise.

Another look at the rock and dirt walls made me certain I was underground, which narrowed things down. Antarctica's ice sheet has thinned from global warming, but there aren't too many spots with accessible cave systems. Most are buried beneath fifty feet of ice or more.

I'm not that far down. Nowhere close. Light is filtering in from translucent places above me. I squeezed my eyes shut to rest them for a moment. Now that I was up and moving, I was determined to explore every aspect of my prison. When I first regained consciousness, I'd screamed my lungs out, but no one answered. Or if they did, I couldn't hear them over the roar of rushing water.

Where were the seventeen other researchers from my boat? How about the twenty seamen who'd piloted it?

Whoa. Rein it in.

I buried my face in the high neck of my suit and took a few deep breaths of warm air. Panic was close to the surface. Too close, and I couldn't afford to make any mistakes. I have a good mind. It's always been one of my saving graces, and it was past time to put it to use. There has to be a way out. I was tossed in here—or carried—which argues there's a way out as well.

Oblong rocks lined one wall. Odd shapes, the distribution didn't look natural, but maybe my head injury was worse than I thought. I scrunched my forehead, sorting possibilities, but then realized my mind was wandering. Mostly to force a way past the inertia gripping me, I walked toward the closest group of rocks.

Breath caught in my throat before my stomach doubled up in rebellion. Between the two, I had a hell of a hard time breathing. Not oblong rocks. Bodies wrapped in tarps. Horror turned my guts to water. I bit back a shriek.

"Jesus fucking Christ. Get hold of yourself," I gritted out and hurried forward.

Kneeling, I rolled the first tarp over and exposed the body within. I didn't need to check for a pulse to know Brian was dead. He'd been a Scottish chemical engineer with a quick grin and a quirky sense of humor. Heedless of my newly warm fingers, I yanked off my gloves so I could examine him. I had to know how he'd died. Was it exposure or something far more malevolent?

Quick and methodical, I pushed more of the tarp out of the way. Its canvas was stiff and unyielding from congealed blood, but I forced it aside. Gunshot wounds, two of them, sat over his heart. My soul ached at the senseless slaughter, and I pulled his lids over his sightless eyes.

"Aw, Jesus, Brian. I'm so sorry."

Not much point in wrapping him back up, so I moved on to the other forms I'd misidentified as rocks. Horror yielded to numbness, the same dispassionate place I'd discovered as a young doctor. One that allowed me to move forward on autopilot, no matter what was unfolding around me.

I made my way from body to body. After Brian, I didn't expect any of them to be alive. My clinical detachment deepened as I checked each corpse for cause of death. So far, two others had been shot, and three looked as if they'd died from exposure.

"Well, that's six out of seventeen." I was talking out loud again. It made the carnage spread before me easier to absorb. And kept me from dissolving into a helpless muddle of tears. I'd cry at some point, but it wouldn't be today.

I've never minded being alone, but the isolation in that cave unnerved me, haunted me, made it seem as if the walls were moving closer, threatening to choke the life from me too. After a few breaths to steady myself, I crawled to the last body, ignoring sharp rocks that cut through the heavy fabric of my outdoor suit. If I hadn't been dressed for going outside when the men boarded my boat, I'd be just as dead as the rest of my crewmates.

Maybe not from gunshots, but exposure would have done me in.

I rolled the last body onto its side. This one was different. Rigor mortis hadn't yet set in, and it turned easily. I focused on the man's sharp-boned face and hope speared me, so sharp I almost couldn't breathe. Johan Petris, the Dutch metallurgical engineer, was still alive. Dark stubble dotted his cheeks and squared-off chin.

I knelt next to him and ran my hands down his body, assessing for injuries.

Please. Please. Let him be all right. I wasn't certain who I prayed to, but the words ran through my mind like a mantra embedded in a tape loop.

His eyes flickered open. "It is useless." His accented words were harsh. "My leg is broken."

"I can fix it. I'm a doctor." I winced. I sounded like an idiot. He knew about my training, even though there'd been another "official" ship's doctor to tend to the sick and injured.

"I did not forget." He yelped when I touched his upper leg, finding the broken femur easily. It had bled like a bitch, and a huge knot pressed against his insulated bib pants.

"Steel yourself. I have to realign the bones—"

He grabbed my hand, clamping his fingers around my wrist. "Leave me. Even if you line up the bones, I have lost blood. A lot of blood. You can get out of here, Erin. I am dead weight. The cold will do me in soon."

He focused very blue eyes on me. "If you stop moving, the cold will get you too."

I ground my teeth together. I wanted to shake Johan, tell him he had to try, that giving up wasn't an option. Besides, it set a terrible example for me. Hadn't I flirted with curling up in a corner and giving in to a death that felt inevitable?

"I propose a deal."

"Really? Here at the end of our lives—or mine, anyway—you want to turn into a gypsy trader?"

"I'll realign the bones. You tell me what happened. They knocked me over the head before I even got into a raft. Do you know more about what unfolded after that?" I sucked in a ragged breath. "Do you know where we are?"

"Yes to both, but a bargain presumes you have something I want. I already told you there is no point setting my leg."

"Your opinion, not mine," I said tightlipped. What I didn't say was I couldn't bear to let him die. Despite my brave thoughts about not minding being alone, I did mind. A whole lot.

I repositioned myself at his feet and grasped his boot. Before I pulled hard and then twisted to get the splintered bone ends to mesh, I said, "This will hurt like nobody's business. Go ahead and scream, but do not fight me. And try not to move."

I didn't give him a chance to respond. I wasn't at all sure I'd be strong enough to manage this without a traction splint, but I'd give it my best shot. The same calm, quiet place I always found once I settled on a decision surrounded me.

Pull and twist.

Yeah, I know, I told my inner instructor, the one who'd sat on my shoulder since medical school.

Johan grunted, but it turned into a long, tearing shriek. He tried to sit, no doubt to rip my throat out, but the motion gave me what I needed. I felt the femur ends slide together.

"Goddammit, Erin, Stop. Stop! I would rather die." He flopped back into the dirt, squealing.

"Done. All done now. Breathe. The pain will slow down." I was panting with the effort it had taken. "Going to take time for the lump to resolve, but it will now that the bone isn't bleeding into your thigh."

For long moments, the only sounds were him and me gasping for breath. "Yeah," he managed through a grimace. "It is better. Still doesn't mean I'll live, though."

"No. It doesn't." I kept my tone neutral and even. Lying to patients has never been part of my gig. "What happened after they clubbed me over the head?"

"Yeah. That was the quid pro quo, was it not?"

I nodded. "It was." I rocked back on my heels and stuffed my hands into my gloves. "You must have heard me yelling when I finally woke up in here. Why didn't you answer?"

He managed a shrug. "I could not get to you. Figured you would be dead soon anyway, just like everyone else."

His explanation made sense in the grim, eerie half-light of the cavern.

"I have been listening to water for hours. Can you get to it?"

I staggered upright, grateful to have something to do beyond running the odds of his survival through my medical algorithm trained mind. "Yes. I'll bring you some, but I need to find a container. Bet you're thirsty from losing all that blood."

"I am. There is an empty water bottle in my suit." He pulled off one glove. Scrabbling with his zipper, he reached inside and withdrew a quart bottle.

I took it and kept my voice crisp when I said, "Put your hand back inside your glove."

Johan made a face, but he also picked up the glove he'd discarded to fish out the bottle. "Yes, Mother."

Hustling to the water, I filled the bottle. It was tough to keep a lid on my elation because I wasn't alone anymore, but I needed to be realistic. Johan's assessment of his prognosis was accurate. Absent someplace like the boat's infirmary, his odds of living were virtually nil. He needed antibiotics, for one thing. And warmth. And fluids.

My survival hung in the balance too, if I couldn't find shelter and food soon. I wouldn't check out as fast as Johan, but neither would I be all that far behind him.

I squatted next to him while he drank in huge gulps. He handed the empty bottle back to me. After two more trips, he set the bottle down. "It is enough for now."

"Tell me what happened. Do you know who boarded our boat?"

He hooded his eyes. "Yeah. That Russian group. The ones intent on gold and uranium. You might not have known because you do not speak Russian and you also did not hang around on the bridge, but Mikhail was really worried about them. A few hours before they boarded the

Darya, the other two ships in this sector left for their home countries."

"Do you suppose they had advance warning, or something?"

He paused to take a deep breath before going on. "Who ever knows about these things? Mikhail predicted problems and suggested we leave, but no one took him seriously."

I pictured our tall, rawboned Russian sea captain with his short dark hair, intense dark eyes, and ever-present beer. "Hmmm. He's Russian. They're Russian. Do you suspect they were in cahoots?"

"No way in hell. Mikhail was a good man." Johan's face scrunched in pain. "Besides, he is dead. He refused to leave the ship, so they shot him."

"He's not here." I waved my arm to encompass the collection of bodies.

"Yeah. I know. They dropped him off the side of the boat after they killed him."

I sucked air through my teeth. "How'd Brian and Ted end up shot?"

"They attacked the men herding us to this cave." Johan shook his head. "I am fading. Adrenaline is not going to last much longer. Let me tell this in order."

I gripped one of his hands, nodding encouragement.

"Ten men boarded the boat. They radioed ahead, said they had critical scientific data to share about the uranium deposits we'd mapped the previous day." Johan's nostrils flared. "Mikhail warned us. Told us we should not let them board, but everyone fluffed it off, teased him about acting like a scared old woman."

"Go on."

"You were there when they boarded, saw it unfold when they ordered us off the *Darya* and into the Zodiacs. They killed a few dissenters after they clubbed you. After that, everyone else marched down the gangway and into several rafts. Some of ours and their two. Half of the Russians remained on the *Darya*. God only knows what plans they have for our ship."

He closed his eyes, breathing through parted lips.

I removed a glove to capture his wrist and check his pulse. It wasn't as strong as I would have liked, but it could have been worse. "Would you like more water?"

"No, but maybe you can refill the bottle before you leave."

I opened my mouth to protest I wouldn't leave him, but shut it fast. I'd leave because one of us had to. Perhaps I could find help before the rugged Antarctic climate killed us both. It was December, Antarctic summer, but that didn't mean a whole hell of a lot.

"The Zodiacs split up. I have no idea where the other ones went, but we are inside the chromium dig site. They probably picked it because the ice is only a few inches thick here."

"So we're still on the Palmer Peninsula," I murmured. We'd only traveled a few miles from where the *Darya* had been moored in the bay next to King George Island. "Maybe I can get to one of the research stations."

"How?" He eyed me through eyes pinched with pain and fatigue. "I am certain they would not have left a Zodiac on the beach."

"Overland, how else? Is there a way out of this cave?"

He nodded slowly. "Yes. Just keep walking that way." He pointed. "You will have to climb at the end, but it is doable."

"If it's doable, how'd you break your leg?"

"You missed your calling, Erin. You should have been a lawyer. I ducked and ran before they could shove me in here. They caught up with me and bashed me hard enough to break my leg."

I swallowed around a painful place in my throat, thinking about the force behind that blow.

"Get that look off your face. It was stupid of me, but that was when they shot Brian and Ted. Only reason they did not shoot me was they knew I could not walk anywhere."

"How long have we been here?"

He shrugged. "Maybe thirty hours. Enough time for everyone but me—and you—to freeze to death. The others were not dressed to be outside."

My heart ached for him. He'd been lying in the middle of a sea of dead and dying bodies for two days, but hadn't complained once. I felt small, petty, and vulnerable. I'd barely been conscious for a couple of hours, and I'd already contemplated cashing in my chips.

I pushed to my feet and returned to the bodies that had been wearing down jackets and pants. Methodically, I stripped off layers of insulation and carried the garments to where Johan lay.

"What are you doing?" he asked.

"Hang on. I'm making a warmer place for you."

He didn't say anything while I dragged three tarps close, doubling them to make a rough shield against the cold, damp dirt. Once they were laid out next to Johan's prostrate form, he moved his upper body mostly onto the sheets of canvas. I lifted his hips and legs, slowly and carefully, taking extreme caution not to disturb his broken femur. Once that part was done, I piled the down clothing I'd collected beneath and on top of him, tucking it in.

"Erin." His voice was weak, thinner than it had been.

"Don't try to talk."

"You need to go while your strength lasts."

I placed a jacket beneath his head and snugged his hood around his gaunt, whiskered face. The hard truth was I couldn't bear to walk away from the only other survivor from our ship. I knew I had to, but it was tearing me up inside.

"Just a little more, and then I'll work on rescuing us." I stressed the *us* part. Hope was often the only element standing between living and dying, and I'd be damned if I'd extinguish his.

Another search through the dead turned up belts and extra clothing. I fashioned a rough splint around Johan's injured leg to stabilize the break. Lucky for us, I also found two more water bottles. A quick trip to the waterfall, and I filled both and left one alongside the half empty one next to Johan.

I tucked the other one inside my suit where it wouldn't freeze.

Johan seemed to have slipped into a doze, but it could just as easily be a coma. I patted his upper arm, but he didn't stir. Poor bastard. I draped another two tarps over him to hold in what heat they could and started in the direction he'd indicated. All my thrashing around had thawed my extremities. Thank God, the grinding pain was gone.

I reached the end of our prison fast. A jumble of rocks—that were really stones and not bodies, this time—angled upward. I tested one. It held. The next two rattled downward the moment I put any weight on them. Shit. Crap. I'd need to watch myself if I didn't want to end up with a twisted ankle —or worse.

I'd never wanted out of anywhere more than I wanted out of the chromium dig site, but I forced myself to slow down and assess the tangle of rocks. Some of them were big enough to do a lot of damage if the whole pile avalanched. I moved to the side of the rockfall, thinking perhaps it would be more stable than the middle.

The waterfall sounded different. I angled my head, trying to hear better. Had it changed course? Was it threatening the cocoon I'd made for Johan? Minutes ticked past as I listened. I was on the verge of going back to check when I sorted musical notes from the characteristic rush of water.

Crap! Had I started hallucinating? The specter of my head injury rose to taunt me. The central nervous system could appear fine and go south really fast if pressure—or bleeding—built up where it didn't belong.

I scrunched my eyes shut and listened again. This time, the notes stood out. Single chimes running up and down the scale. Fear made my teeth chatter. Or maybe it was the cold. I had to be hallucinating, and it didn't bode well for my future. No way a musical instrument could be within a hundred miles of here.

Maybe it's the Russians, and they set up a camp on the beach.

Impossible. They'd want to be gone as quickly as possible. Before some other ship showed up and hailed them. The *Darya* and its research staff had been a permanent fixture in Antarctic waters for months. We'd become friendly with several other research expeditions.

Surely, the Russians knew as much.

The music wrapped around me, soothing and urging action, but it was just as impossible as Russians having set up shop outside the chromium dig site. Determined to get outside, see the lay of the land and what I had to work with, I ignored the music and started to climb.

Narrowing my focus to one step at a time, I tested each one before committing my weight to it. It was maybe a hundred feet to the top, not far at all. I was close. Only half a dozen steps from victory when a roaring filled my ears, and I knew the precarious pile of rocks had let go.

It took a moment before I started to fall. Amid crashing and creaking and pounding and choking dust, I tumbled into darkness so profound no light penetrated. Instead of hitting with enough force to break every bone in my body, I floated the last few feet.

Floated and touched down gently.

That freaked me out more than falling and dying on the spot would have.

And how the hell could I have fallen farther than the hundred feet from the cavern floor to the top of the rock pile?

I should have panicked, but my first thoughts were for Johan. He must have heard the rock avalanche, and he'd assume the worst. That I was dead, buried beneath tons of rubble.

Without me, there was no hope for him, either.

"Hang on," I yelled. He wouldn't hear me, but maybe, just maybe, he'd pick up on some random vibration of knowledge that I wasn't dead.

Not yet, anyway.

CHAPTER 2

I got to my feet, cursing my burned-out headlamp. My eyes were useless, so I extended my arms in front of me, determined to find a way out. Part of me—hell, most of me—was convinced I was doomed, but I muffled my inner pessimist until I'd done everything I could.

Staring into the blackness, I willed some sliver of light from somewhere, anywhere, to pierce it. My gloved hand touched something. A wall studded with sharp objects? I didn't push hard, afraid of another unstable stack of rocks, but I worked my way along a barrier of some kind. As I moved, I realized it was warmer down here. A whole lot warmer than it had been above.

Another impossibility. It was tough to estimate how far I'd actually fallen, but even if I'd tumbled five hundred feet, which seemed unlikely, there should only be a few degree difference between where I'd begun and here.

I was starting to sweat, which made no more sense than anything else. I stopped moving and took stock of my body. It actually felt stronger than when I was scaling the jumble of rocks.

"Erin!" The word bounced off everything, reverberating all around me.

I cupped my hands around my mouth to project my voice upward. "I'm fine."

"You can't be."

"I am. Aw crap, Johan. You moved. You probably fucked up your leg again."

"I didn't. I was careful. It stopped hurting, and I feel stronger."

I closed my teeth over my lower lip and bit hard enough to hurt, so I wouldn't lecture him about leaving the nest I'd created. Protection that would have wrung a few more hours out of his life—if he'd remained where I left him.

"I'll do my damnedest to get back up there."

"Do not take risks on my account. You know how stupid that would be."

I waited, but he was done talking. I could only imagine how much dragging himself seventy-odd feet to the end of the cavern had cost him. He only thought he felt stronger. It had to be an illusion borne of wishful thinking, pain, and a buttload of adrenaline.

"Did your dig have a second level?" I hung on, heart thudding against my chest. If he and the team had excavated down here, it meant ladders or a series of ledges with ropes.

"No." Johan hesitated before a string of words emerged.

"I took readings and found nothing except solid earth beneath the cavern. Where you are should not be there. How is it you did not injure yourself in the fall?"

"I have no idea."

"Can you see this?"

I tilted my head back, staring upward. Impossibly far above me, a light winked on. "Yes."

"I am going to drop a flashlight. Try to catch it. It may not survive otherwise."

"All right. Ready." I kept my gaze glued on the light as it plummeted downward. The same ground cushion or other weird geothermal phenomena that had halted my fall, did the same for the flashlight. I scooped it easily from the air and swung it in an arc, examining where I was.

"Got it," I yelled.

Breath stuttered in my throat. Crystals surrounded me, thousands of them. I was in a circular space lined with uneven crystalline formations. They reflected every shade of the rainbow as I played the flashlight over them. Were they the source of the heat? I loosened the zipper down the front of my suit and pushed my hood back.

"Erin?"

"Yup. Still here. This place is incredible. A geologist's paradise."

"Tell me later. You are at least a hundred feet down. Do you see a way out?"

"Hang on."

Now that I had a light, I made a quick transit of the space. It wasn't very big. Back in my not-so-idle youth, I'd enjoyed free climbing. One spot had enough nubs and knobs I thought I could make it back to where Johan was.

"I'm going to try to climb out of here."

"Odds?"

I smiled at the scientific detachment in that one word. We played odds in medicine too, but even decent percentage points in your favor were a disappointment if you happened to be one of the 10 percent who didn't respond to a particular intervention.

"I honestly don't know. They'd be better without these clunky boots, but I'd be worse than a fool to leave them behind." I glanced at my bulky polar footwear. No laces, or I'd have tried tying them together and looped them over a shoulder.

"Go for it," he called down to me. "I will attempt to locate a rope. We had a supply chest in here."

"Stay put," I screamed.

"Erin. My leg is better. Your job right now is to climb. Do not worry about me."

His leg couldn't be better. *Better* would take weeks.

Yeah, and I should be dead. Falling a hundred feet should have done me in, but here I was. This was not the time or place to think too hard or too deeply about anything. Johan had a good mind. Once we got out of this, we'd establish what had actually happened.

My eyes opened wider. Somewhere along the way, I'd started expecting both of us to survive. How had that happened when I'd been dead certain our lives could be measured in hours, not days?

"Everything will keep," I lectured myself. Answers wouldn't be forthcoming. Not in the bottom of this pit.

I removed my heavy gloves and attached their lanyards to my suit. No way I could climb with them on. Pushing everything but the path beckoning to me aside, I attached the flashlight to my suit, angling it so it illuminated the wall and started to climb. I should be clumsier, yet I moved not fast but with more grace than I believed myself capable of.

My earlier exhaustion faded, giving way to enough energy to find the next hold. My boots that I'd been certain would trip me up and send me plummeting back down gripped the rough wall far better than I'd expected.

Was our luck finally turning? Or was I riding high on adrenaline and not thinking straight?

I kept my gaze glued to the wall. A route showed itself where I needed it, sharing secrets one at a time, like a Chinese puzzle box. Darkness reigned below, so it was tough to judge how far I'd come.

I also had no idea how long I'd been at this. My sense of time passing had deserted me. The next two moves were hard. I was certain one of them would be the end of me because it was such a long reach to the next hold. Breath whistled through my teeth, and my heart pounded from tension.

Small chips rattled down around me from places the wall wasn't as solid as I'd hoped. Shit! Would this be like trying to leave the upper cavern? Where I got close enough to taste freedom only to lose everything?

I stopped and forced myself to breathe. Deep and easy. I

didn't know if I had it in me to do this again, which meant I had to make it work this time.

"Just a little more," Johan called from above me, his voice much nearer than it had been before. "You are maybe two meters from the end of a rope I have secured around a boulder."

Rope? A rope?

Hope jabbed me so vigorously, it made my stomach hurt. I started to lean my head back to look, but it nearly unbalanced me. I bit down on my lip hard enough to hurt to force myself to keep going. Two meters may as well be fifty if I couldn't get there.

I saw a hold, but I'd have to jump for it, so I scanned the wall, hunting for something more conservative. I looked three times, but nothing showed itself. Frustrated, I glanced down to see if I could improve where my feet were.

Yes!

I'd have fist pumped the air if I wasn't hanging on with everything in me. Curling my fingers around their holds, I carefully moved my right foot several inches upward. Once it was stable, I moved my left.

I was panting from effort, but the higher position allowed me to grasp the two holds above my head. I flailed around some but located two more footholds. Christ! Where was the rope. I was certain I'd climbed six feet.

Stop it! My inner voice was harsh. Before I knew there was a rope, I was only counting on myself.

One move at a time. Maintain three points of attachment. Keep breathing.

Instructions from long-ago teachers ran through my head. They steadied me, and I inched upward. Enough light filtered in from above I no longer needed the flashlight, but I couldn't reach over to shut it off, either.

I saw the rope now. It was close but still beyond the range of my arms. Sweat ran down my face, making my eyes sting. I blinked it away.

"Erin. Come on," Johan urged.

"No more holds." I gasped out the words even as I searched desperately for one more protrusion, even a small one.

"Here. This will help."

The rope snaked down another few inches.

I checked my footing and swiped a hand upward. My fingertips brushed the end of the rope. "I need a little bit more," I muttered.

He must have heard me because the rope descended enough for me to grasp it. I'd love to have tied it around me, but I didn't have enough slack. Not yet. "Climbing," I yelled before I put my weight on the rope and used it to force my way upward.

My boot soles skittered off holds, but it no longer mattered. Once the end was long enough, I stopped and looped the rope around myself. It gave me what I needed to polish off the last few feet. I paid attention, though, and I was damned grateful for the rope. Without it, there were spots I would have been stymied. No way up, and I certainly couldn't have downclimbed my ascent route.

Finally, puffing and panting and screaming my victory to

the skies—probably damned stupid if the Russians were outside—I dragged myself over the lip. Rather than being located within the tumble of rocks at the end of the cave, the hole began on the cavern floor a few feet from the rockfall.

I looked for a gash extending into the rockpile but didn't find one. How could I have fallen through a spot twenty-some feet above me, and have it form a crater here?

Johan sat with splayed legs, the end of the rope wrapped around his torso. He'd belayed me. Goddammit. I could have unbalanced him.

"You said a boulder," I protested.

"Yeah, that was before you needed more rope."

"What the hell?" I staggered upright, pulling the rope behind me so I could coil it, but first I retrieved my gloves from where they dangled and slid my frozen hands into them. Then I looped the rope into neat coils, working on autopilot.

He grinned up at me. "No thank-yous?"

"Okay." I was still panting hard enough, it was tough getting words out. "Thanks. Now, what the fuck?"

He shrugged, unwinding the rope from his chest and shoulders. "I heard music. Odd notes that floated about me as I was working my way to this spot." Shaking his head, he said. "Everything is so bizarre, the least I can do is relay the events in sequence. I heard the rockfall. It jolted me out of whatever place I had sunk into. I listened hard, expecting to hear you scream.

"Never happened. So I worked my way out from under all that shit you wrapped around me—not an easy task as depleted as I was. Once I was free, I rolled onto my belly and used my arms to drag myself toward where you had to be. That was when music surrounded me."

He exhaled, breath whistling through his teeth. "At first, I figured I was hallucinating, that my mind had launched a diversionary activity to protect me from being so incapacitated by pain I would have to stop."

I'd finished coiling the rope and dropped it between us, my gaze alternating from his face to his thigh. The one where there'd been a visible lump. "Go on," I urged, and dropped to my knees next to him where I could run a hand lightly over the fracture site.

"Before I do…" He nailed me with his blue eyes. "What did you find just now?"

"Uh, I'd have to remove your suit and mid layer and long johns to be certain, of course, but—"

"Erin." He dropped a hand on top of the one I still had resting on his thigh and pressed downward. "It doesn't hurt. I can walk on it."

"I wasn't wrong about it being broken." Defensiveness bloomed, heating my face.

"Never said you were. I may be a lowly engineer, but even I know my leg was broken. I felt the ends slide together when you reduced the fracture." He paused for a beat. "I also know it healed. The music coincided with me feeling stronger and…"

I understood why he'd run out of words. No matter how many he ginned up, he'd never explain his unprecedented recovery. One I'd been certain would take a month—if we lived that long. Reaching into my suit, I extracted a water bottle and took a long drink.

"I heard music too. Just before the rock pile caved in."

Johan inspected me through narrowed eyes. "How is it you did not sustain an injury? You fell far enough to kill you."

"I'm sure it was just some odd geothermal phenomena. It was warmer down there. A whole lot warmer, and—"

"That is not an answer. You should have broken every bone in your body."

I'd been casting the occasional glance his way, but I finally looked him square in the eye. "Some type of ground cushion softened my fall. I sort of floated the last few feet. It's how I got the flashlight too. It fell slower toward the bottom. A lot slower."

Johan tucked his legs beneath him, a motion that made me wince, but it didn't appear to bother him at all. "Fascinating. Could you feel warm air blasting upward?"

I shook my head. "Nothing like that. Maybe the air was thicker, or—" Or, what? I'd studied physics, and rational explanations didn't fit, but I wasn't willing to say that out loud.

Unexpected noise filtered in from outside the chromium dig site. It took me a moment to sort the sound bits into rough male voices spouting Russian. "What are they saying?" I kept my voice very low, a ragged whisper, and cursed my lack of ability to learn any language beyond English—and the Latin I'd needed for chemistry and physiology classes.

Johan held up a hand and cocked his head to hear better. He drew his brows together and stood, making as little commotion as possible, while motioning for me to do the same.

The buzz of voices from outside grew louder. Maybe four men judging from the conversation flow back and forth. What were they up to? Had someone gotten cold feet? Made sense. This was an established dig site for chromium, a valuable mineral. Since it was already excavated—and included in reports we'd sent to our respective countries— chances of it remaining undisturbed were low.

Sooner or later, a new team would work their way in around the rockfall area and find a bevy of dead bodies. It was cold enough to discourage much in the way of decomposition. But remains were still remains. They wouldn't go away on their own, and it didn't take a forensic pathologist to determine some of the corpses had resulted from foul play.

Nothing like a bullet hole or two. Just in case anyone was in doubt.

I followed Johan to an alcove off to one side. Several chests had been butted together. After laying a finger over his mouth, telling me to be silent, he pried one open and handed me a big bore, high-powered automatic rifle with a scope.

"Ever shoot one of these?" His mouth was right next to my ear.

I shook my head, and he took the rifle and handed me a pistol. I've never been much for firearms, but this was a revolver. Seemed more manageable. He slapped a magazine into the rifle's stock and handed me bullets. I fumbled around before finding the release catch that let me spin the cylinder so I could load the gun. It was awkward, so I pulled off my outer glove. After that, the weapon felt cold and menacing. I was sworn to do no harm. Could I shoot someone if I had to?

Guess I was about to find out.

Meanwhile, Johan threaded his way behind the chests. I joined him. They were constructed from heavy gauge steel. It should keep us safe enough from Russian gunfire.

I hoped.

Rocks grated against one another, clinking, clanking, and falling. The men were digging their way inside. Should clear the way for us to leave.

Yeah. Once we kill them...

A bucket of ice water over my head wouldn't have been any more sobering. It was a shorter road than I'd ever guessed from the Hippocratic oath to premeditated murder.

Unlikely my whispers would carry over the racket, so I leaned close to Johan. "Is it the same bastards who dumped us in here?"

"No, but they work together. This batch is the cleanup crew. I heard enough the first time to suspect they'd send someone back. This might be the ass end of the world, but a bunch of corpses would be reported to the Antarctic Treaty Organization."

"They'd send multi-national militia to investigate," I murmured.

"Precisely, which would have put a crimp in all the illegal mining."

"Why didn't you say something?"

"What for? If Dame Fortune smiled on us, you would have been outside in a spot you could have hidden."

I rolled his answer around in my mind. "Not very many hiding spots. You might have suggested I bring a gun."

A soft sigh rattled from him. "Erin. I was barely holding on. The pain was so intense, I am surprised I remembered anything."

I touched his arm. "Sorry."

"Kneel like I am. Rest the muzzle on the chest to stabilize it. Line up the sights and pull the trigger nice and easy. Be ready for the kick. Keep the weapon in a steady plane."

While I was digesting the information, he went on. "We should not need your firepower. My plan is to wait until all of them are inside. This baby"—he patted the barrel—"will cut a swathe through a battalion. It will be loud, though."

"Got it." My stomach burned from bile, and adrenaline coated the back of my throat with a sour taste. I was surprised I had any left after climbing out of the hole.

"I bet they will have a Zodiac on the beach. Once they are dead, we will take it, and—"

"Whoa. Where there are Zodiacs, there are ships." The specter of a Russian vessel loaded with long-range rifles and scopes scared the crap out of me.

"Some risks cannot be helped. We are not far from the Argentine base, Belgrando. It is just around the headland. We are more maneuverable than a ship."

"Unless they send a second raft. Plus, that base is often empty."

He placed a hand over where mine felt like it had frozen to the gun. "One step at a time. Ssht. They are inside."

I'd been intent on our conversation, but he was right. The cascade of displaced stone had nearly stopped. Disquieting thoughts sent a fist into my solar plexus. The cleanup crew would notice the canvas tarps had been disturbed. Surely, they'd been told how many bodies to collect. Coming up two short would initiate a search.

None of it mattered. Johan planned to gun them down.

A burly man, his head covered by a thick hood, strode into my field of vision. A rifle was slung across his back. He hefted one of the bodies as if it weighed nothing, carted it to where I couldn't see him any longer, and yelled something in Russian.

"Fuck!" Johan mumbled.

I didn't need Russian to understand the men had set up a grisly assembly line. One carried the corpses to some kind of sling setup. Other men up top winched the dead guy to the surface. Or dragged him if they didn't have a mechanical assist.

The hooded man returned for corpse number two. If the out-of-place tarps bothered him, he gave no sign of it.

"What do we do?" I hissed, louder than I meant to.

The Russian stopped dead and shouldered the rifle, turning in a full circle. Someone from outside yelled at him. He yelled back and slowly put the gun down, but he didn't sling it around his back. He set it where he could get to it and grabbed another body.

I wanted to ask Johan what the exchange had been about. Instead, I focused on holding myself absolutely still. We were so screwed. If we shot the guy ferrying bodies back and forth, the noise from the gunshot would bring the other ones down here on the double.

Or maybe they'd just chuck a grenade into the hole and call it even. Double duty. It would obliterate evidence and kill us at the same time. The music started up again. Stray notes just like when I was nearly out of this hellhole. Next to me, Johan jumped as if he'd been struck.

Odd golden light glittered around the Russian. He crumpled to the ground with his neck bent at an unnatural angle. The body he'd had over one shoulder in a fireman's carry skittered forward a few feet, landing with a *thunk*.

I scrambled from our hiding place, intent on making certain he was as dead as he looked. Johan leapt over the collection of chests, covering me with the rifle. Fear pricked me, but I bent over the fallen man. He opened his mouth, but nothing came out. His eyes rolled back into his skull.

He was dead, but how? Nothing to trip on. If he'd had a cardiac event, he'd still be clinging to life. I glanced at Johan and shrugged. We needed a plan, and right now, I had zip squat.

The men outside shouted in Russian.

"They want him to hurry," Johan said.

The musical notes hadn't abated. They were more pronounced, more melodic than before. The shimmery light returned, and I swung my revolver up. I'd be damned if whatever killed the Russian would get us too.

The music shaded to a man's voice. Strangely accented, it said, "Welcome to my realm, humans. There is nothing for you above but strife."

Johan's eyes widened until white showed all around his dark blue irises. "What the unholy fuck?"

"You took the words right out of my mouth," I mumbled.

The music turned into a veritable orchestra. In a repeat of my earlier plunge, the earth beneath our feet opened, and we fell into darkness. At least this time, I wasn't expecting the precipitous descent to crush the life out of me. Still, fear and a deep sense of foreboding made me want to puke. Death was something I understood. Disembodied voices weren't. Nor was music that had no source.

CHAPTER 3

Konstantin exchanged a pointed look with his sister. He'd hoped for joy, relief, or at a bare minimum, curiosity, after revealing his presence to the humans. Particularly after he'd obliterated one of their problems.

What he hadn't expected were anger, outrage, and fear. "Perhaps choosing these two was a mistake," he muttered.

"No going back now," Katya pointed out. "You've already dumped them in the crystal cave. Plus, it is far too soon to make any sweeping proclamations about failure."

"But I killed their problem. The man threatening them. They should be looking for me, ready to lay their undying fealty at my feet."

"They don't understand such is true, Brother. They have no idea you—or I—exist. All they know is their adversary died—under strange circumstances." She gripped his lower arm briefly, offering support.

"The circumstances could have been far stranger." Smoke swooshed from his open mouth. "I could have burned him to ash where he stood."

"What you did was better."

"Why do you think so?" Konstantin trusted his sister's instincts, but often didn't understand her reasoning.

Steam from her mouth and nostrils wove with his, creating a captivating pattern. "Humans, the good ones, are easily frightened by events beyond their reckoning. You made it appear the man's neck was broken."

"It was," Konstantin sputtered. "I sent magic in just the proper spot to separate two of his upper vertebrae."

"Yes, yes." Katya waved her hands in front of her. "My point was that in the human world, broken necks mean death."

"And immolation doesn't?"

She thinned her mouth into a frustrated line. "You asked for my opinion. Do you want it, or was your plan to pick my thoughts to shreds?"

"Sorry. Of course I want to hear your views. Is it because the path I employed was less...dramatic? Did that make it easier to accept?"

"Maybe not easier to accept, but less frightening. If you'd turned the man into a blazing inferno, I have no idea what the other two would have done."

Far above them, in the cavern he'd just cleared of the man and woman, shock waves blasted his sensitive hearing.

Goddess damn humans and their bombs and weapons and destruction.

"I shall return presently," he told Katya.

"Shall I welcome our, erm, guests?"

"No. Let them wander in circles for a while. Maybe then they'll be happier to see us when we lead them to someplace more commodious than the crystal cave."

Konstantin visualized a sheltered cove out of sight of the stretch of beach in front of the cavern. Perhaps revealing himself for what he was would be ill-advised, but he was furious. These men had killed their own kind for sport, and now they'd returned to desecrate the dead. He'd listened to their talk, words skulking behind the blast waves, and they made him ill.

Incendiary devices blowing up the cavern above his realm were the final indignity.

These men did not deserve life, and he, Konstantin, once a prince among dragon shifters, would see they never drew another breath. Deep within him, the dragon's joy at its freedom filled him with love for the creature who shared his body. His soul. His dragon had shining black scales, where Katya's was golden from head to tail.

His sister was ashamed her dragon had deserted her. That was why it had taken her so long to admit its absence. Now that he knew about it, though, he and his dragon could address the problem.

And they would. He had faith his dragon could coax hers from wherever it had taken refuge and talk sense into her.

He emerged into a day marked by brisk wind and cloudy

skies and summoned shift magic. Bones stretched and altered, skin reformed and grew scales. His jaws elongated, and he clacked his double rows of teeth together.

Fire spewed from his mouth. He flexed his talons, beat his wings a time or two, and jumped into the air. He didn't hesitate once he crested the spit of land separating him from three men standing around shouting at each other. He'd give them a reason for all that racket.

Bugling furiously, he aimed a strip of fire right in front of them. The men's heads tilted skyward, and they began screaming as they ran for a black raft a few meters away. Konstantin spewed fire until it encompassed the raft in a sheet of flames. It took a moment before fire engulfed it, burning in smoky gouts.

With their escape route cut off, the men turned to face him and dragged rifles to their shoulders, firing at him like madmen. Cretins! Apparently, they had no idea his scales were impervious to bullets. And blades. Everything else too.

Dragons were immortal.

He waited, fanning the air with his wings and raining fire down on the men until they tossed their useless guns aside. No more ammunition, not that what they wasted before they ran out did them any good.

Konstantin wasn't a bully by nature, but these men were. He was an excellent judge of character, whether the bearer was human or dragon or some other iteration of magic wielder. After inscribing a lazy circle in the sky, he dropped low, intent on landing.

The men weren't trying to escape, but where would they

have run to? The icy shoreline gave way to snowfields marked by deep fissures. Even with skis or snowshoes, the men would have found travel painstakingly slow as they worked their way around ridges and troughs.

His hind legs brushed the beach, and he folded his wings, regarding the trio staring back at him.

"You can cast your costume aside," one of the men said in Russian. Like the others, he was garbed in a bulky black suit that covered him from its hooded top to his green rubber boots.

"What if it isn't a costume?" Konstantin countered in the same language. He spoke all human languages, plus one specific to dragonkind.

The center man doubled up a fist and shook it his way. "Do you take us for fools? I admit your getup is clever enough to conceal an engine of some kind, but—"

The first man made a chopping motion and leaned closer. "I represent a wealthy company. We would pay handsomely to know your secrets. You would have to sign the rights over, but once you've done that..." He shrugged and offered a disingenuous smile.

Konstantin decided to play along, for a short time, anyway. He folded his forelegs across his scaled chest and aimed his whirling eyes at the man who'd spoken. The man made a good faith effort to meet his gaze, but gave up.

"To what do you attribute my eyes?" he asked. "Another clever motor?"

"It has to be something," the man standing in the middle muttered. "Technology gets better every day."

So far, man number three had said nothing. Nor had he looked at Konstantin. A bit of smoke and ash were in order, so he puffed them around the third man until he was lost in a thick, choking haze.

The man stumbled out of the cloud, coughing and sputtering. "Enough. I see you for what you are. Kill us and be done with it."

The other men erupted in outraged shrieks, telling their companion to shut up.

"You see me for what I am, eh?" Konstantin repeated the man's words. "And what might that be?"

The man twisted his neck and trained bloodshot brown eyes on Konstantin. "Any fool can see you're a dragon."

"He's mad," the man in the middle yelled.

"Don't encourage him," the first man chimed in.

"Who is deranged?" Konstantin asked coolly. "Your compatriot or me?"

The men clammed up fast.

"What are you doing on my headland?" Konstantin selected another tactic, more to see what they'd say than anything.

"We were told to clear dead men from there." The first man waved a gloved hand behind him.

Konstantin puffed more smoke. "Interesting. How did they die? I haven't killed anyone. Not lately." He spread his jaws in a parody of a smile—and to show off his teeth.

"They, uh, were stealing from our company," the man in the middle replied.

"We had to set an example," the first man added.

"What were they stealing?" Konstantin pressed. "Anything of worth in this region is part of my hoard."

Three sets of eyes widened. "It, um, it didn't happen here," the first man said.

"N-no," the second agreed. "A long way from here. Our associates moved the bodies here from that other spot."

"And now you're moving them again. Quite poor planning, if you ask me," Konstantin wasn't exactly enjoying himself, but he was warming to his role as tormentor.

"These things are difficult to anticipate," the man standing in the middle muttered.

"Anyhow"—the first man extracted something that looked like a radio from within his suit—"we'll alert our ship to send another raft, and we'll be out of your way quite soon."

Konstantin resorted to magic instead of fire. The black plastic oblong box exploded, showering the man with sharp bits that left bloody tracks down his face.

"Idiots!" The third man located his tongue. "You're bigger fools than I imagined. That is a dragon. We angered it by trespassing on its land. It's toying with us, but none of us will leave this place."

"How is it you know about my kind?" Konstantin asked, genuinely curious.

"My great-grandmother saw a dragon when she was a small child. It wasn't black like you, but green."

"Did it speak with her?"

"*Nyet.* She hid in her family's grotto, but the story was passed down in our family. I was certain it had to be true."

"Why?"

"Because the old woman helped raise me, and I never knew her to lie."

Konstantin rocked from one hind foot to the other. "One of you believes I am more than smoke and mirrors."

The first man flexed his hand, and the remains of the radio clattered to the ground. "Whatever you have in mind. Get on with it."

Nothing like an open invitation. Anticipation swelled as his dragon embraced the moment. It loved killing, lived for it.

"Step back five paces," Konstantin ordered. The man walked backward, never taking his gaze from the dragon. Before he came to a stop, Konstantin let fire blast from his mouth. It surrounded the man, burning quick and hot. So hot, the man never got a chance to scream.

"Brother, what is taking you so long?" blasted into his mind.

"Nothing. I'm fine," he answered Katya.

"Our prisoners, uh, I mean guests, grow restless."

"Back soon."

Konstantin focused on the other skeptic, who stared at him with mulish defiance. The last man, the one who believed in dragons, scuttled out of the way, anticipating what would happen next.

Konstantin didn't disappoint him. He sent another volley of fire to consume the man who'd once stood in the middle. Hatred and disbelief blasted from him in waves, even as his flesh liquified. Both pyres added a burnt smell to the clean, marine air.

Konstantin turned to the last man, undecided regarding his fate.

He knelt on ice-coated rocks, head bent, waiting for the end of his life.

"What are you thinking?" Konstantin demanded.

The man kept his head down. "That if I must die, I am grateful to have laid eyes on one of the world's wonders." He raised his head. "I have done horrible things, aligned myself with wickedness. I deserve death as much as those two." He waved a hand in the direction of the smoking pyres.

"This grandmother of yours, would she approve of how you have lived your life?"

The man's features scrunched in sadness. "Great-grandmother, and no, she would have dragged me to church with her every day to better pray for my tarnished soul."

Konstantin scoured the man's mind with magic to assess if he was telling the truth. The others, the ones turning to ash, had been beyond redemption. This man retained a conscience. "I will not kill you this day, but I would extract a promise."

The man bowed his head once more. "Anything."

"Consider this a second chance. You will craft expiation for your wrongdoing and make your family proud of you."

"I will. I promise."

"Stand up."

The man scrambled upright.

"We will ensure you do not sustain blame for your associates' deaths. Come close, and I shall toss you onto my back. We will fly near enough your ship the others see us, and then I shall drop you into the sea."

"Thank you. This is far more than I hoped for. I will keep my end of our bargain."

Konstantin skewered him with his whirling eyes. "You will, indeed, for if you do not, I will know, and the death that did not claim you this day will find you."

"If I welch, I deserve to die." The man ran close.

Konstantin lifted him with magic until he straddled his broad back. "Hang on." Spreading his wings, he circled to gain enough altitude to spot a ship. It was the only one in the area, and another of the infernal rafts had just left the lowered gangway.

"This is good," the man informed him. "You won't have to fly as far, only to the raft."

Konstantin set a path to intercept it. Before he got very close, bullets zinged past them. They couldn't hurt him, but they could injure his passenger. He blasted a path in front of him, frosting the air with flames. The man kneeling in the raft, rifle raised to his shoulder, stared at the fiery trail above him and lowered his gun.

Distant shouts reached him. Konstantin banked and circled. The man on his back was close enough to call to the two in the raft. Good. Meant they wouldn't waste more ammunition trying to drive him out of the skies.

A slight course correction, and he hovered a few feet above the raft, looking down on faces scrunched in panic and horror. The man who'd been riding him leapt sideways, landing sprawled in the bottom of the raft.

Konstantin flapped his wings hard, intent on putting distance between himself and the raft. He'd done enough damage for one day. Revealing themselves to humans was frowned on, except who would call him to task? For all he knew, he and Katya were the only two dragon shifters left on Earth.

Besides, if he hadn't ferried the man back to his ship, no one would have believed his stories about seeing a dragon. No. They'd have blamed him for the deaths of the other men. He'd have probably been shot and dumped over the side of the ship.

This group of men had an ungodly fascination with guns and death. For the barest moment, Konstantin considered returning and blowing up the ship. It was well within his capabilities to set fire to the machinery that powered the vessel. The dragon was all for anything that smacked of destruction, but Konstantin pulled him back.

Killing everyone on the ship would be grand sport, but it defeated the purpose of sparing the man whose great-grandmother had glimpsed a dragon. And now, two more men had seen him as well. They'd have no doubts about what he was. Not after the one who'd ridden him was done.

This way, a few sailors would keep tales of dragonkind alive on the lips of men. It was vain of Konstantin, and probably misguided, but he didn't want the memory of those like him to die out.

A spate of rapid-fire Russian faded behind him as he flew fast and sure back toward the spit of land where he'd emerged from his underground lair. His dragon's delight at being airborne lightened his soul. They'd killed today, but they'd also extended compassion.

His dual nature was both boon and challenge. The dragon would merrily kill anything in its path, but the man's task was to provide wisdom and a modulating effect. All shifters fought the same fight. When the animal nature took over the partnership, the elders sat you down and had a heart to heart.

A warning before they banished you to a distant borderworld where the harm you might do would be minimal.

Konstantin touched down and rebuked himself. No more elders to keep overly enthusiastic shifters in line. He and Katya were on their own. Had been for centuries.

As he summoned shift magic and reclaimed his human form, excitement thrummed hotly in his chest. Was the alone part about to change? The human woman was comely. Surely, she'd wish to welcome a dragon and become immortal. What person could resist such an offer?

And then he remembered her reaction to the gift he'd offered. A gift with no strings at all when he'd directed magic and killed the man in the cavern. Gratitude hadn't even made the list. She'd been shocked, frightened, outraged, and confused.

His certainty about her reaction to his glorious two-fold nature faded, replaced by caution. If she proved too much trouble, he'd keep his word and plunk her and the man back on the beach. Let them figure out their own way back to what passed for civilization in a badly flawed human world.

"I've returned," he called to Katya as he waited for fingers and toes and skin to replace scales and talons.

"And not a moment too soon."

He started to ask what in the Nine Hells that meant, but decided not to. He'd find out soon enough.

CHAPTER 4

"Engage the safety," Johan yelled at me as the dirt beneath our boots crumpled.

I fumbled with the gun and discovered I'd never released the mechanism that would have allowed the revolver to fire. Determined not to mention that part—no reason to—I waited for the cushion that had broken my fall last time.

And prayed like hell it would still be there.

It was, and I righted myself toward the bottom, landing on my feet.

"Well." Johan grunted the word. "I know why you did not die the first time, but Christ, there is something horribly wrong here."

"You think?" I angled a glance in the direction of his voice. Remembering the flashlight still clipped to my suit, I turned it on and gasped.

"What is it?"

"Wait a moment." I stayed put but turned in a full circle, playing my light over the thousands of multifaceted crystals I remembered all too well. The small, rounded enclosure sure as hell looked the same, but it couldn't be. Last time, I'd fallen from a spot seventy-five feet away. The cave wasn't anywhere near that in diameter. Thirty feet tops.

Maybe there were more than one of these places. That had to be it. I hustled to the area where I'd found a climbing route in cave number one. There wouldn't be one here. There couldn't be.

Because the caves had to be different.

As I blitzed past landmarks, I remembered them. I didn't want to, but I did. Shit. Breathing way harder than my level of exertion required, I shone my flashlight over familiar territory. This was where I'd climbed out of the other cave. Scuffs from my boot soles marred the lower crystals.

Johan had activated a second light. He must have stuffed a flashlight in his suit after he'd tossed one down to me *Good man. He thinks ahead.* Maybe he sensed I was thinking about him because he clamped a hand around my upper arm.

"What. Is. It?" He inserted spaces between the words this time, and I knew he wouldn't let me off the hook until I told him something that resonated as true.

"This is the same cave I was in last time," I said dully. "It violates every single law of physics, but these"—I ran a gloved finger over a place the crystals had broken beneath my weight—"happened when I was climbing out of here."

"Many physical laws have fallen today," he said in a

carefully neutral tone. "Why are you so distraught about this one?"

"I am not distraught—" I began and clamped my mouth shut. My lips were trembling, and I did not want to cry. My hyper-emotional state was stupid, ill-timed. The only important thing was escape.

I'd no sooner thought about fleeing, never mind I had no idea how we'd manage it without the rope, when an explosion rocked the chamber above us. Johan threw me on the ground with his body on top of mine; rocks rained down around us. None did any damage because the mysterious layer of thicker air that had protected us, slowed the rocks too.

"Appreciate the thought," I gritted out, "but you're crushing me."

"You have a difficult time with thank-yous, Madame Doctor. Better me than rocks." He moved off me, ended up in a crouch, and rolled his eyes. "If I had been thinking, I would have realized they wouldn't fall hard enough to hurt us."

"Thanks for trying to protect me. Crap on a cracker, can this get any worse?" I used hands and knees to move off my belly and into a sit.

Aftershocks rolled through above us, sounding like giants engaged in a bizarre bowling match. Dust filtered through both holes. The one I'd fallen through, before—and the new one.

"To answer your question, our situation could be far worse than it is. We could be wounded," he pointed out. "Like I was. Or dead."

I winced. I hadn't been thinking about his broken leg—and subsequent miraculous recovery—because the whole thing creeped the hell out of me. "Even if we could climb out of here..." I scanned him, assessing the reach of his long arms and legs, and decided he could probably manage free climbing.

The corners of his mouth twitched. "Have you found a way to determine if someone has climbing skills without asking them?"

I felt my face heat. "Uh, no. Besides, it's pointless. Even if we got back to where all those chests are, it would take us days to dig our way out. We have no food..." Because our prospects were dim enough to unnerve me, I opted for a question. "Was that a grenade?"

"Maybe. Might have been plastique, which does a hell of a lot more damage." Johan hesitated. "We do have food, Erin. Perhaps not what you would rather eat, but beggars cannot be choosers."

I opened my mouth to ask what but closed it in a hurry. Every story I'd ever read about survivors of cataclysmic events resorting to cannibalism roared through my mind. We weren't lacking for dead bodies. All we had to do was excavate them out of the rubble. My gut clenched, and for long moments it was nip and tuck whether I'd vomit.

When I looked up, Johan's gaze was fixed on me almost as if he were willing me to get hold of myself. "Stay here and take a break for a few minutes."

"Where are you going?"

"Obviously, not far. I will perform a methodical circuit of

this space. Perhaps there is a way out that does not require steep climbing."

"I'll be here." I nodded glumly, feeling like a chump. Hunting for an easier way out had never occurred to me. Oh hell, no. I'd been all about proving how tough I was. A couple of my sketchy moves had nearly gotten me killed when I'd climbed up the series of knobs and marginal holds.

Or they could have been the end of me in a normal world, one where a safety net didn't catch me at the bottom.

I clicked my light off to preserve the batteries. They were the extra-long-life ones, meant to perform in sub-zero conditions, but even the heartiest battery gave up eventually. Johan's boots made little scraping sounds as he worked his way along the base of the wall, scanning upward with his light every few feet.

If we couldn't find an alternate escape hatch, we'd have to return to the upper cavern. This was starting to feel like a twisted version of *Groundhog Day* where we started over a gazillion times. I tried to remember how the movie had ended, but couldn't.

It was a bad sign I couldn't connect the dots. Was my head injury creating internal problems like bleeding or intracranial pressure from cerebrospinal fluid leakage? Issues that would slowly worsen until they killed me?

I squeezed my hands together, willing the pressure, palm against palm, to calm me. If I hadn't been a doctor, I'd never have had any idea about maladies like Talk and Die Syndrome.

Well, maybe I'd have known about that one since

someone famous had died from it, but I definitely would not have known about the cavalcade of possible disasters lying in wait if my central nervous system failed. So many complex parts. A whole lot could go wrong.

Yeah. Easier to think about medical shit than eating corpses.

I ground my teeth, shamed by my thoughts. I had to stake a claim to the dispassionate place I lived when I stood in the OR for ten hours performing an intricate surgery. I'd been a master at not getting too far ahead of the curve, of focusing on the problem in front of me, of pivoting on a dime if something went south. I'd always prided myself on my flexibility. My unflappability.

What the hell had happened to that woman? I needed her back. Her absence wasn't acceptable.

"Erin!"

Johan's summons rocked me out of the funk I'd fallen into, and I jumped to my feet. "Yes. Did you find something?"

"Maybe. It's not quite big enough. Help me dig it out." Scraping noises followed his words.

He stood on the far side of the space, maybe twenty feet away. I took the most direct route, not bothering with following the curved walls. The ground was uneven enough, I flicked on my light, angling it to illuminate the bumps ahead of me.

One spot looked funny, concave where everything else was more-or-less level. I didn't understand why, but I picked up a rock and chucked it at the center of the dip. The ground shuddered, and the rock vanished, accompanied by two or three of the same musical notes I'd heard earlier.

I didn't want to disturb Johan. Not yet, anyway. I looked around for a stick. Of course I didn't find anything nearly that convenient. Then I remembered the rifle. Johan had left it back where we'd been sitting. I retraced my steps and picked it up. The weapon felt heavy and alien in my hands, but I schlepped it back to the spot I wanted to test.

"What is keeping you?" Johan called.

"I may have found something. Be there in a flash."

"What kind of something?"

"Not sure. Hold on." I crouched as close to the odd place as I could, making certain my boots were on solid ground. I remembered how the rock had vanished, so I wrapped one arm around a conveniently placed good-sized boulder and poked the center of the declination with the rifle's barrel.

Something sucked hard on the gun. Hard enough, it took all my strength to yank it back into the cave. I knelt there, panting.

"What are you doing?" Johan joined me. He picked up a rock and tossed it into the same spot that had tried to seize the gun. Naturally, it vanished. "Well, well." He swayed back on his heels and cast an appraising glance at the concave spot. "I did not hear the rock hit bottom. Did you discover Alice's secret path into Wonderland?"

I dropped my head into my hands and rubbed my aching temples, wishing I'd had the foresight to bring my medical bag, the one I kept packed and ready despite not being the ship's official doctor. Right about now, I'd sell my soul for aspirin, or Tylenol or ibuprofen.

My mind was wandering. Badly. I'd been unconscious

when they carried me off the *Darya*. No way to bring anything, much less medical supplies. Meanwhile, Johan reached around me and grabbed the rifle, repeating my experiment. Without any instructions from me, he instinctively hung onto a convenient rock with his other hand.

"Definitely a gateway of some kind," he muttered.

"Huh?" I raised my head and gazed at him bleary-eyed.

He offered me a sheepish expression. "Reading science fiction is one of my secret vices. Granted, things get wonky this near the southern pole, but the magnetic pull of that place"—he pointed, and I noticed he'd removed his heavy mitts—"suggests an electrical imbalance between where we are and wherever that leads. It isn't natural, so I suspect someone constructed it to discourage entry."

"Entry to where?"

"I have no idea. Want to spend a little time seeing if the gap in the wall leads anywhere? This vortex is not going away. We can always jump through it."

"Into what?" My voice emerged as a croak, and I waved a hand his way. "Never mind. I'm not expecting you to know."

"You are trained as a scientist. What do you think it is?"

In truth, I hadn't gotten that far. Nowhere close. "I don't know. Maybe a black hole, except aren't they formed by dying stars?"

He nodded. "They are, but it is not a quantum leap that a meteor may have plowed into Earth in this area and formed the same type of electron trap a dying star would make."

"You did some kind of study of this site, didn't you?"

"Yes. And this place where we are did not show up. My graphing equipment displayed a solid layer of earth extending a long way down. Until you reach a string of subterranean lakes."

"How far underground were they?"

"Nearly four kilometers."

I did a quick conversion and came up with roughly two-and-a-half miles. His off-the-cuff comparison to Wonderland stuck in my head. It seemed we weren't that far beneath Antarctica's surface, but nothing else down here acted like I thought it should.

I sure as hell hadn't climbed more than a hundred feet to exit this cave, but the cave could have moved for all I knew.

I got to my feet and gestured toward where he'd been standing. "Let's exhaust the spot you found, first. Maybe we'll stumble across something."

"And if we do not?" He raised one dark brow.

"We'll talk about it then."

He pushed upright and followed me across to the space he'd been widening between two large boulders. If I turned sideways, it was close. Another couple of inches, and I'd be able to squeeze through. For the next span of time, we worked in silence. Dirt fell into the hole nearly as fast as we removed it, so we didn't make rapid progress.

Bending forward, I scanned the far side of our excavation, reaching my light as far as I could. Darkness bounced back. No reflections off anything, almost as if something was sucking the energy out of my LEDs and giving nothing back. No crystals in whatever lay through the narrow spot. Apparently, nothing else, either. I unzipped my suit and opened the panels beneath the arms and across my thighs. It didn't help very much. I was still overheated.

"It should not be this warm," Johan commented.

"Same thing I thought the first time I ended up here." I pushed one shoulder through the space we were working on and wriggled it. "There. I can fit. Stop digging so nothing falls and traps me in there."

"I can do better than that. Once you step through, I will stand in the space and ensure it remains open."

I could have hugged him, but if I hesitated I might lose my nerve. I wished for the rope to tether myself to him. As weird as this place was, who knew where I'd end up once I left the crystal-lined cave. With my heart beating faster than it should and my mouth dry as a desert, I flipped on my flashlight. After waving it about like a madwoman trying to spin gold out of dross, I'd turned it off since Johan's provided enough light to see by.

The back of my insulated suit caught on something, but Johan freed it, and I stepped into the unknown. Part of me expected there not to be a floor, but there was, and it was the same level as it should be. Crouching, I shone the light in a semi-circle. Rocks dotted the ground. If there were walls— and there pretty much had to be—they sat well beyond the beam of my high-powered flashlight.

Except I already knew that. Why had I expected anything would change?

Because there should be a wall. My inner voice was implacable. *The one shared by the crystal cave,* it added in case

I was confused. I turned until I faced Johan. He was almost close enough to touch. Aiming my light beyond his form yielded blackness. The wall that had to be there wasn't.

I spun back around before I turned into a blithering ninny. Staring hard at the ground, I took a few tentative steps. I wanted to make damn good and sure I didn't miss one of those concave places and vanish into God knows where.

"Angle either right or left," Johan suggested.

It was good advice, so I did, counting steps as I went. Quick glances behind me showed Johan illuminated by his flashlight. I didn't want to put any more distance between us, but I kept going, anyway. Something about this darkness bothered me. It didn't feel as safe as the cave I'd left behind.

When the fine hairs on the back of my neck twitched, I took a deep breath and told myself to get a grip. I was fifty paces from where I'd entered this place with no end in sight. No walls. Just the rock-strewn ground. Something about the rocks bothered me, so I stopped long enough to kneel and examine them. Rather than a mixed bag, like normal rocks, these were all roughly the same size. And they were rounded, almost as if someone had filed them or put them through a machine like the polisher rock hounds use to smooth agates.

Seventy-five steps. Still nothing.

A single musical note reverberated around me. Maybe I'd imagined it, but that goddamned music had presaged my initial fall, and the death of the Russian and maybe our second descent as well. I couldn't remember.

I tried to keep moving. Truly I did, but I could not force myself to travel one inch beyond where I stood. Sweat gathered across my back and breasts and dripped down my body. I played the beam of my light around me, but I may as well have been in the bottom of a vast black pit.

Another note blatted against my ears. This one held a menacing aspect, but maybe I'd imagined it. The next noise wasn't musical. It was a roar from no animal I'd ever heard before. Guttural and threatening, it sent me scuttling back toward Johan and his light. Puffing and panting and trying my damnedest not to scream, I wasn't watching my feet. I hit one of the perfectly shaped rocks and fought to not sprawl face first onto the dirt.

The enraged animal roar died out replaced by Johan. "Take your time, Erin. Do not panic."

Easy for him to say. I reined in bitterness and aggravation. I was in full-blown fight-or-flight mode and embarrassed to be caught out. My forehead joined the sweating party, and I wiped it on a shoulder. Forcing myself to follow the path my light illuminated, I covered the remaining distance. Once I got close, I noticed dirt had fallen on Johan's head. He appeared to be cemented into the opening by clods of earth.

Before I could say anything, he extended a hand. "Grab onto me. On my count of three, we will combine our strength and push back into the place we started."

I gripped his hand. It was warm and dry next to my cold, clammy one. "Ready." My voice shook.

"Erin. We will not get a second chance. Butt your body up against mine to give you leverage."

I didn't ask how he knew about no second chances. At least the fucking music had stopped, but I expected a pissed-off dinosaur to come blasting out of the darkness, triple rows of teeth bared in rage.

"Ready," I said again, trying my damnedest to project confidence I'd be the partner he needed, not deadweight.

"One. Two. Three." He jerked the two of us so hard my shoulder popped.

I did my part and threw my entire weight after his. We fell in a heap on the floor of the crystal cave. Dirt rained around us as the hole we'd worked so hard on slammed shut as surely as if it had been a door.

I untangled myself and sat, rubbing my shoulder.

"Did you see anything at all?" Johan asked.

"Yeah. All the rocks were the same size."

"You only thought they were."

I grabbed his arm. "No. They were uniform in size. It bothered me, so I got close enough to examine a bunch of them, but that doesn't matter. Did you recognize that screech?"

"No."

"This will sound paranoid"—I floundered for words —"but something didn't want me in there."

"Same conclusion I came to."

If a mule had kicked me in the chest, I wouldn't have been more surprised. "Why aren't you telling me I'm full of shit?"

"Because, the farther you went from me, the more dirt fell. I was worried about being trapped, but if I moved, you would never have found your way back."

"Why didn't you say something?"

"If it had gotten any worse, I would have." He patted the hand I still had curled around his forearm. "Only one thing left to do."

A shudder racked me. "No. I don't want to jump into that thing."

"We do not have any other choices. Something does not want us to leave this place." His voice was neutral, but steel sat behind it. In the face of his determination and courage, how could I act like a mewling wimp?

"We could try to climb out." I neglected tacking *again* onto the end of my sentence.

"Before the explosion, we might have. Even if we made the upper chamber, despite having food, we would still be stuck."

The bomb. I hadn't exactly forgotten about it, but neither had it been in the forefront of my mind.

"Okay. I guess it's not something where one of us can go and look around and report back."

"No, it is not." He pulled a water bottle out of his suit and took a long drink, swiping the back of his hand across his mouth. "The vortex may not be as big a longshot as all that. Something appears to want us to remain alive."

"It sure as fuck didn't feel that way when I was over there." I waved a hand at the spot we'd clawed our way out of. The opening we'd widened had been obliterated, filled in with rocks and dirt.

"Maybe not." Johan got to his feet and offered me a hand up. "The dirt could have crushed me, yet it stopped short. Whatever that beast was could have shown itself."

"None of this is making me feel better." I followed him to the edge of the concave spot and tossed one more rock into it, checking. The stone vanished just like the other two had.

"Put your arms around me, Erin."

"Why?"

"This is not an ill-timed seduction scheme. We must not get separated. If this is a magnetic anomaly or a type of black hole, I want us to come out the other side still together."

I suspected the vortex was as likely to rip flesh from bones as to deliver us safely anywhere, but I kept my mouth shut and put my arms around him. He held me tight. So tight, I felt the thud of his heart against my ear.

"Here we go," he said and jumped dead into the center of the declination.

Golden light shimmered around us, and the music blared. Not single notes but a barrage of discordant pitches where each bit of sound battled its companions for ascendency.

I clung to Johan, and we plummeted downward. Too late, I realized we'd left the guns behind.

CHAPTER 5

Konstantin's shift didn't happen as quickly as he would have liked. Probably because he was in a hurry—and had expended more magic than he'd used in a while killing the Russians. Finally fully human, he teleported into the heart of the lair he and Katya had carved out for themselves.

After the other dragon shifters left, he and his sister had made many changes. Since there were only two of them, and magic wasn't limitless, they'd altered many of their systems to be self-sustaining. The last of the seedlings had withered to dust many seasons ago, so they no longer expended any effort growing things. He missed vegetables, but there wasn't much he could do about it.

Other than relocating to a more commodious climate. Somewhere amenable to growing crops.

He and Katya had discussed importing seeds and

starting over, but he feared the same fate would meet new crops too. Something about the soil didn't lend itself to farming. It was probably far too alkaline, but he'd never tested his theory. Instead of fancy lab equipment—although he could have snuck inside one of the research bases that had sprouted across Antarctica like cancerous growths—he trusted his dragon senses.

The fact that all light had to be created by judicious use of magic and reflection probably didn't help the crop situation. Living underground wasn't ideal. Not for dragons. Not for crops. Probably not for much of anything beyond the blind fish that populated the eerily beautiful subterranean lakes.

The grand hall where he'd left Katya rose around him, and he splayed his toes across the marble flooring. It was always pleasantly warm from its proximity to the earth's crust.

Katya raced to his side. "You were gone for a long time. What happened? Did you kill anyone? Did anybody see you? Did—?"

"Stop! First off, why did you say my return wasn't a moment too soon?"

She raked curved fingers through her coppery hair. "Because those humans are more trouble than they're worth. First, they tried to dig their way out of the crystal cave."

"So what? Nowhere they can go."

"Of course, there is." Katya pursed her full lips into a grim line. "One of them—the woman—made it into a side channel. If she'd followed it, she'd have come out in the middle of Level A."

"I'm still not seeing the problem." When there had been a full complement of dragons here, they'd divided the land into six levels with roughly eight dragons assigned to develop each one. They'd built dwellings and cleared fields near enough to the freshwater lakes to simplify irrigation.

Katya shot an irritated look his way. "The human would have found an empty house, and shed. She would have seen the last batch of dead crops and known someone used to live there."

"But we planned to reveal ourselves to them, anyway."

Fire puffed from her mouth. She didn't appreciate being corrected. "Planned to reveal limited aspects," she growled. "Not our entire history. Not until we were certain they would embrace our offer to become like us."

He eyed his sister. If she was panicking about discovery, it was probably a good thing to get his confession under way. "I did not employ stealth after I left. Enough humans saw me to shit themselves. Rumors of dragons will come to life again."

Katya grabbed his arm. "Damn it, Konstantin. We're supposed to remain hidden."

"Yes, well, that was before humans set the wheels in motion to destroy Earth. We live forever. They do not. If seeing me breathes new life into the superstitions that kept humans from mowing through resources as if they were limitless, I did a good and decent—"

"I'm not seeing the relationship between the two," she broke in.

He tried to come up with a snappy retort, but couldn't, mostly because he was making excuses for doing something he'd wanted to do for a long time. Dragon shifters were a proud race, not accustomed to skulking in shadows.

He uncurled her fingers from his arm. "The woman. Did she get to Level A?"

"No. I scared her. Made her run back to the man."

Alarm seared him, and he realized he'd already begun to view Miss No Name as potential mate material. "What did you do?"

"Used my dragon voice. And made certain the man almost got stuck in the opening they hollowed out."

He frowned. "I thought your dragon left."

"She did, but I can still bugle with the best of them." Opening her mouth, she blasted sound all around them.

He bugled back. "If you can still do that," he told his sister, "your dragon can't be buried too deep."

"Do you really believe so?" Her golden eyes sheened with hope.

Konstantin nodded. "How long ago did you chase the humans back to the cave? Have you checked on them since?"

"Not long, and no." She hesitated. "How is it I answer your questions, but you walk around mine?"

"Fair enough. I killed two men. The third one believed in us, so I let him go." Smoke billowed from his mouth and nose."

"There is more," Katya prodded.

Her mirror may have dulled, but his sister's sixth sense about when something had been left out was as acute as ever. Konstantin nodded. "I feared the man's compatriots would accuse him of killing the other three, and—"

"I thought you said two."

"I am also counting the one in the cavern who met his fate first."

"All right. I'd forgotten about him. Go on."

"I may have given the believer a ride back to his boat."

Katya screeched long and shrill, obliterating the last of his words. "You took a human onto your back? What in the Nine Hells is wrong with you?"

"There is nothing wrong with me," Konstantin said stiffly. "I wished to ensure his safety, and so I returned him to his people in such a way his tale of a dragon killing the others would be credible."

Katya rolled her expressive eyes; steam and smoke huffed through her nose and mouth. "I suppose you were so hungry for evidence we've not been forgotten, you took his story on faith."

"I most certainly did not." Anger tightened his belly, and a flame or two shot from his mouth. "I tested his words. He had a grandmother, no a great-grandmother, who had actually seen one of us."

"Pfft."

"Do you accuse me of lying, Sister?" In all their time together, they'd never had a serious disagreement. It appeared that was about to change. Konstantin planted himself right in front of Katya.

"No." The word held a sullen note. "Merely of not looking too deeply when something that pleases you surfaces."

"I was already in a good mood before the man, who acted differently from the other two, told me about his great-grandmother. Days when I rid the earth of bad men are always grand days."

The tension that had been sitting between them like an overstretched bowstring broke, and Katya smiled indulgently. "Some men need killing."

"These certainly do. Anyway, the ship had launched another raft, and I dropped my passenger squarely into it."

"They must have shot at you."

He shrugged. "For all the good it—"

Her pleasant expression darkened, and she pounded a palm with the other fist. "Damn it all to hell."

Goddess be damned, indeed. One of many magical markers he'd set to warn them if their borders were breached blared as surely as any alarm would have. The fucking humans must have steel balls. They'd jumped through a trap door, one-way gates constructed to ensure once someone was snared they'd never find their way back out.

Surely, they'd tested the odd-looking spot and knew it held a gravitational pull. His dragon wanted out, but he kept it contained. Plenty of room for it in this grand chamber with twenty-foot ceilings, but it was in a rowdy mood. The deaths they'd meted out fed a primitive part of the beast, and preserving the upper hand might prove difficult.

Smoky flames poured from his mouth. The dragon was not pleased, but its ire reinforced Konstantin's decision.

However it happened, he intended to talk with the humans. That task would be far harder if most of his mental strength was diverted to ensure the dragon didn't slip its bonds.

"They're almost here." Katya's voice was tense, and she balanced magic, arcing it back and forth between her raised hands.

"They cannot hurt us," he reminded her. "Sheathe your power. It will only make them nervous because they won't understand its source."

"I know, but they have guns, and this could get...unpleasant."

"Our job is to ensure it remains cordial."

The notes—music was part of many of his castings—grew louder and more discordant. Konstantin stood next to his sister, watchful but relaxed. He was more curious about this duo than anything else. How was it they'd survived where so many of their companions were dead?

Light splashed across the far end of the chamber, first golden and then a clear blue-white. When it cleared, the humans faced at right angles away from him and Katya, clutched in one another's arms and breathing hard.

Konstantin added a touch of a don't-look-here spell because he wanted these moments—before they noticed him and Katya—to study them.

"Do you think this is the bottom?" the woman asked. Her

voice was low and melodic, but a catch in it betrayed her nervousness.

"Yes. Or we would still be falling." The man let go of what looked like a death grip on the woman. He wore thick, black winter clothing. Clearly a lot of layers from how bulky his garments were. His hood was thrown back displaying longish black hair, a gaunt face with a square chin and high forehead, and shrewd, blue eyes. Black stubble dotted his cheeks. Konstantin felt certain not much got past those eyes.

The woman groaned and shook out her arms once she'd let go of the man. Dressed similarly to him, her hair was as fair as his was dark. It vanished down her back inside her clothing, so it was impossible to tell how long it was. Her eyes were a clear, pale blue and her facial features matched her Norse coloring with high cheekbones and a well-formed chin.

Both of the humans wore clunky green boots that were probably constructed of dual or triple layers of neoprene.

Next to him, Katya stiffened. Konstantin didn't understand what it was about two puny humans that would frighten her, but she was definitely uncomfortable. He decided to push things along, so he brushed his spell aside and stepped forward. "Welcome. This is not how I envisioned meeting you, but—"

Both the man and woman squawked and twisted to face him. "Who are you?" the man demanded.

"You're naked," the woman yelped. "How is that even possible?"

Konstantin eyed them, keeping his temper in check. He'd

expected gratitude, relief, or at a minimum, mumbled thanks. "Have manners fallen out of fashion among your kind? This is my house. How I clothe myself is my choice. Your job is to introduce yourself. Once I hear your names, I shall decide if I wish to offer mine."

The man growled something unintelligible.

The woman inclined her head, and said, "I've got this." She took a step toward him and Katya and pushed her shoulders back, facing them squarely. "My name is Erin Ryan. My companion is Johan Petris. We were part of an Antarctic research project. My task was assessing the effect of extreme cold on the human body."

"You said were," Katya commented. "Not are."

The man, Johan, moved to Erin's side. "Physiology was Erin—Dr. Ryan's—job. The rest of us were mapping precious metal deposits. Mapping, not mining."

"The Russians took matters into their own hands," Erin said, "and decided to cash in on our efforts since we'd already done the spade work."

Johan nodded. "You can guess the rest. They boarded our boat, killed the dissenters immediately, and stuffed the rest of us in what used to be our chromium dig site just up there." He pointed.

"How is it the two of you survived?" Konstantin asked.

"They knocked me over the head and assumed the blow would kill me," Erin replied. "It damn near did."

"They broke my leg," Johan said. "Erin patched me up, but somehow, the bone fixed itself in record time."

"The other reason we didn't die of exposure is we were

both suited up for winter." Erin patted the chest of her thick black outer garment. She narrowed her eyes. "It's warm in here, but not that warm. How can you get by without clothes?"

"I ask the questions," Konstantin said firmly.

"We answered yours," Johan pointed out.

"You will be offered information in due time," Konstantin muttered. His dragon was kicking up chaos. Muffling fire that wanted out singed his throat and mouth.

"Drop the sparring match." Erin's words tangled with the tail end of his comment. "Can either of you help us get out of here?"

"We could, but such is not our intention," Konstantin replied. Before they could react, he added, "I am Konstantin. This is Katya, my twin sister."

Despite offering his name, just as the man had requested, it didn't appear to mollify him. "Do you plan to hold us against our will?" Johan asked in a deceptively smooth voice.

"Harsh words," Katya murmured.

"Forcing us to remain where we do not want to be is also harsh," Erin said. She unzipped her suit a few inches and drew her hair out from beneath it. One long braid hit her at ass level. After blowing out a breath, she spread her hands in front of her. "Look. We've been through hell. God knows what happened to the *Darya*, and—"

"What's that?" Katya asked.

"Sorry. Our ship," Erin replied. "Our best bet would be to

go to the Polish research station, but it's a little way from here on King George Island in the South Shetlands."

"Why that one?" Konstantin asked.

"It's manned year round, and we have friends there," Johan answered.

It annoyed Konstantin. He'd asked the woman, not Johan. Yet rebuking him a second time for a lack of manners would scarcely endear him to the man.

He scanned their visitors with what he hoped was a subtle shot of magic. Both of them were nervous, the woman more than the man, yet she didn't allow her trepidation to bleed through. Good for her.

"What would this Polish base do for you?" he pressed, still seeking information about how their world worked.

"Several things," Erin replied. "First, they would alert the authorities about our ship. Our research firm probably knows it's missing by now, and they will do whatever is required to get it back."

"Beyond that, our friends will see we have transport home," Johan added.

"So this ship, it is not your permanent residence?" Katya raised a copper brow.

"Oh my goodness no." Erin smiled. It lit her face, made her eyes glow a deeper blue, and dropped a decade off the worry that had stamped itself into her features. "I'm a doctor, actually a surgeon. I live outside Seattle."

"Is this a holiday for you?" Konstantin asked, still not quite understanding how she'd ended up in the Southern Ocean.

"Kind of. I was sick of a whole lot of things, and so I took a leave of absence. My practice partners were great—for once. I'll return to my office and my other life after I'm home."

"And you?" Katya turned her burnished gaze on Johan.

He did a doubletake, nearly stumbling. "Your eyes. They are gold. What are you? Human eyes do not come in that shade."

"I told you, I ask the questions," Konstantin cut in. He masked a smile. No one had noticed his eyes, but Johan was interested enough in Katya to be observant. It might bode well.

"Fine," Johan snarled and turned to Erin. "Do not say another word until we figure this out."

"I'm not sure it's the best way to proceed—" she began, but he chopped a hand in front of her face.

"They are dredging for information. I have no idea why or what they will do with whatever we tell them. If you look from this angle"—he tilted his head—"their bodies are glowing."

"It has to be a trick of the light," Erin murmured.

"I do not believe so. They are naked, yet not shivering. Both of them have golden eyes with green centers. Have you ever seen a human with—?"

Erin flapped her hands his way. "Stop. Fine. So they're not human. They're out best bet—our only bet—of getting out of here."

Konstantin considered lauding her for common sense, but it might be better to keep his mouth shut. Where would these two humans go next? Clearly bright and resourceful, they would probably try to bargain with him—except they had nothing he wanted that didn't include their continued presence.

Erin crossed her arms beneath her breasts and regarded him and Katya. "Us being here isn't accidental, is it?"

"Yes and no," Katya replied.

"You couldn't have anticipated our presence at the chromium dig site," Erin went on, "but once you realized we were there, you decided to shanghai us. Am I close?"

"What does shanghai mean?" Katya asked.

"Kidnap." Johan bit off the word. "It is when—"

"I know that word." Katya cut him off, looking hurt by his assumption she was stupid simply because she lacked a single word in English. His sister spoke hundreds of languages. Konstantin bet the human man only knew a handful.

"Let's not get sidetracked," Erin spoke up. "Since you sensed us, or however you figured out we were up there, you've been pulling puppet strings."

The implication rankled enough, Konstantin's next words lurched past the protection of his throat. "You overreach. I have been occupied killing the men who *shanghaied* you from your boat. The *Darya*, wasn't it?" He stressed the word shanghaied to pound home the point he understood its meaning.

Erin's eyes rounded, but she held her ground. "The dead Russian up there"—she jabbed an index finger at the ceiling

—"was your doing? How the hell could you murder him if you weren't in the upper cavern?"

"I told you." Johan smirked. "These two, they are not human. God knows what they can do." He staged half a bow. "Thank you for killing however many you did away with. Those men were a scourge. Death was too good for them."

"And that is one place you and I are in agreement," Konstantin said and rocked back on the balls of his feet. His dragon was delighted by the compliment, and a bit of smoke escaped through his nose.

Johan nudged Erin and jerked his chin toward the smoke spiraling above Konstantin's head. She shrugged and muttered, "I already told you, I don't give a shit what they are."

"What happens next?" Johan asked unfastening parts of his winter clothing, presumably because he was hot.

"You will remain with us," Katya said.

"Get to know us," Konstantin added.

"While we appreciate the honor of you wanting our company," Erin said, "we respectfully decline."

Johan shot her a side-eyed look that clearly said he disagreed with her approach. He set his mouth in a tight line. "If we are your prisoners, we have certain rights."

"You are our guests." Katya added a calming spell to her words.

"Bullshit." Johan looked as approachable as a cornered hyena. "Guests are free to come and go as they please."

"You will show respect toward my sister." Konstantin strode close to Johan.

"It's not a good idea to antagonize them," Erin told Johan.

"Groveling is not doing us much good, either," he shot back.

"I wasn't groveling. I was making a good faith effort to be polite."

"Yes, well, regardless, it did not work. We are still their *prisoners*"—he stressed the word, breaking it into syllables —"and as such we are entitled to—"

"You are entitled to nothing," Konstantin roared. He was sick of riding herd on his dragon. Fire spewed from his mouth. "You are fortunate to be alive. I"—he turned the full force of his hypnotic gaze on them and amped up the juice —"killed several of your problems. Have you thanked me?"

"Yes. I did," Johan reminded him. "What can you do besides produce fire?"

"Who cares?" Erin screeched at him. "Fuck your scientific objectivity. We have to get out of here. Before they turn us into dinner—or whatever they had in mind when they dragged us here."

Konstantin's dragon pushed hard against their bond. He wanted to show the woman his glory. Prove to her she was wrong, that dragons did not eat humans—unless the human in question was unworthy and the only food source available.

Katya joined him, staring at the humans with blood in her eyes. "We saved your pathetic lives. Perhaps some time alone will improve your attitude. Come, Brother." She hooked a hand beneath his arm.

He shook her off. He was all for putting some space

between himself and the arrogant humans, but first, he'd give them grist for the mill. He loosed his hold on his beast and it burst forth, altering form faster than he expected.

Katya's approving laughter as she teleported out of the grand hall warmed him. Predictably, both humans cowered in the face of eight feet of black-scaled magnificence. He shot fire upward in great gouts and bugled menacingly before he teleported out of the chamber, following his sister.

Ha! Let Erin and Johan wrap their feeble minds around magic and dragons and other things neither of them believed existed. Next time he and Katya showed up, the humans would bow to them. Kiss their toes. Be cognizant of the honor bestowed upon them.

Very few humans had ever been rescued by dragon shifters.

Damn few.

In truth, he couldn't think of any.

He materialized on the same spit of land where he'd shifted last time. Katya waited for him. "Give me a ride," she demanded. "Perhaps it will present my beast with ideas."

"More likely, your dragon will be outraged you've chosen to ride on another. It might be just the thing to draw it back to your control. Hop on, Sister. Let us determine if the ship I saw earlier has left yet."

CHAPTER 6

Smoke stung my eyes and lungs as I stared at where the dragon had stood. Christ on a fucking crutch. A dragon. It had to have been real. It was breathing fire. No number of props could mimic a display like that. Speaking of breathing, I was having a hell of a hard time talking my lungs into cooperating. They'd forgotten what they were designed to do.

Move air into my body so the rest of it didn't die.

Johan was muttering in Dutch. I started to tell him to switch to English, but what difference did language make in the face of what I'd just seen? A thought slammed into me so hard, I doubled over.

Maybe I was dead. That had to be it. My head injury had killed me, and everything else was random neurons firing, making me think I was still here. It didn't exactly explain Johan, but he could be dead too. When he'd done all that

89

work sliding across the rough dirt floor and dropping a flashlight down to where I'd fallen the first time, he must have torn his leg up again. It had bled, and he was gone right along with me.

It didn't exactly explain how I'd crawled out of the pit. Or the rope. Or Johan moving around, walking on the broken leg, but I might have dreamed the whole thing.

Breath whooshed out of me, the cadence I'd tried so hard to maintain forgotten. I didn't need to breathe. Not anymore, so I stopped paying attention to forcing air into my lungs. Maybe my central nervous system could get on with dying, and I wouldn't be presented with impossibilities like dragons or glowing naked humanoids who puffed smoke and fire.

Arms wrapped around me from behind. I was so shocked, I shrieked.

"Erin. Get hold of yourself. We need to strategize." Johan spoke sternly. "We must assume they can hear everything we say."

I twisted in his grip. "But we're dead," I protested. "We have to be. It's the only explanation."

He grabbed my chin in one hand hard enough to hurt and made me look at him. "We are not dead."

"Yeah. Go on. Keep telling yourself that." I tried to pull out of his grasp, but he held tight. "Jesus, Johan, you're hurting me."

"That, Madame Doctor, is far from the worst of our problems. For one thing, it proves you are very much alive. I need you. All of you. Front and center and thinking." After a final squeeze, he let go.

I rubbed my jaw a little gingerly. "I liked my explanation fine. What's yours?"

"I read a lot of science fiction. Fantasy too. I have for a long time."

"I suppose you're going to tell me your stories have come to life?" I didn't bother tempering my sarcasm.

"Hear me out before you mock me."

Shame ran hot. On the off chance we weren't dead—and I still wasn't totally convinced about that—we were in this together. I nodded mutely.

"Good woman. All right. Similar to the topic of alien visitation, enough common threads exist in speculative fiction, I always suspected someone had run across humans who took animal forms and vampires and witches and faeries."

"Why stop there?" I clapped a hand over my mouth. "Sorry."

He looked askance at me. "Many, many humans have detailed alien abductions where they were taken into ships or to other worlds. All of them could not have been mentally ill."

"Why not?" Damn it. I couldn't seem to keep my mouth shut. Apparently, my lungs were working fine even absent me riding herd on them.

"Because there are too many of them. I have read Carl Jung's theories about a collective unconscious that gives us common memories, but when hundreds of people from every culture imaginable all recount similar incidents, there must be something to them."

Sweat poured down my body. I dragged my arms out of the sleeves of my suit and unzipped the layers beneath it. Johan swiped a finger across my forehead. "The dead do not sweat."

"Yeah. All right. So we're not dead. It was easier when I thought we were."

"Only because it excused you from doing anything beyond standing here." His tone was implacable, and I wanted to punch him.

"What do you think Konstantin and Katya are?"

"Dragon shifters. At least he is since he showed us. She is his twin sister. Presumably, she has similar abilities."

Most of my pleasure reading was romance novels, but I'd be damned if I'd admit it. "What do you know about shapeshifters?"

"Obviously, they came from somewhere other than Earth. I have no idea why they're here, how long they've been here, or what they want with us."

"I figured they saw us as food," I mumbled.

"You are not thinking. Antarctica has plentiful fish and bird populations. Penguins taste better than we do."

"And you know this, how?"

Johan grinned crookedly. "I have eaten penguin. Never humans, though, but I suspect we'd be tough."

Jonathan Swift's *A Modest Proposal*, where he tongue-in-cheek suggested the Irish eat children, danced through my mind. I shut it down fast. "Let's take a walk and see if there's a way out of here."

"I was about to suggest the same thing. Do not get your

hopes up, but we can familiarize ourselves with what we have to work with."

"We fell a long way through that vortex thing, huh?"

Johan nodded. "I was working on calculating our rate of descent, and I believe we are three or four kilometers lower than we were."

"No wonder it's so warm."

"But not warm enough for them to be naked." He didn't have to clarify whom he was talking about. "It was my first clue they had to be something other than human." He copied my actions and slipped his arms out of the sleeves of his suit. "Come on."

We walked the length of the large room with high, rounded ceilings. No wonder it was so big if it had to accommodate dragons. Now that my hood wasn't in the way, I reached up with one hand and palpated the lump at the base of my skull. Dried blood had pooled beneath it, but it wasn't particularly tender to touch, nor was it as big as I'd imagined.

Perhaps it had gone down in the days since it happened. More evidence I was alive, although I'd reluctantly abandoned my death theory in the face of all the evidence to the contrary.

We passed impressive multifaceted crystals and what might have been veins of gold and silver threaded through the walls. Was there even an "outside" here. "I understand we're underground," I began, not quite sure how to phrase the question in my mind.

"*Ja*, that explains the minerals in the walls. This chamber was hollowed out of rich ore veins, probably because dragons value gold, silver, and gemstones. Hey! I see stairs ahead."

The idea of miles of dirt above me, pressing in on me, made me claustrophobic, but I'd felt that way the first few days aboard the *Darya* too. Obviously, not because of dirt but because the ship was small and the ocean impossibly big. We trotted up two flights of stairs. The next level up held what looked like a kitchen with a table, twenty chairs, and a stone countertop constructed in a U-shape along three walls.

"There must be more, erm, dragons." I pointed at all the chairs.

"It would appear so, but where are their food stocks?" Johan strode the length of the room pulling mostly empty cupboards and drawers open.

"Why would they need them? Can't they turn into dragons and kill whatever they need to sustain themselves?" I winced, not believing I was speculating about the culinary habits of dragon shifters.

Just like the level below, ore ran through the walls. Bright and shiny, it almost made up for the lack of windows. I had no idea where what appeared to be daylight was coming from. I hadn't seen any lamps, yet both the lower level and this one were illuminated by some cunning means.

"All this light. Where's it coming from?"

Johan unclipped his flashlight and played it over a wall. The surface sparkled. "Bioluminescence? Something in the walls both produces and reflects light. My guess is it's some type of lifeform."

I understood bioluminescence conceptually, but even single-celled organisms with reflective capability required an external light source. Absent one, there'd be nothing for them to mirror. Arguing was pointless. I didn't know enough, and neither did Johan.

One of the core differences between the sexes was I'd be far more willing to admit my ignorance.

He left the kitchen and mounted the next flights of steps. Our second stop was a level that looked to have sleeping spaces. Several rooms opened off a central hall with skylights, suggesting we were close to a subterranean surface of some kind. Each room had a generous pallet spread across the floor. No blankets, but the dragons probably didn't need anything to keep them warm.

Wooden chests lined the walls in two of the rooms. When Johan knelt and opened one, it was full of archaic clothing. He turned to me and held up a fur-trimmed tunic. "This suggests they leave here occasionally."

"And that they know they need to be dressed to escape unwanted attention."

I felt weird snooping through the dragons' home, so I hustled back to the stairs. The next flight stopped abruptly in front of a double stone door. I expected it would be locked, but when I pushed on it, it opened easily, swinging outward on silent hinges. I had no idea what I thought I'd find. Surely not blue skies, yet what hung above me certainly looked like sky, but in a pale violet shade.

Grayish dirt spread in every direction, interrupted by occasional rocks and boulders. In the distance, the blue-green waters of a lake sparkled. I still couldn't figure out where light was coming from. We were too far underground for the sun to penetrate, yet a dim, cozy purple glow surrounded us.

It was how I've always imagined a back-to-the-womb experience would be.

Johan burst through the door and hustled to my side. "Wow!" A long, low whistle escaped him. "I want to take a look at that lake. I am sure I mapped it, and once we are closer, I might know more or less where we are."

We walked as fast as our clunky polar boots would allow, but the lake was farther away than it appeared. I was soaked to the skin from sweat by the time we got to it. Kneeling, I pulled off my gloves and tested the water with a couple of fingers. "It's warm."

"Of course. Everything down here is. It is also freshwater. Go ahead, lick your fingers."

I did, not because I doubted him, but because I was curious. "Do you suppose it's safe to swim in?"

He nodded. "I was considering the same thing, except I do not particularly want to be naked when our hosts return. And they will return. Look over there." He jerked his chin to our right.

"What am I supposed to be looking at?"

"It used to be a tilled field, but the crops died a long time ago. If this were on the surface, the evidence would have been obliterated by wind and weather, but those are not a consideration here."

I crouched by the water's edge, still trailing one hand in

the tepid lake. "I understand how anything subterranean is protected from weather, but how is it we can see? Your bioluminescent theory has holes in it. Big ones. Where is the light coming from? Did you figure out where we are?"

"*Ja*, we are roughly under Brown's Point—a few degrees offset to the southeast. This is one of hundreds of lakes down here, but it is one of the larger ones. In terms of the illumination, I do not know. You might want to ask our hosts."

"You mean our jailers." I rolled back onto my butt. "Why did they drag us down here?"

Johan sat next to me. Rather than answering, he asked, "Do you have a working theory?"

"No, but the music seems related to them. It blasted me before I fell the first time, so I suspect they didn't want me to leave the chromium dig."

"Interesting. You did not mention that."

"Yes, I did."

"Perhaps so. A lot has happened in a short time."

I shivered as the implication of us being here sank in. "What do you suppose would have happened if we hadn't jumped through the vortex?"

"They would have met us in the crystal cave." He blew out a noisy breath. "Because it appears to move around, it is probably a gateway to where we are."

"What about the place on the other side of the cave? The one where I got so scared I couldn't move, and you were preventing the entry from caving in. Were the dragons responsible for that too?"

"I am far from certain, but perhaps you trod too near another entrance, so they scared you off. That horrendous animal sound we could not identify had to be a dragon bugling."

"So it was. I hate to agree with something that esoteric, but there's nothing quite like hearing the same racket from a dragon standing ten feet away." Another shiver clawed up my spine. "I don't like any of this. They've been manipulating us ever since the Ruskies chucked us into the chromium dig site."

"We need the dragons, Erin. Without them, we will never get out of here."

His words pounded nails into a coffin I'd already acknowledged, but they were still tough to hear.

"You asked why they captured us," he went on. "I believe it is just the two of them. The dead field suggests they have had struggles here. The chairs in the kitchen indicate there were once more dragons in this location."

"But why us?" I bit hard on my lower lip as I tried out reasons, discarding them as fast as they surfaced. None fit our situation well enough to examine further.

"I do not think it was us, specifically, but we showed up in a place that brought us to their attention. Rather than leaving us alone—something they must have done to countless Antarctic explorers—they zeroed in on us."

"That doesn't make me feel any better."

"I am not trying to. Our task is to figure out as much as we can, so we will be prepared when they return."

"Prepared for what?"

"They will offer us a proposal." He hesitated. "We will have no choice but to accept it."

I got to my feet. Sitting still was grating on me. I left my gloves where I'd dropped them and paced in a tight circle. "What do you mean by *no choice*? Will they kill us if we refuse?"

Johan shrugged. "I have no idea. I suppose it is a good thing neither of us has a spouse or children back home."

Home. The thought of the Pacific Northwest with its greenery and perpetually gray skies made a thick place form in my throat. "Where are you from in the Netherlands?"

"Leiden. It is south of Amsterdam."

"I've been through there. It's a beautiful old city."

Johan smiled softly. "It is, indeed. I miss it. I taught at the university in addition to working for Leistadt, my engineering firm."

I took a chance, although not much of one. I'd avoided personal relationships with everyone aboard the *Darya*. I didn't plan to be there beyond my six-month stint, and I didn't want complications.

Wimp.

I looked away so my expression wouldn't give me away. I'd been on the rebound from a predictable breakup when I boarded the ship, and I didn't want to be tempted into anyone's bed. Not that I'd been brokenhearted or anything, but it was simpler not to start something with someone who lived hallway around the globe from me. I'd been doing fine with my "ask me no questions, and I'll tell you no lies" stance—until I was kidnapped.

"It's none of my business, but how is it you don't have a wife and little ones waiting in Leiden?" I asked.

"There was never any time. I am away for more months of the year than I am home. Most women prefer a partner who is more present. I told myself I would stick closer to the Netherlands, but an intriguing proposal would present itself, and off I would go." He shrugged. "Years have a way of passing. To borrow one of your American phrases, I dug myself into a rut."

"You must not have wanted out very badly."

He laughed. "I was under the impression you were a surgeon, not a psychiatrist."

I laughed too. It broke the tension that had been sitting on my shoulders like a million-pound weight. I looked at the water again. I hadn't had a bath in months, and my last shower was nearly a week ago. "I'm going to take a swim. If the dragons come back, I'll cut it short."

"I shall join you. I can smell myself. My clothes will not be any cleaner, but at least I will be."

I sat on the shore and levered off my boots. Next I peeled off two layers of stinky socks. My suit came next, and then my down layer. And then the two layers beneath the down pants and jacket. I'd never thought much about all the garments I'd become used to wearing, but there were a lot of them. The pile next to me grew until I was down to a sports bra and panties. I decided to keep them on.

Next to me, Johan was buck naked. He stood and walked into the water until it eddied just below his shoulders. "Christ, it feels heavenly."

I changed my mind about my underwear. I'd rinse it once I got out. As bare as him, I charged into the water. It closed around me, surrounding me with warmth. Tilting my head back, I let water stream down my filthy hair. I should have taken the braid out, but this was good enough for now.

Johan set off in an efficient crawl, swimming laps back and forth, but remaining within about fifty feet of the shoreline. I joined him. It felt good to move my body without all the clothing weighing me down.

He ducked and swam beneath the surface. When his head popped up, he showed me a black, wriggling fish clasped in one hand.

"What is it?"

"Near as I can tell, a relative of the Mexican blind cave fish. They will be good to eat. Dive with me. Lots of them down there."

Half an hour later, we crawled out of the water next to a respectable pile of fish. We hadn't been greedy. We'd only taken enough to feed us a meal or two. Gritty dirt stuck to my wet skin, and I sacrificed one of my long john shirts to use as a towel. My clothing smelled like stale sweat. Fear sweat was the worst. Bitter and rotten, but if I washed my shirts and pants, I'd have nothing else to wear. I did rinse out my underwear. Once my bra and panties dried, I'd put them back on.

The clothing chests.

They were full of possibilities, but I couldn't help myself to garments that didn't belong to me. Resigned, I pulled my clothes back on, a layer at a time, stopping after the down items. I couldn't bring myself to drag my heavy insulated one-piece suit on.

"Ready?" Johan stood and tossed his outer suit over one arm. He'd washed out his shorts, and laid them over his suit.

"Yeah." I bent and gathered the fish.

"I can take some of them."

"Nah. They're not heavy. I hope there's a heat source in that kitchen. I didn't see one."

A snort burbled past Johan's lips. "Dragons make their own fire."

"Maybe they'll show up in time to provide cooking materials." I set a reasonably quick pace for the house. Before we got there, light flared in front of us. I stopped dead, not as surprised as I would have been before, but a familiar tightening in my gut told me it would take a lot more than a few hours before I developed a comfort zone around supernatural creatures.

Things that shouldn't exist.

Sure enough, Konstantin and Katya emerged from the brilliance. No longer frozen with fear, I took a good look at both of them. Konstantin was a beautiful man with hair the same copper shade as his sister's. Where hers fell to her waist, his ended at his broad shoulders. The glow Johan had noticed was more pronounced, setting off defined musculature rippling beneath his golden skin. His Greek-god chest led to a flat stomach and long, well-shaped legs. Between them, nestled in a mat of copper curls, was an enticing phallus. It hung far enough down to suggest it would be enormous erect.

The direction of my thoughts added to the tightening in my stomach, but this time apprehension wasn't the driving force.

"Erin?" Johan glanced back at me, and I realized I'd stopped dead.

"Be right there," I called and yanked my gaze away from Konstantin. The last thing I needed in my life was a roll in the hay with him.

We'd eat something, bide our time, figure out what the dragons wanted, and hopefully talk them into returning us to the surface. No time to lose. Another month or two, and the season would turn first to autumn, and then to the three months of dark that marked Antarctic winters. It would be far more difficult to get home once winter set in.

Perhaps impossible.

My nipples rubbed against my long john top. My thighs were slick against each other as I walked. *Come on, move past this,* I urged silently. If there was ever a time not to get lost in misplaced lust, this was it.

Konstantin and Katya did not look overly pleased. Johan had reached them, and they pointed at me.

"What?" I trotted to where they stood, my clunky boots making sucking sounds as they slapped the dirt.

"You have violated our lake," Konstantin said.

"Sorry, we won't swim in it again," I murmured.

"Swimming isn't the problem. It's the fish," Katya clarified.

"We cannot put them back. They are already dead," Johan spoke up, adding, "We were hungry."

"We will provide for you. Why did you leave the house?" Konstantin asked.

Pretty man or not, my anger flared. "We have a right to look around."

"Whatever rules you used to live by"—he nailed me with those odd eyes of his—"none of them apply here. Inside. Both of you."

"Leave the fish," Katya instructed. Before I could lodge a protest, a jolt of something hit me, and the fish flew through the air, landing at her feet.

It pissed me off. "Next time," I bristled. "Ask, don't just take."

She looked at me as if I were an intriguing specimen pinned beneath a microscope. "This was more efficient." The glow around her expanded to include the fish, and they began to wriggle again. My skin prickled like it would have if I'd walked next to a high voltage wire, and the fish vanished.

My mouth gaped open. "What? Where?" I stammered

Johan grabbed my arm and angled his head toward the stone doors. I got the message. Don't ask questions. Don't talk back. Don't piss them off. Arranging my face in what I hoped were neutral planes, I let him steer me back inside. The fish had reanimated—and disappeared. For some reason, it rattled me more than when Konstantin had turned into a dragon.

short while earlier

Konstantin's dragon was delighted. After months of being quashed, he was flying again. And killing. Life didn't get much better than that. When they took to the skies with Katya aboard, he decided to show off, swooping and plucking a nice, fat seal from the water.

His human half didn't rebuke him, but one seal was enough. Chewing, swallowing, and flying consumed the next span of time. A few choice bits fell into the sea, but not many. By Y Ddraigh Goch, it felt right to stretch his wings, to sink his teeth into tender flesh and savor hot, salty blood splashing down his throat. So long as he was on a roll, he sent out a mental summons, bugling through time, space, and other worlds, to Katya's missing dragon.

She might be in a snit, but she couldn't evade her human partner forever. The bond was permanent, not something to toy with. She had to come back sometime, and it may as well be sooner rather than later.

KONSTANTIN ENJOYED INDULGING THE DRAGON. His beast fed a primitive, feral part of him, kept it from withering. So he loosened the hold he usually tethered it with, allowing it to swoop and dive, to hunt and kill prey. Earth wasn't quite the paradise he'd hoped for. Scarcely a place dragons could fly free. Far from a Mu replacement, it had forced dragonkind into a holding pattern.

"Do you suppose our kinfolk located lands better suited to our needs?" he asked Katya.

"I hope so. There is little enough for us here, yet leaving is risky. We could end up someplace worse."

He didn't see how, but he didn't say so. Nothing like tossing out a gauntlet, one the universe would be delighted to slap him down over.

"What are your plans for the humans?"

"We already discussed this," he told his sister.

"So we did, but they do not appear particularly tractable. The man is quite attractive, though, and I like it that he has spirit."

Konstantin didn't reply. The woman, Erin, was beautiful. Tall and stately with a self-possession he didn't expect in human females. Not that he'd spent much time around humans in general, but the women he'd met before all appeared somewhat timid.

Katya whooped, a wild, joyous sound that could only mean one thing. The weight on his back vanished. Katya's golden dragon burst through a diaphanous veil, her eyes whirling with happiness. She puffed steam; his dragon puffed back until both wyrms were surrounded by clouds of mist.

He draped them in an invisibility casting to allow their play free rein. He hadn't spotted the Russian ship, but nor had he looked particularly closely. Now was a time for celebration. Katya's dragon was back. He suspected his beast might have had something to do with its return, but it would never reveal its secrets.

The dragons had their own world, their own society, both barred to human bondmate entry. They decided which shifters to bond with, but they were loyal. The bond was forever, so they chose wisely. That Katya's dragon had been gone for years spoke to how miserable it had been hidden beneath kilometers of dirt and ice.

Some animals, like the blind fish in their lakes, belonged beneath the southern continent. Dragons were not blind fish, requiring protection so they wouldn't die out. Dragons demanded open air and boundless skies. The more Konstantin thought about it, the worse he felt.

They couldn't remain sequestered beneath tons of rock and ice. The ones who'd left were the wise ones, although he hadn't believed it at the time. He'd been lost in self-righteous indignation and had labeled the others as quitters. The reality of leaving, of seeking a better home for themselves, put a huge crimp in his plans for the humans.

They didn't need to create new dragon shifters. Not if they planned to relocate. He had no idea what they'd find elsewhere in the universe of worlds, but bringing two newly minted dragon shifters, created from humans who had never wielded magic, was a very bad idea.

Every dragon shifter he'd ever known had been born, not created, which meant they were born to magic. Born to sharing their skin with a beast. Perhaps the transition would be too much for someone who'd begun as merely human. Even if it weren't too rigorous a journey, it would take more time than he was willing to devote to the task. Simply learning magic would consume at least a century. By then, his dragon would be in full rebellion. Katya's was happy now, but that was because it was reunited with her.

All too soon, the reality of being stuck beneath an endless glaciated landscape would rankle once more. As he thought it through, he wasn't at all certain any dragon would link its essence to a human living in such appalling conditions.

Katya's dragon flew high. His chased after, grabbing her tail in his teeth playfully. They'd gained enough altitude for him to have a clear view of the Russian vessel he hoped would be long gone. Another ship bobbed on moderately rough seas a few meters away. He scanned the other ship, focusing his sharp, dragon eyesight on writing splashed across the bow.

Darya in Russian characters.

So this was the ship the humans had come from. The one stolen by whoever was in charge of the second ship.

Konstantin pulled rank, wrested control away from his dragon and quit playing with Katya's.

"Look over there." He could have spoken out loud, but telepathy was easier.

Katya's dragon flew a figure eight before settling in next to his. *"Two ships."*

"One belonged to the humans."

Fire flashed from Katya's dragon, lighting the cloudy skies. *"We can kill it."*

He matched her fire with some of his own. *"The operative term is sink, not kill, but we gain nothing."*

"It might be fun."

His dragon pushed hard against their bond, clearly in agreement. Destroying anything was sport. Never mind the ship wasn't alive. Odd waves formed between the ships, swells that didn't match the rest of the sea.

"Something is down there."

"Yes, two ships." Katya's dragon bugled laughter.

"Look between them."

Konstantin flew to one side, hoping for a clearer view, but maintaining enough distance to evade detection. His invisibility spell should still protect them, but he didn't care if it wasn't absolute. He hated the Russians who'd invaded his territory with death and incendiary devices.

Maybe sinking their ship wasn't such a bad idea.

And the *Darya* too. He knew enough to understand that dropping Erin and Johan back on board wouldn't do them any good. A ship that size required crew, and from the sound of things, the Russians had gotten rid of them.

A long, sibilant hiss came from Katya's dragon. He focused his attention on the strip of ocean that wasn't behaving properly. Probably a whale—or a school of them. A blast of unfamiliar magic shot from the heaving sea, followed by an even stronger flash.

The sea turned shades of deep violet before it took on a brackish, black hue.

Not whales.

What in Y Ddraigh Goch's name was down there? Suddenly, he cared a whole lot about his invisibility casting and made an effort to strengthen it. *"Sister. Remain close."*

Men poured out onto the decks of both ships, high powered rifles raised and ready as they stared over the railings. Shots rang out. Konstantin fanned his wings, holding his position.

Men were worse fools than he'd imagined. Who fought magic with bullets? It was a contest they were certain to lose. An enormous black triangular head broke the surface, followed by thick coils.

Goddess's breath! A sea-serpent.

It opened its mouth and sprayed poison in an arc at the stupid fools leaned over the side of their boat. Konstantin could smell the taint from where he hovered, perhaps half a kilometer away. It was harsh, acrid, and it burned his eyes and nostrils. His dragon closed its third eyelid, the transparent one, to protect itself.

A second serpent joined the first, and then two more emerged from the unsettled waters. Men fell over the sides of the boat or collapsed on the decks. A few, the ones with brains, tried to run back inside, but it was too late. Sea-serpent toxin was not only deadly, but airborne. Anyone near enough—anyone human, that is—would die a slow, painful death as skin sloughed from bone.

He'd seen plenty. Wheeling, he led the way back to their protected spit of land. Katya didn't give him any problems. Sometimes, she defied him, but not in the face of such a threat. He summoned shift magic as soon as his talons dug into the dirt. By the time Katya landed, he was mostly back in his human form. He waited for her to craft her own transformation. They had to talk, and the sea-serpents could intercept telepathy.

Any magical creature could, and the serpents were unspeakably ancient and powerful.

Katya's fingers and toes were still forming when he said, "Thank you, Sister. I understand you'd rather have remained in your dragon's body for longer."

She inclined her head. "It's all right. Both she and I understand the need for haste and secrecy. Do you think they saw us?"

He hunkered behind the headlands. Once she'd joined him, he said. "About seeing us, I'm not sure. They didn't glance upward, nor did I sense their magic directed our way, so perhaps we escaped detection. Where do you suppose they came from?"

She shrugged. "Same place we did? Not Mu obviously, but their own world must have become an inhospitable place, and—"

"What makes you think this isn't some kind of power grab on their part?"

"I don't know." Breath rattled through her clenched teeth. "Remind me about them, Brother. You were always fascinated by mythology."

He put an arm around Katya and drew her close. "This tale is painful. It is one we had to learn, yet I understand why many of us chose to forget about it."

She twisted her neck and glared at him. "Skip the lecture. I remember something about them and us having common roots, but that's where my recollection ends."

"Long ago, much farther back than when we settled on Mu, dragons and sea-serpents were once one and the same. We shared the air and the seas, rulers one and all over everything on every world. They had wings, and our dragon bodies were longer, more sinuous and better suited for swimming."

Konstantin unclenched his jaw. "Y Ddraigh Goch had a sacred shrine on a distant world. It contained his hoard, and he and his mate set their children to guard it while they ruled over dragonkind.

"Several sea-serpents hatched a plan to steal from Y Ddraigh Goch's collection of gold and gems. I am not certain, but I believe they only meant it as a prank. It went terribly wrong. Two of Y Ddraigh Goch's children were disfigured protecting their father's treasure. One lost a wing, the other a foot."

"Surely, they grew back," Katya protested.

He shook his head. "They were severed with magic, dark

magic that ate away at the children until they went mad. Let me tell this in order, Sister."

Katya nodded, her golden eyes filled with pain. "No wonder I didn't remember the rest of this tale. It's very unsettling."

"Y Ddraigh Goch and his mate heard their children's cries and hurried back to the faraway world. The sea-serpents fell on their bellies and cried, repenting what they'd done, yet they had revealed that they commanded dark magic.

"Such is forbidden to us under our Covenant. Y Ddraigh Goch banished the serpents and cursed them so they would lose their wings. From that day forth, they were limited to swimming in the seas."

"What happened to the two brave children? The ones who went mad."

"Y Ddraigh Goch moved them to a hidden world to live out their immortality. I have heard it is a paradise with plentiful food and water. Our dragon god sealed the world off from the universe. No others may enter, nor may his children ever leave."

"Have you ever heard about sea-serpents on Earth before?" Katya asked.

"No, and it worries me. We cannot allow them to remain."

"How will we stop them?"

"I don't know yet." He pushed his shoulders back amid bones cracking, but it didn't release the tension dogging his muscles. "I had decided to return the humans to their world, but we cannot do that. Releasing them now would be tantamount to signing their death warrants."

"What about one of the research bases? The woman, Erin, said it was where they wished to go. Other humans reside in those spots."

He shook his head. "They are at risk too. Erin and Johan are safer with us than they would be elsewhere."

Katya squinched her eyes to slits. "They won't see it that way. Furthermore, they won't believe you—us—about any of this."

He furled both brows. "And why not? I revealed my dragon to them."

"And then we left." She snorted. "What do you suppose they've done with that information during our absence?"

"Hopefully, come to terms with it."

"Or perhaps they ginned up some scientific flimflam explanation. Like smoke and mirrors and pulleys or something."

"I doubt it. Faced with incontrovertible evidence, surely they would have..." Would have what? He had no idea. They couldn't escape, but they probably weren't sitting around, either. He stood and summoned a light spell to return them beneath the surface. "We should go back."

"I agree. What will we tell them?" Katya got to her feet and wove a bit of magic in with his.

"I'm not sure. It depends on how amenable they are to listening."

She laid a hand on his arm. "The way I see it, they're useless to us as human. To themselves as well."

"They may not have a choice. I was thinking about that while we flew. Earth is not the best choice for dragonkind. Even if one or both humans express interest in becoming dragon shifters, I'm not at all convinced any dragon would want them."

"Maybe so," she murmured. "Too many downsides, but we will need more of us if we challenge the sea-serpents."

"Yes, but not brand new dragon shifters. We need some of our erstwhile kin to heed our call and return."

"How will you manage that?" Katya pursed her lips into a frown.

"I have no idea. Telepathy might work for Y Ddraig Goch across worlds, but it won't work for you or me. If I broadcast a call for aid too loudly—checking to see if any of us are elsewhere on Earth—the sea-serpents are certain to hear me."

"Maybe they just got here. Perhaps they don't plan to remain."

"A whole lot of unknowns. It's not as if we can overfly them and engage them in a discussion."

"Why not?"

"Because if we asked the real questions, like what they're doing here or anything to tease out their intentions, they'd either not answer or lie. We may have been a single race once, but that was a very long time ago."

Katya nodded slowly. "I suppose they don't like us any better than we like them."

"Worse, since our god is who banished them."

"Makes us righteous, and they've had millennia to fan the flames of being wronged." She rolled her expressive eyes.

"About the size of it."

A cracking sound dragged his head around. Beyond the headland, brash ice had filled the bay, the pieces shuddering against one another. Konstantin loosed the magic he'd summoned and walked to the shoreline, squatting to touch the water. Not that ice was an unfamiliar aspect of polar waters, but this ice had materialized between the space of two breaths. Odd since the wind had died to almost nothing.

Katya joined him. "What?"

"Ssht." He leaned toward the water, employing his dragon's ears to listen intently. It took a few moments before he heard an insidious chant, driven by arcane energy. What were the serpents up to? The ice had to be their doing.

He straightened and strode back the way they'd come, drawing a subtle spell as he did so to encompass them both. Before his sister peppered him with questions, he swept both of them into a casting to move them through kilometers of dirt, rock, and ice to their home.

His spell still flickered, losing steam but not quite gone yet, when he saw Erin and Johan. They'd clearly been in the lake. Their hair was wet, and they carried some of their heavy clothing across their arms. A closer look revealed fish sitting on top of Erin's pile of outerwear.

Damn it all to hell. They'd been fishing? He and Katya hadn't been gone for more than a couple of turns of the glass. He tried to muffle his displeasure but didn't do a very good job of it. He had other problems—ones far more significant than the two pesky humans.

Johan reached them first. He'd been smiling, but it faded fast. Mercifully, he kept his mouth shut.

Erin trotted up, her boots making sucking sounds as they struck the dirt. "What? Why do the two of you look like you just ate broken glass?"

"You have violated our lake," Konstantin said.

"Sorry, we won't swim in it again," Erin muttered.

"Not the swimming. It's the fish," Katya clarified.

"We cannot put them back. They are already dead," Johan spoke up, adding, "We were hungry."

"We will provide for you. Why did you leave the house?" Konstantin made a grab for equanimity, but it escaped him. Too much had happened.

"We have a right to look around." Erin tossed her head defiantly.

Katya nailed her with a stony glance.

"Whatever rules you used to live by," Konstantin said gruffly, "none of them apply here. Inside. Both of you."

"Leave the fish," Katya instructed. Not giving Erin a choice, she chased her command with magic that left the fish flopping at her feet.

"Next time," Erin growled. "Ask, don't just take."

Katya made him proud when she didn't snipe back, merely noting, "This was more efficient." Konstantin understood what she meant to do, and her actions clinched it. Magic flowed from her, reanimating the fish so she could return them to the lake.

Erin's mouth gaped. "What? How in the hell—?"

Johan grabbed her arm and half-dragged her toward the doors. They vanished within.

Katya nudged him. "She was right about your expression. Be gentle. Our world is as alien to them as theirs is to us."

When he pushed out a breath, fire came with it. He forced himself to take several long, deep breaths until only steam accompanied them. Once he was confident he wouldn't storm inside and immediately dress the humans up one side and down the other, he followed their path.

"Stop in the kitchen," Katya said. "We could all do with something to eat."

He wasn't hungry. The seal his dragon had eaten had been plenty, but this wasn't about him. Johan had said he was hungry. It was why he and Erin had gone fishing. Maybe it wouldn't have been the end of the world to let them have the blind fish.

Konstantin pulled the doors shut behind them, sealing the entrance with magic. The likelihood of sea-serpents finding them was remote, indeed, but caution was never wasted. They trotted down one level to the kitchen. Erin and Johan were already there.

Good, it saved hunting them down.

Erin faced them, hands on her hips and the pile of her clothing laid across one end of the table. "I'm happy to cook, but we couldn't find anything in here to eat." Strain carved lines into the skin around her eyes, but she was trying.

Katya waved an arm to one side. Cupboards that had been hidden with magic shimmered into view. "Let's look together, shall we?" she invited Erin. "That way we will all be happy with the result."

Erin joined her, appearing skittish but pointing out items in response to Katya's queries.

Johan's eyes had widened at the casual display of power that made edibles appear. He swallowed visibly and dropped his armful of clothing next to Erin's. "We appreciate your hospitality," he began, "but we do not belong here."

Katya angled a pointed glance his way; Konstantin nodded to let her know he'd handle this. "You're absolutely correct," he told Johan. "But in the time since you chose to violate one of our gateways, things up there"—he waved a hand above his head—"have changed radically."

"How?" Johan asked. Before Konstantin could answer, he charged on. "We have accepted the loss of our ship, of our research project. All we require is transport to the Polish research station, and then you will be rid of us."

Konstantin nodded and speared Johan with his unwavering gaze so the man would see truth hovering behind his eyes. If humans could even sense such things. "I had come to the same conclusion—that it was a mistake for us to reveal ourselves to you, although you made things damned difficult when you forced your way into our world."

"We did not know," Johan protested.

"If we had—" Erin began.

Konstantin waved both of them to silence. "Many things happened that were beyond your control, and your choices sprang from not having any others. I understand that. Unfortunately, now something has occurred that is beyond my control, and if we can't figure out how to deal with it, I fear your precious Earth will turn into something unrecognizable."

"You're just saying that," Erin pronounced defiantly.

Foodstuffs clattered from Katya's hands, and she rounded on Erin. "My brother does not lie. Apologize. Immediately."

Erin stared long and hard at his sister before dropping her gaze and mumbling, "I'm sorry."

"Tell him, not me." Katya's tone was implacable.

"It's not necessary," Konstantin cut in. "How long before a meal is ready?"

Rather than answering, Katya snarled accompanied by a few plumes of fire.

Konstantin walked to a chest in a far corner and withdrew a flask. It contained lake water he'd coaxed into a fermented blend that was mildly alcoholic.

"Sit," he invited and took his customary place at the head of the table. "We shall share a drink, and you will listen."

"To what?" Erin asked.

"Sit." Johan pushed her gently toward the table and settled her into a chair, taking one across from her.

Rattling platters told Konstantin that Katya had risen above her ire and was once again working on a meal. "It is impossible to impart every detail," he began, "but I will tell you something of dragon shifters. Listen carefully. This information will be critical as you evaluate the options available to you."

"Thank you," Johan said.

"For what?" Konstantin inquired. "I haven't said anything yet."

"As you pointed out, our last choices went badly," Johan clarified. "I appreciate you offering us an opportunity so perhaps our next ones will work out better."

"Me too," Erin said and sounded as if she meant it.

Konstantin took a long drink from the flask and handed it to Johan. Even though these two seemed naïve and childlike, underestimating them was a mistake. After Johan offered the drink to Erin, Konstantin had decided where to begin.

"You may view Earth as the only inhabited world, yet many, many others exist both within this solar system and others. Dragon shifters are far from the only magical creatures, yet we are one of the more ancient ones..."

CHAPTER 8

We passed the flask around as Konstantin recounted a tale that belonged in a children's story, except it had a bloody aspect. Maybe more like Grimm's Fairytales in the original Germanic version. I'd suffered through it during one of my many attempts to master something beyond English.

Not unlike most of my med school classes, there was too much information flowing from Konstantin to absorb and process, so I focused on the highlights. Other worlds. Other races, mostly with magical underpinnings. The bit that was hardest for me to wrap my head around was that supernatural beings—not unlike the ones on *Supernatural* and *Grimm* and other television series I'd sucked in for diversion, were real.

Theoretically.

Apparently.

Impossibly.

"So how long have the two of you been here by yourselves?" Johan asked. He wore an expression I'd come to recognize from our days aboard the *Darya*. I'd privately dubbed it his "scientist look," because his body was angled toward the speaker, eyebrows slightly raised, and the corners of his eyes scrunched the tiniest bit.

We'd been inside long enough for our hair to have mostly dried. Somewhere along the way, Katya had plopped a couple of tureens on the table with spoons. The expectation was we'd all eat out of a common bowl. It got my medical ire up, but I didn't want to risk alienating Katya any further than I already had by fishing where we shouldn't have.

And by suggesting her brother had twisted the truth to suit his fancy.

Still listening to a very different version of history than I'd ever heard before, I picked up a spoon, set it down, and grabbed it again. Tugging the nearest dish closer, I took a tiny mouthful, surprised when a pleasing mixture of flavors exploded on my tongue.

Even that small amount reminded me how famished I was, how long it had been since my last meal aboard the *Darya*. Three days, give or take a few hours. After a laughably brief struggle, hunger won out. I overlooked all the ways food can kill you and dug in.

Everyone else was eating too. I thought about asking exactly what Katya had used for ingredients but decided I was better off not knowing.

"It has been at least fifty annums since the other dragon shifters, who also lived here, left in search of a more commodious home," Konstantin was saying.

Katya shook her head. "Closer to a hundred, Brother."

He shrugged. "It might be as much as that. We have no reason to mark the passage of time."

I supposed not. If they were immortal—and I was still having a hell of a hard time accepting they were—what were a hundred years on one side or the other of some imaginary line?

"Do either of you have more questions about what you've heard so far?" Konstantin asked. He got up, retrieved another flask, drank, and passed it around.

I rolled my eyes. "Yeah. Of course. Who wouldn't? But probably none of them are more than idle curiosity. Are there things you left out in the interest of expediency that we need to know to understand whatever you plan to tell us next?"

He shook his head.

"I have a question." Johan sat straighter. "I understand we triggered some kind of gateway that dumped us down here, but if we had not done so, would you have shown up in the crystal-lined cavern?"

"Yes, we would have."

"I suspected as much," Johan said. "My next question is, "Why? What did you want with us?"

"It wasn't you, specifically," Katya began.

Konstantin held up a hand. "If it is all the same to you, Sister, I would prefer to tell this, since it was my idea."

I expected Katya to tell her brother to piss up a rope. Instead, she nodded pleasantly. Apparently, dragon shifter females deferred to their male kin.

And why shouldn't they? It's the same way humans operated until very recently, I reminded myself.

Johan edged his brows a notch higher, but stopped shy of suggesting Konstantin get on with it. He'd been eating like a starving orphan, just like me, and perhaps having food in our bellies for the first time in days had a modulating effect.

"When we first became aware of you," Konstantin went on, "Katya's dragon was not precisely missing, but nor was she present. The dragons hate it here because they can't fly free whenever the mood strikes them. Her dragon had pressed her to leave long ago. When she refused, it vanished."

"But that's terrible," I murmured and looked at Katya.

"No. It's understandable," she corrected me. "But my dragon has returned, and her absence no longer presents a problem."

"But she was gone when I decided we needed more dragons if we were going to stay here," Konstantin continued his narrative.

"Why?" Johan asked.

"We do better when we are part of a society. Dragons were not born to live alone," Katya answered him.

"Yes, and it wasn't wise to leave without Katya being able to access her dragon's body because we would have been venturing into the unknown, and she could not fly. Our only other option was to strengthen ourselves, develop our missing community, by creating more dragon shifters."

"Are you born or made?" I asked. Maybe he'd told us when he was deep into his magical history retelling, but I'd jettisoned a good deal of it in an effort to keep the most important parts straight.

"Both," Konstantin said.

"We believe both," Katya spoke up. "Our legends suggest dragon shifters can be created, yet neither of us have ever known such to occur."

"If the lot of you don't stop asking questions and engaging in side conversations, I'll never get through this," Konstantin groused, sounding as if his patience was wearing thin.

I zipped it and smiled his way.

"As I said before, it wasn't the two of you specifically," he went on. "But we needed a way to enhance our numbers. Your genders were convenient, and—"

Forgetting all about my commitment to remain silent— one I'd only made a few seconds before—I blurted, "You planned to have sex with us? Use us as some kind of esoteric breeding stock? How the hell would that even work? She"—I jerked my chin at Katya—"might do fine giving birth to...to whatever your young look like. But I probably wouldn't. How do you even know my body would be capable of—"

"Silence!" Konstantin was on his feet, towering over me. So close the sheer maleness of him stole my breath and my wits and a whole lot of other things.

I made a grab for the flask and drank so fast I choked,

spitting out the alcoholic beverage as I fought to clear my lungs.

"Were you planning to give us a choice?" Johan's voice, even and neutral, shamed me. I was acting like a teenage drama queen.

"Of course. I would have left you back on the surface if you were not amenable," Konstantin replied. "What do you take us for? We are not animals that force others to our bidding—or our pleasure."

"Sorry," Johan said. "You cannot expect us to understand your thought processes, which is what makes questions so important." He took a breath and blew it out. "You should welcome questions rather than assumptions."

"I should, should I?" Konstantin turned his head in time to divert fire that blasted from his mouth.

Katya flowed to her feet and gripped her brother's arm, dragging him a few feet from the table. "They are not like us. You can't expect them to react like another dragon shifter. We haven't spent enough time around humans to understand them any better than they understand us."

Another blast of fire scored the far wall. I suddenly understood the importance of most of this dwelling being built of rock. Good, old non-flammable stone could withstand a whole lot.

I opened my mouth, but nothing came out, so I took a far more cautious swallow from the flask and tried again. "You said you'd take us back to the surface. I can't speak for Johan, but I'd like to leave. Whenever is convenient for you, of course," I added hurriedly. No point in Konstantin and his sister thinking me even ruder than they already did.

He yanked free from Katya and spun to face me. His eyes glittered dangerously, their deep golden color incredibly hypnotic when paired with the forest-green centers.

"That option is no longer open to us."

I absorbed his words. Before I could find a subtle way to determine why he'd changed his mind, Johan asked, "Why not?"

"An unexpected scourge materialized. If we moved you to the surface now, it would mean certain death. For you."

I got heavily to my feet, the meal I'd just eaten sitting in my stomach like a congealed lump of undigestible material. I hoped I wouldn't puke it back up. No matter how upset I was, I needed calories.

"It's the Russians, isn't it?" I asked dully.

Last to stand, Johan moved to my side and draped an arm around my shoulders. "Probably not. You are not thinking. Those two"—he tipped his head toward the dragon shifters—"could kill anything human and not look back."

"We only kill for good reasons," Konstantin said stiffly.

"You're goddess damned fortunate he killed the one in the upper cavern with you." Katya rounded on me and Johan. "Furthermore." She took a step nearer to us. "I'm who fixed Johan's leg."

"I wondered how that happened," I mumbled, grateful to have something to glom onto instead of the likelihood of spending the rest of my life miles beneath Antarctica.

"Thank you." Johan inclined his head.

Konstantin seemed to have recovered his equanimity. At least the fireworks had slowed. "When Katya and I were aboveground just now, we saw both the Russians' ship and the *Darya*. We also ran into an old nemesis. Several of them, to be precise. They were killing the men on the Russian ship in droves."

"Serves them right," Johan said darkly.

"Killing them, how?" I asked, wondering if Johan and I could manage the *Darya* on our own. Probably not for a blue-water sail, but I was confident we could guide it around the headlands to the Polish research station on King George Island. Failing that, we could launch a Zodiac—assuming some were left aboard.

"Poison," Katya said succinctly.

"It is airborne and kills on contact," Konstantin added

"Um, how come you're not dead?" I blurted, and then shook my head and mumbled, "Never mind."

"For once, you asked a decent question," Konstantin said in a more moderate tone. "We are impervious to their venom because back at the beginnings of time, they were related to us."

"They still are," Katya said. "Unfortunately. Them being banished by Y Ddraigh Goch did not sever our familial link."

"I suppose you're right," Konstantin grumbled.

"Who is *ydraikgoc*?" I bungled the word because I couldn't visualize it.

"Y Ddraigh Goch is one of several dragon gods," Johan answered.

I stared at him, open-mouthed. "And you know this, how?"

"I told you. I read a lot of sci fi and fantasy. Mythology too." He narrowed his eyes and asked Konstantin, "So your god did something to another branch of your family, and now they have arrived to exact revenge?"

"No. Nothing like that," Katya cut in.

"It's unlikely they know we're here," Konstantin added. "Although that could change very quickly."

"Our god exacted punishment millennia ago," Katya said. "Long before Konstantin and I were born. We had no idea any of our...relatives were on Earth."

"How many of these, erm, kinfolk are there?" I asked.

"Same thing I was wondering," Johan said. "Any chance we could slip out of here after dark? Maybe if they do not see us, we might get to the Polish base."

"Now it is you who aren't thinking." Katya tossed Johan's words to me back in his face. "Our senses are far more acute than yours. The only reason our distant relatives didn't figure out Kon and I were in the air watching them was because they were intent on killing the sailors aboard that boat."

"And probably eating them," Konstantin muttered. "No point letting all that meat go to waste."

The nausea that had threatened earlier swept over me in a wave. Bile splashed the back of my throat in a burning cascade. I swallowed hard to keep my stomach's contents where they belonged and not splattered across the stone floor.

Johan tightened his grip on my shoulders. "Steady," he breathed into my ear.

I inhaled to the bottom of my lungs, blew it out, and did it again. Half a dozen breaths later, I wasn't on the verge of puking, but it was about all I could lay claim to. I didn't feel very sanguine anymore. My belief we'd get through this somehow was fading to a dull hopelessness.

Johan let go of me and flexed his fingers in front of him. "You have conveniently avoided naming what it is you saw outside. Am I correct they are like you? Dragons?"

Konstantin pushed his shoulders back as if a heavy weight sat atop them. "No. Not dragons, but sea-serpents. Once we shared a similar form. After Y Ddraigh Goch banished our kin, he stripped them of their wings. They can no longer fly."

I pinched the bridge of my nose between my thumb and forefinger. Why the hell were they making us drag information out of them? "Why not just tell us?" I asked. "The whole thing. Not dribs and drabs."

"Probably because we're still sorting out what it means," Katya said.

"If you had magic, you would see the truth in our words," Konstantin spoke up. "As it is, you'll have to take our word and not presume we've made up a tale to hold you here." Walking forward, he splayed his hands on the tabletop. "We have told you the truth. Certain death lies above. If you still wish me to, I will transport you to the Polish research station and leave you, but everyone there will be dead soon enough."

"If they aren't already," Katya said.

"Why?" The word tore out of me.

"Because our sea-serpent kin hate humans," Konstantin replied. "When Y Ddraigh Goch expelled them, it was to several distant, mostly abandoned worlds where they could do no harm."

"We are of two minds," Katya broke in. "I believe it may be accidental some of them are here. They may have ended up on Earth for many of the same reasons we did. Their planet imploded or became uninhabitable."

"And I don't believe in coincidences," Konstantin growled. "They are here for a reason that has nothing to do with losing their home and everything to do with expanding their power base."

"I guess you can't ask them," I mumbled.

"Not without revealing our presence." Konstantin shot an unreadable look my way. "Right now, the fact they don't know we're close is a point in our favor." He seemed to consider his next words. "The simplest course for Katya and me would be to leave. We had decided to expedite our departure before we were drawn into your problems."

"Leaving Earth behind is no longer viable. Not with goddess knows how many serpents infesting its waters," Katya said. "I shouldn't care. This hasn't been a particularly good home for my brother and me, yet I do. It isn't right for us to leave while the sea-serpents mow through this world and its resources."

"Humans did a fair job stripping wealth and disturbing

eco-systems before these serpents of yours showed up," Johan said.

"We know," Konstantin replied. "We have no control over humans, and despite being related, the intruders are not 'our serpents.'"

"Sorry. Poor choice of words." Johan's nostrils flared. "If you remain, how will you fight this threat?"

"With more of us," Konstantin said. "I was about to do what I could to put out a call to see if other magical beings are close enough to help."

"That won't work," Katya spoke up. "The serpents would hear your telepathy. I did have an idea, though. And I put it into action."

"You might have said something, Sister." Konstantin turned his intense gaze square on Katya.

"When would I have had a chance? I sent my dragon to hunt for others who may be nearby. They know who is here and who is not."

A smile altered the grim planes of Konstantin's striking face. Part European royalty. Part Hollywood star. I could look at him for the rest of my life and never get tired of the view.

Christ on a crutch. Where the fuck had that come from? Besides, looks only went so far. He might be gorgeous, but he was also a righteous, self-absorbed bastard.

From what I'd seen so far.

I cleared my mind as much as I could. No way did I want either of the dragons helping themselves to my thoughts.

"Brilliant." Konstantin clapped Katya across the back.

"Why, thank you. My dragon liked the idea too."

"You did say the serpents can't fly, right?" Johan asked.

"Correct. Nor do we swim particularly well anymore," Konstantin replied.

"Do they have a human form like you?" I looked from him to his sister.

"I believe so," Katya said.

"The particulars of their exile were never shared with dragonkind. Only that they were wingless henceforth. And gone," Konstantin said. "But that isn't important. The two of you must decide if you will remain with us or if you will go. You must both chose the same option. One of you remaining while the other one leaves is not possible."

I wanted to ask why, but didn't.

"We will leave you to discuss your fate," Katya said. "You have a little time, but not much. My brother and I have a war to plan."

I did a doubletake. "You sound happy about it."

She grinned with zero warmth and a whole lot of teeth. "I am. Dragons live for battles and victory. It's been far too long since I had a worthy goal to sink my talons into."

With that, she and Konstantin shimmered to nothing, leaving me staring at Johan. "What do you want to do?" I clasped my hands behind me and paced to the far end of the kitchen.

"I might ask you the same question," he countered.

I turned to him. "It's not much of a choice. Not really. They believe we'll die if we return to the surface."

"We may die anyway," he pointed out before blurting, "I want to stay. This is like all the stories I have ever read come to life. I cannot believe we are here, and this is happening, but since it is I cannot walk away. At least, I do not wish to."

"You feel pretty strongly about it." I kept my tone as neutral as I could.

"I do, but I would hear your desires." He rocked from foot to foot, watching me.

"You mean besides curling up into a ball and telling one of those dragons to just kill me now?" Bitterness spilled from me. "None of this is fair. I was only going to be gone for six months, not a lifetime. If I'm away for too long, I won't be any good in an operating room anymore. My surgical skills will fade."

I shook my head, feeling like an idiot. Who the hell cared if I could wield a scalpel with any level of precision?

"No. None of it is fair," he agreed, being diplomatic enough not to mention I was focused on the wrong things. "The question before us is do we die with our own kind, or do we take our chances and help the dragons in whatever way we can?" Before I could answer, he added, "We may die either way. Nothing I heard ensures our safety."

I snatched the flask from the table and drank, welcoming the burn of the alcohol as it coated my throat and stomach. I'd always seen myself as adventurous, but for once an adventure too big to grasp had found me.

All of my control-freak genes were activated, and not in a good way.

"Talk with me, Erin," he urged. "What bothers you most?"

"Like it's just one thing. Let me see." I extended a hand,

counting on my fingers. "One, I have no control over my future. Two, I dropped into fairytale land. Three, I probably will never see my home again. Four, I..." My voice ran down mostly because tears were really near the surface.

"You do have control over where you end up. I want to stay here, but if you feel strongly about returning to the surface, I will acquiesce."

"Aw shit." Tears spilled over, running down my cheeks. "Why do you have to be so deucedly decent?"

He shrugged. "You call it, Erin. Let's figure out which pony we will bet on."

I scrubbed my cheeks with the backs of my hands, snuffling back my pain and indecision and confusion. "Okay," I said when I could talk again. "We'll stay here."

A shocked look bloomed on his face. Clearly, it wasn't the answer he'd expected. "Just like that? Why?"

"We know nothing of magic. Well, to put a finer point on things, I don't. You seem to have a passing acquaintance with it. If we go to Arctowski, the Polish base, obviously no one there believes in magic, either. We'd be helpless in the face of...of the fire and other shit we've seen the dragon shifters produce. Or poison from the serpents. But so would every other human."

Crap. I was rambling, but Johan was letting me roll with it, so I plowed ahead. "Judging from the brief look I got at Konstantin, dragons have scales. I'm guessing the serpents do too."

At Johan's nod, I went on. "So probably bullets can't penetrate. We know their bodies don't burn, and they're immortal." I turned my hands palms up. "Earth might not be their home, but it is ours. Maybe what little we can do against the sea-serpent threat would work better here where we have the dragons to guide us."

He shut his eyes for a moment. When he opened them, he said, "Thank you."

I started out of the room, but he called, "Where are you going?" after me.

"To tell the dragons."

"Come back, Erin." Johan chuckled. By the time I rejoined him, he was laughing outright. I grabbed his arm and shook it. "What's so funny?"

"I am sure they already know. With magic like theirs, they probably listened to every word that passed between us."

Heat traveled from my chest upward. My face must have turned bright red. I'd picked a path. Made my bed. Now it was up to me to pull my head out of my ass and be more than a nay-saying albatross.

But I don't believe in magic, my inner voice lodged a protest and was shot down by a second one pointing out that from now on, I was a total convert. Time to drink the Kool Aid, suck it up, and fall headfirst into fairyland.

CHAPTER 9

onstantin strode from one end of the great hall on the lowest level of their home to the other. He had no idea which outcome he hoped for. Each of them had downsides. As if she'd read his thoughts—and she probably had—Katya asked, "What do you want to do?"

He stopped pacing and turned to his sister. "Now that your dragon is back, nothing is holding us here."

"Nothing except honor," she agreed. "Y Ddraigh Goch would not be pleased if he knew we identified a threat—a serious one—and turned our backs on it to save ourselves trouble."

"Mmph. There is that." Smoke puffed from his mouth and nose. "The humans complicate things. I wouldn't have set things up so our paths would cross if I'd known about the serpents."

"Why not? Your reasons are still valid. We're still alone, and—"

He sliced one hand downward. "Because you were absolutely correct when you said we didn't understand them any better than they understand us. I haven't spent much time at all around humans. I had no idea they'd be so..." He searched for a word and came up dry.

"Opinionated?" Katya supplied, followed by, "Strong willed? Mouthy?"

"Yes. Now that you mention them. All those things."

She tilted her head, regarding him with an arch expression. "What were you expecting?"

Ash and smoke marked his annoyance as he stared at his twin. "Obedience? Compliance? Recognition we know more than they do?"

"Pfft. You view them as children, but they aren't."

He opened his mouth to protest, but shut it quickly. As usual, Katya zeroed in on the heart of the matter. He did see both Erin and Johan as moldable clay, and their resistance infuriated him.

"You could tell them you've changed your mind," Katya tossed out.

"Huh? About what?"

"About them having a choice." She moved closer to him. "You might simply say you and I discussed it, and the best place for them is with their own kind."

"But I already told them plopping them back on the surface is a death sentence," he sputtered.

"Remaining here doesn't guarantee survival for them,

either," she pointed out. "Of course, we would do our best, but we cannot be here every second. We might become entangled in a battle on the surface and be unable to return for them. Then they truly would be stuck down here. Eventually, they could starve. If they ran through all the fish." Katya turned her hands palms up.

He nodded and walked to a wall, placing a hand on a rich vein of platinum. The metal warmed beneath his touch and soothed his troubled places. The woman, Erin, was beautiful in a way that had crept up on him. She was tall and had a direct way of looking at him out of her clear, blue eyes that he respected. Her hair reminded him of grain growing beneath Mu's twin suns: white-gold, thick, and unruly. But she still relegated magic to an illusory realm, even after all the pains he'd gone to explaining their history to her and Johan.

He'd thought her intelligent, but maybe she wasn't as smart as all that if she could listen to him and discount his message. And then he remembered how his body had stirred to life when she and Johan were walking toward them, hair dripping from the lake and arms full of fish and discarded clothing. Her breasts had been clearly outlined beneath her top, the nipples large and round as ancient coins. Her lips were lush and full. They'd been parted over very straight, very white teeth, and he'd imagined her mouth sinking over his shaft.

Just recalling that moment sent a jolt of sensation straight to his groin. If Katya hadn't been in the room, he'd have wrapped a hand around his jutting appendage. It wouldn't take much to slake his lust since he couldn't recall the last time he'd come.

Katya tilted her head. Magic flickered around her. Was she leaving to offer him privacy?

Rather than disappearing, she looked straight at him. "Too late."

"For what?" His brain was muddled by lust. How could it ever be too late to bring himself to orgasm?

"I was listening in. Erin changed her mind. They're staying."

He wrenched his attention away from his swollen cock. "Why? What changed?"

"I missed some of their earlier discussion, but it appears she believes she can do more good with us to guide her than she can do back in her usual surroundings." Katya took a breath. "She knows enough to recognize humans lack effective weapons to fight magic, and Johan wanted to stay here. Why'd you tell them it was all-or-none?"

He clasped his hands behind him to resist the temptation to fondle himself. It would be perverse in front of his sister. "Because if they both went back, I would obliterate their memories of having been here. What they do not recall cannot be revealed in case the sea-serpents smelled magic on them and dug deeper."

"I understand that, but you could have done that to the one you sent back if the other had wished to remain. I rather like the man, and he clearly wanted to stay. Magic fascinates him."

Konstantin nodded. Thank the goddess his cock was

deflating. "I told them they had to agree because they need community in the same way we do. Had only one remained, it would have just been a matter of time before he—or she—demanded to return to the surface. And then, explanations to their companions—assuming any yet lived—would have been much harder."

"I see what you mean," Katya murmured. "There would be questions about why one showed up and where the other one had been in the intervening weeks or months before they popped back into plain view."

"Exactly." He glanced down to see if he was decent. Not quite.

"Returning to our earlier topic, now that they've made their choice, will we allow it or tell them we've rethought things?"

Konstantin considered her question. The immediate future would be far less complicated without the humans to worry about. If they were obedient, followed orders without question, he wouldn't hesitate. He needed to consult his source materials for the spell to turn willing humans into dragon shifters, but once he had it in hand, he and Katya could proceed. If their efforts bore fruit, soon there would be two more dragon shifters, albeit green-as-grass ones. It would take time, but their dragons would teach them magic —if they listened to them any better than they listened to him.

"Well?" his sister prodded.

His groin throbbed dully, cock still at half-mast, but he was used to repressing the sexual side of his nature. "Try to impress upon them that they must follow orders—at least until they've become dragons."

Katya puffed steam his way. "I'm not sure turning into dragon shifters—or mating with us somewhere down the line—is included in their plans. Only in ours. I will return to them and see what I can discover. Take your time."

Before he could protest, tell her he should be there too, she was gone. Katya understood. The lack of sex had grated on her as much as it did him, but they'd come to terms with it long since. It didn't make the longing for another's body any less pressing, though. As if it understood he'd kicked the floodgates open, his cock rose in a column against his belly, hard as it ever got.

Coming would take the edge off, make it possible to be in the same room with Erin without having to first stop upstairs and find clothing to cover himself, although it wasn't a bad idea. Clothing got in the way when he shifted forms, but the humans might be more comfortable with both him and Katya if they were covered.

Konstantin made his way to a sheltered alcove at the far end of the room and wrapped a hand around his erect phallus. It shuddered when he touched himself. His heart beat faster and breath steamed through his teeth, mixing with steam as he pumped his hand the length of his shaft.

He shut his eyes, not knowing which erotic scene would fill the dark canvas. He had a few favorites, but none of them materialized. He tightened his grip on himself. This wasn't a time to tease his hunger. This was a time to get down to business and get things done. Dragons mated in the air, amid noisy, brawling lust. His dragon had quit nagging about its lack of mating privileges a long while back. Once the other dragons had left the sub-Antarctic lair, there hadn't been any possibility of sex—for either himself or his bondmate.

He thrust into his hand. Steam thickened around him as his breathing came in panting gasps. The dark vista behind his closed eyes took on a wet, glistening aspect. Erin came to life, but a very different side of her. This Erin was prone with pillows beneath her head and hips. Her legs were spread, giving him a view of a mat of golden curls and swollen labia.

Like him, her eyes were shut. Golden hair cascaded around her. One hand was buried between her legs. The other pinched a nipple. She groaned, rotating her hips before settling into thrusting against the fingers sunk deep into her body. Her other nipple pebbled into a stiff peak. Color splashed across her breasts, shoulders, and face. She shrieked and moved the nipple hand to her clit, rubbing furiously. Her entire body vibrated as a climax spun her around and wrung her out.

The vision got him hotter than hot. His balls tightened, and desire roared through him as semen jetted from his cock, splashing against the wall before it dripped onto the flagstone floor.

Panting, gasping, and laughing, he sank to a crouch, fingers still curled around his hard-on. He was aroused enough to come again, but he'd indulged himself sufficiently. The imagery of Erin shattered the moment he opened his eyes. It had been so vivid. More tangible than most of his erotic fantasies. Maybe because she was real. Alive, breathing, and only one floor above him.

He shook the remaining drops of semen off the tip of himself and stood. A well-aimed shot of magic obliterated his seed. Someone like a sea-serpent could do a great deal of damage if they captured his jism.

They couldn't kill him, but they could make him damned miserable.

He raked his hands through his hair, shoving it behind his shoulders, and trotted across the room toward his library. Maintained with magic, the chamber had neither windows nor doors. Once he'd slithered through the illusion holding the room apart from the rest of the lower level, it didn't take long to locate what he wanted. He took a few moments to consult two moldering scrolls, memorizing the incantation. And an alternate in case the first didn't work.

Satisfied he was as prepared as he could be, he called a short teleport spell to take him to the room with his clothing chests. Feeling light, buoyant, and far better than he had before he came, he squatted in front of his chest and selected a pair of buff-colored leather breeks, soft lace-up boots, and a dark-green tunic, woven from lambswool, that had always been one of his favorites.

Suitably attired in centuries-old clothing, he walked nimbly downstairs to the kitchen. Everyone sat around the table, and the food dishes were empty. Katya glanced his way, her eyes widening. "Oh my. We've become formal." She pushed back from her seat. "I'll just run up and get dressed too."

"Do not bother on my account," Johan stood and half bowed.

Konstantin laughed. "Never tell a beautiful naked woman to cover herself, eh?"

"Something like that." Johan sank back into his chair.

Even though they may have already answered a similar question from his sister, he asked, "Why'd you toss your lot in with us?"

"Your sister asked the same thing," Johan murmured.

"What did you tell her?"

"We have different reasons," Erin replied. "Quite different, really. Turns out Johan has always had a fascination with magic. I never believed it existed."

"But you do now," Konstantin said.

She pushed her shoulders back, accentuating the swell of her breasts beneath her top. "Rather difficult not to when you turn into a dragon in front of me. And your sister waves a hand over our fish and they vanish. Either I actually saw the transformations, or I imagined them. Or I was dreaming or dead or suddenly took a nosedive into mental illness."

"I take it you discarded the other options?" Konstantin furled his brows.

The corners of her mouth twitched. "I tried to convince Johan we were dead. He wasn't buying it."

"Good man." Konstantin nodded Johan's way. "Other than nurturing a secret belief in magic, why'd you decide to remain? You never did answer my question."

"Proximity to magic was my primary motivation." Johan met his direct gaze. "I finally stumbled into something I had suspected was real for most of my life. To walk away before I could delve into it, learn as much as I could, would have crushed part of my soul."

"And you?" Konstantin turned toward Erin.

She laughed. "I'm afraid my motives aren't nearly as pure as Johan's. Part of my medical training is triage. It means I go where I'm needed most. From what you said, it appeared we'd be throwing our lives away if we returned to the surface. I didn't fancy standing by while people died in droves around me from a poison I had no antidote for."

She drew her brows together. "I'm assuming since the toxin is magical, nothing crafted by humans would counteract it."

Konstantin nodded. "Sea-serpent venom is malleable. It changes depending on how they choose to employ it. So even if you stumbled on something effective against it—which is unlikely—they would simply alter the formulation."

Breath hissed through her teeth and she muttered, "Got it," tightly before adding. "I figured I could do more good here than watching people die. Maybe you'll come up with something, a way to fight the serpents. I probably won't be much good in any kind of battle capacity, but I can patch up wounds."

He muted the smile that wanted out. Her willingness to help in any way she could boded well.

The ether glistened, and Katya shimmered into view. She'd donned a long black skirt and a soft-looking sweater in tones of cream and blue. Her coppery hair was drawn back into a queue that hung down her back.

"Did I miss anything?" she asked and slid into a chair next to him.

"Not really," Johan answered. "We basically told him the same things we told you. About why we opted to remain."

Konstantin stood and walked to the end of the table where he could see everyone easily. "All right. I will not lie to you. I expect you to do what Katya or I request without question. No matter how you feel about it."

"What kind of requests?" Erin sat straighter. "Give me an example, please."

"Say we are on the surface and it becomes necessary to take our dragon forms; we may instruct you to mount us."

"Very cool!" Johan made a fist and punched the air.

"Ride a dragon?" Erin's voice shook a little.

"Yes. We hate having anyone on our backs," Katya replied, "so we would only order you to ride us if it wasn't safe to leave you."

"Other examples," Konstantin continued, "include any reasonable request. You must trust if we are asking, it is necessary."

Erin shook her head. "I'm not sure I can do that."

"Why not?" Konstantin asked.

She spread her hands on the table. "We don't understand you, but nor do you understand us. I'm close to forty years old, which is probably nothing to you, but in human terms I'm edging toward middle age. I haven't been in a position where someone has told me what to do—and forced me to comply—for a long time."

"Not precisely true," Johan said.

"But they're proposing to treat us like children," Erin protested.

"Hear me out," he urged. "You do have people shaping your behavior. Your medical board, for instance, has standards. If you deviate from them significantly, they have the power to pull your license. Aboard *Darya*, we had many rules we had to follow. Most were for our safety and the convenience of the crew. I did not agree with all of them, but nor did I argue, and neither did you.

"As an engineer, I am held to certain standards as well. Unlike you, I do not have a license that can be withdrawn, but if I venture too far beyond accepted scientific methods, no one will hire me."

Konstantin focused on Johan's words. Perhaps he'd been misguided to assume the humans had to conform to dragon-shifter standards. They could learn from each other, which offered value beyond creating new dragon shifters. A topic he hadn't yet raised.

Erin nodded slowly. "You've made excellent points. I got so spun out by feeling like my freedom was being encroached upon, I didn't move the lens out far enough."

"Is freedom very important to humans?" Konstantin asked. "And what did you mean about a lens?"

"I can only speak for myself," Erin replied, "but personal freedom is critical to me. The lens analogy was from a camera." At his blank look, she went on. "It's a device that creates a likeness of something, rather like painting a picture. Depending on where I stand with my camera—and what kind of lens I have—I get very different perspectives if I stand closer or farther from the thing I want a picture of."

"Do you have one of these things with you?" Katya asked.

Johan sputtered something that sounded like a dismissive grunt. "All our gear is aboard the *Darya*, assuming she is still floating."

"A big assumption," Katya said. "The serpents may have scuttled both boats."

"Back to freedom"—Konstantin skewered Erin with his gaze—"what would make you feel yours had been violated?"

"There's no easy answer." She held his gaze. "I told myself I have to open my mind, be more flexible." Color rose to her cheeks. "Um, one of the downsides of being a doctor in the States is we believe we're at the top of a whole lot of heaps."

"States?" Katya asked.

"The New World," Konstantin told his sister. "North America is split between three countries, Canada, the United States, and Mexico."

"Thanks. Even though we speak English," Katya went on, "some of your phrases are confusing. I understand being on top of something, but how does it relate to being a healer?"

"Doctors in the States have a privileged position in society," Johan told her. "This is not so much true in Europe where they are salaried workers like the rest of us."

"What I tried to tiptoe around"—Erin picked up the conversation she'd let drop—"is I'll do my damnedest not to let my belief I'm special—something that's drummed into every newly minted doctor—get in the way of being a team player."

"So, healers believe they deserve more freedom than everyone else?" Konstantin was still trying to understand.

"Maybe not so much freedom as latitude and respect. Anyway, I'll work on getting over it, but I can't guarantee I won't ask questions if something makes no sense to me."

"And if I tell you there's no time for an answer?" Konstantin pressed.

"Then, I guess I'll accept it and move on."

It was good enough. "So long as you do not balk and refuse, all will be well."

"*What about new dragon shifters—and mating?*" Katya asked in telepathy.

"*Too much information right now,*" he told his sister. "*We can save that part for later.*"

"*But it's the main reason they're here.*"

"*Later.*" Konstantin closed off their private channel.

"Were the two of you talking?" Johan's gaze slid from him to Katya. "I felt something electric flicker between you."

"Yes. We can converse in mind speech," Konstantin said. Fascination shone from Johan's dark eyes. He'd probably warm to turning into a dragon shifter, but Erin was skittish as a newly hatched youngling. She was putting up a brave front, but apprehension rode close to the surface.

Katya's eyes widened, and she stood and began stripping out of the clothing she'd just put on. "My dragon is back. She says for us to meet her at the surface."

Konstantin started removing his clothing as well.

"I want to come with you," Johan said.

"So do I," Erin spoke firmly. Flowing to her feet, she picked through the pile of garments she and Johan had heaped at the end of the table and layered them on top of what she was wearing.

Johan mirrored her actions and glanced at Konstantin. "We can join you, right?"

Erin had levered off her boots so she could put on a thick outer suit, but she stopped and looked at him too.

Konstantin juggled his concerns, laying them aside for now. Either the four of them were allies—or not. While it was far more convenient to leave the humans beneath the ice sheet, it wasn't fair to them, nor would leaving them behind teach him anything about how willing they were to play by dragon-shifter rules.

"All right. Hurry and dress. Once you're ready, we'll go and meet Katya's dragon."

"Can both of you be visible at the same time?" Johan asked as he tossed clothes on.

Katya shook her head. "We are two consciousnesses, but it is either her form or mine. Never both."

"Intriguing," Erin said. "I want to hear more about how that works. Okay. I'm ready."

"So am I." Johan strode to a spot near him and Katya. "How will this work?"

"We will include you in our spell," Katya told him.

"It will seem strange," Konstantin cautioned, "but do not fight the sensation."

"Strange like the passageway that chucked us in your living room?" Erin asked.

He smiled. Erin could no more not ask questions than she could not breathe, but it was hard to fault her for curiosity. "Exactly like that." Before she could formulate any more questions, he called power. Once it crackled around them, he provided their destination.

A familiar surge of enchantment swept them into its maw. He found himself hoping Erin would embrace the feeling. He wanted her to welcome magic in all its manifestations, but it would take time.

Time they might not have now that the sea-serpents had come calling.

CHAPTER 10

The bite of Konstantin's magic rippled around me. It was, indeed, very like the sensation that had pounded against me after we jumped through the black hole-esque thing in the crystal cave. Rather like a mild electric shock paired with the scent of baked clay and a piquant herb I couldn't quite identify. Maybe rosemary or cilantro.

It hadn't taken very long for Johan and me to cover the miles between the cave and the dragons' home, so I wasn't surprised when an icy blast of air announced our arrival on the surface. I zipped my suit to my chin and cinched the hood cord. Despite the nearly half a year I'd spent in Antarctic waters, I was never quite prepared for the cold that hit me like a wall, stealing breath and freezing my lungs.

Konstantin and Katya were naked. How the hell did the well-below-zero chill not bother them? The magic shielding us dissipated. Icy sleet mixed with snow spilled from skies filled with gunmetal-colored clouds. The wind must have been gusting to forty miles an hour. I had to plant my feet to not get swept off them.

Waves crashed against the ice-crusted shoreline.

A blast of light so intense I clapped my mittened hands over my eyes died away almost as soon as it flared. I pried my eyes open, shielding them against the wind with hands and hood, and saw a golden dragon. I don't know why I expected Katya to look like her brother, but her dragon was totally different. Not just in color, but in proportions.

Katya was smaller—if you consider seven feet an improvement over eight—with more delicate proportions. Except I wasn't sure "delicate" applied to any dragon. She might have different-colored scales, but her eyes were the same, whirling gold with deep-green centers.

She was perched on a chunk of ice with Konstantin standing next to her. Light flickered around them, adding a golden glow to his phenomenal physique. Not that it needed any help. Was he why I'd caved and said I'd stay? A rather guilty yes formed in my mind.

He might not be the whole reason, but he was a big part of it. He'd as much as said he'd imported Johan and me to make new dragon shifters. That might mean sex. A small spark of heat began in my belly and traveled downward.

Or it might be anchored to magic and have nothing to do with the "normal" way babies happened.

"It is good to be aboveground," Johan said, his deep voice breaking into my thoughts.

I wrenched my gaze away from Konstantin's Apollo gorgeousness and nodded. It was a relief to be outside. Something about knowing miles of dirt sat above my head would have bothered me—if I'd allowed myself to focus on it. As it was, I'd had plenty of other items to occupy my mind.

Konstantin walked to where Johan and I stood. I scanned him for patches of frostbite, blue lips, ice clinging to his eyelashes and found none of the above. I may have included his genitals in my visual exam, but only for clinical reasons. Regardless of my pathetic rationale, the inescapable conclusion was his body temperature had to be a whole lot higher than 98.6.

"Are you warm enough?" he asked.

"Yes." Johan smiled.

"I am going to take my dragon form, and Katya and I will fly a reconnaissance to see if the ships are still nearby. Or the serpents. You may remain here, accompany us, or I can return you down below."

"I will come with you," Johan said without the slightest hesitation.

I tried. God knows I tried to say the words that would place me on top of a flying dragon, but they got stuck somewhere between my throat and my teeth. "Okay if I stay here?" I asked brightly. I did not want to end up stuck in the dragon's subterranean lair by myself.

"Probably," Konstantin answered. "Although it's better for us to remain together." He turned one hand so his palm was facing upward and blew on it. I was coming to recognize the feel of his magic, but surprise raced through me when a clear crystalline rock formed, glowing golden in its center.

He handed it to me. "Tuck this inside that garment of yours so you won't lose it. If you run into problems, don't hesitate. Call my name, and I will be here as quickly as I can."

"Thank you." I unzipped one of my chest pockets and dropped the stone inside. It was warm, and its heat radiated through my multiple layers, warming me.

Johan and Konstantin walked away from me. This time, I was proactive about shielding my eyes and managed it a scant moment before Konstantin morphed into a dragon. Seeing him next to his sister reinforced how real all this was.

Two dragons puffing steam and smoke into the frigid air stood not twenty feet from me. Katya waggled a curved reddish talon, and Johan moved right next to her. She bent forward, both forelegs extended, and lifted him easily, swinging him sideways and back until he sat astride her.

He looked like a kid at a carnival, naked joy carved into his face. Jealousy stabbed me, biting deep. I wanted that sense of wonder; it had run off and left me in the dirt so long ago I barely remembered.

Next time, I promised myself.

Next time, I'd gather my courage and ride Konstantin. Especially after I'd pumped Johan for intel on everything about today's adventure. I watched while the dragons extended their wings. It was windy enough, all they had to do was unfurl them and they turned into airfoils, pulling them into the slipstream.

Johan didn't seem to be having any trouble staying astride. The dragons had two protuberances at the base of their necks, which provided something akin to a saddle horn to hang onto. Part of me was sad, another was angry. I didn't have to be such a fucking wimp, but I was still half-expecting to emerge from a coma and be told this was all something my subconscious mind had dreamed up.

I'd sustained a hell of a bump on my head, so my reasoning wasn't all that far out in left field.

The dragons flew higher and higher. Made sense if they wanted to evade detection from the sea-serpents. Presumably, they were stuck in the sea—unless they became human. I scrunched my forehead trying to remember. Either Katya or her brother had said they assumed the serpents could take human form, but they weren't certain.

Despite the minus temperature and the wind, I was enjoying being outside. It couldn't hurt to take a bit of a walk while I waited. Movement would help keep my blood circulating, and I felt the bite of cold even through my triple-layer neoprene boots.

No one knew much about me, but I'd arranged my life very carefully after finishing high school. And I'd taken care to move far from the small town in northern Arizona where I was born. I would say reared, but I more or less raised myself.

I rarely allowed myself to reflect on the years before college and med school. It was as if my life began when I was eighteen and enrolled in a huge junior college in East Los Angeles. I picked Harbor JC on purpose because it had something in excess of 50,000 students. A great place to be invisible. And I was.

I went to class and to work and to the one-room walkup I could afford. Two years later, I transferred to UCLA on a full scholarship. From there, med school at Tulane in New Orleans, and thence to a surgical residency at Northwestern. Once I hit med school, I no longer needed excuses for why I chose not to socialize. Everyone understood I had no time for anything beyond classes, studying, and my hospital rotations.

I shook my head and turned so the wind hit me in the back rather than straight on in my face. I was still being a coward. It was simple to replay my history from my favorite starting point—because it sidestepped the sordid parts. My childhood read like a bad soap opera. Even back in the days when child services rarely removed kids from homes, mine was bad enough to catch their attention.

I tried to hide my situation, but I didn't have many resources when I was six. Showing up to school in filthy, stinky clothes day after day must have led to phone calls. Strangers tried to quiz me, but I was really good at keeping my mouth shut.

One day, I was called to the principal's office. I was so scared, I wet myself, but I smelled so bad anyway, probably no one would notice a touch of ammonia on top of the dirt and grime and sweat. Someone must have figured out how horrible things were at home. It was the only explanation for my summons.

I'd get blamed for telling, even though I hadn't said one word.

I'd be whipped and maybe burned with cigarettes. Usually, Dad's wrath fell on my big brother and sister. They did their best to protect me. They were why I was even in school. They'd never gone and wanted me to have a chance to learn to read and write.

Mom was dead. When Dad was especially angry, he told me she'd died having me, but my brother told me she died from a drug overdose when I was not quite a year old. My father was a right bastard. Drug dealer. Pimp. Addict. Boozer. I have zero good memories of him, but my thoughts were getting off track.

I forced myself to recall walking into the school office that day. A youngish woman with messy blonde hair took one look at me and wrapped her arms around me. When I glanced about, wild-eyed, I saw my brother and sister standing quietly next to one wall.

"What happened?" I cried, sobs obliterating my words.

"Dad's in jail," my brother told me.

"We're going to foster care," my sister added. "No way it can possibly be worse than home."

Brave words from her, but they gave me enough to make it through that day. And the next. I suppose the system tried to place us all together. No one wanted three derelict kids, though, two of whom had never gone to school.

I blew out a shaky breath. Over the next twelve years, I grew a very thick skin; it got me through the worst of things.

Shunted from foster home to foster home, I stopped trying to develop any connections with my families.

What was the point?

Some were worse than others, but none were as bad as living with Dad had been. Obviously, I lost track of my siblings. Last I heard, my brother was in juvenile hall. I have no idea what happened to Sissie. Guilt burned in my guts. I'd promised myself I'd look them up—many times. Except I never did.

School always came easy to me, so I became adept at ignoring my surroundings and focusing on my studies. No one came to my high school graduation, but no one showed up for any of the other ones, either.

I'm many things, but stupid isn't one of them. I fully grasp the connection between how I grew up and my lack of ability to develop much in the way of relationships with anyone. I dated plenty, but as soon as the guy started making noises about wanting anything more complicated than an occasional meal, movie, or roll in the hay, I pulled out my excuse du jour and dropped out of his life. Surgery was a slam-dunk choice. My patients are asleep—for the most part.

Feeling worse than when I'd begun my backward-looking journey, I scanned the skies. The dragons should be back by now. Why weren't they? Wrapping my arms around myself, I shivered. Not from cold so much as fear. If they didn't return, I'd have to fall back on luck and hope to hell if I did see a ship or a raft, it would be carrying friendly folk rather than the Russians who'd boarded the *Darya*.

I clenched my jaw. I was losing it. The Russians were unlikely. If what Konstantin and Katya relayed was accurate, probably all of them were dead. Good riddance, but I still felt hollow inside.

I missed cell phones and the Internet and my cozy cabin aboard the *Darya*. Hell, I missed my home north of Seattle, and my well-curated surgical practice with its blend of plastic surgery that paid in cold, hard cash and patients with decent insurance. Our practice had opted out of Medicaid and Medicare long since.

It wasn't that we were cheap bastards, but standing on my feet for ten hours doing a complicated surgery where the patient's life literally hung in my hands just had to be worth more than the $247 Medicare was willing to pay me. An amount far less than minimum wage when I factored in pre-op visits, paperwork, post-op visits, and everything else required for a reasonable standard of care. One of my exceptions was I did *pro bono* work at Planned Parenthood two nights a month. Far as I was concerned, any woman wise enough to know motherhood wasn't going to work out deserved my help. My family was a living testament to what happened to unwanted children.

I may have clawed my way out of the pit, but the price was high.

I rubbed ice off my cheeks. No reason to think about any of that. My chances of ever practicing surgery again were looking pretty thin. To put a finer point on it, my chances of returning to a life where things like minimum wage mattered were probably nil.

I trotted back to the place the dragons had launched and looked upward once again. Nothing. I tugged off a mitten and dipped my hand inside the pocket that had the stone Konstantin had given me. The one he'd formed from thin air. It was still warm, still pulsing.

Should I call him?

Why did I even believe saying his name would work?

I dropped the crystal back into its pocket and put my mitten back on. I was being stupid. His instructions had been clear enough. To call if I ran into trouble. The only trouble I might run into here would be a renegade elephant seal, and I hadn't seen even one of them.

A wandering albatross winged its way past me, majestic with its better than ten-foot wingspan. Next came a flock of blue-eyed shags. Penguins honked as they trotted up and down the expanse of open shoreline. Normally, I adored the rich variety of bird and sea life. Today, it was tough to give them more than a passing glance.

After checking the wind direction, I hunted for a big enough boulder to shelter me from the worst of it. The entry to the chromium dig site had to be somewhere around here, but locating it wouldn't buy me much. The Russians had blown it sky high. Besides, the jumble of rocks below its entrance hadn't been much of a picnic, either. Although, were it not for a teensy shove from Konstantin, I probably would have made it out of there.

"Yeah," I mumbled. "And Johan's leg would still be broken." Not that it mattered. Had the dragons not intervened, the Russians would have killed me and Johan as soon as they discovered their first attempt to eradicate us had failed.

I found a decent wind screen and hunkered behind it. Penguins trotted close, examining the stranger in their midst. Not being continuously blasted by the brisk, icy wind helped. I leaned against a rock and concentrated on wiping my mind clear of everything. It was almost like a Zen meditation, familiar because I used a variation of the same exercise before I entered the surgical suite.

It settled my mind, blanking out everything but the task ahead. Whether I was nipping and tucking or going after tumors didn't matter. What did was the patient got 110 percent of my concentration.

I liked surgery. There was something clean and beautiful about "see problem, fix problem." Most of the other medical subspecialties were far murkier.

Wishing for a watch, I stared at the sky, hoping for clues about the passage of time. It seemed like I'd been wandering on this beach for about an hour, but it could have been double that, or only twenty minutes.

I was having a hard time not worrying about the dragons and Johan. Konstantin had said they were doing a quick reconnaissance. Quick suggested they'd have been back long since. They must have run into something unexpected. My stomach twisted into an uncomfortable knot.

I wanted to help but had no idea what to do. Sitting wasn't working for me anymore. I scrambled to my feet. Penguins that had settled close to me scattered. The wind hit me hard enough to make me stagger, and I cut a path crabwise into it. Earlier, I'd gone the other way. This time, I traveled to my left along the shoreline. Shoulders hunched, I fought gusts that wanted to send me back the way I'd come.

I tried not to interpret it as a bad omen.

The wind howled, shrilled, shrieked, almost like it was alive. The penguins lumbered into the sea. They might be clumsy on land, but they're exceptional swimmers. Between the wind, the birds, and keeping my head down, I didn't see —or hear—the raft until it was only about seventy-five feet from me, angling in toward shore.

My first instinct was to yell and scream to make sure they saw me. Rafts meant ships and warmth and rescue, but then I came to my senses. I had no idea who was in this raft, and I'd do well to conceal myself until I figured things out. I glanced all around me but didn't see anything big enough to hide behind.

Had the men already seen me? It was likely. My black suit would stick out like flashing neon against the gray-white of the shoreline. I turned around and realized I was a long way from the sheltering boulder that had protected me from the wind. So far, I could barely make it out.

The raft was closer now. Near enough I could make out four occupants dressed similarly to me, but that meant next to nothing. Polar suits were ubiquitous. One of the men raised a hand, which clinched they knew I was here. I guessed the hand's owner was male, but covered up like they all were, some of the people in the raft could have been women.

I had a bad feeling about this. Really bad, and I'd always

had sharp instincts. Honed and developed during my earliest years, they'd saved me from beatings more than once. While I still had the opportunity, I turned my back to the raft and dug out Konstantin's stone. He'd said to call his name, so I did, following it with, "I think I need help."

After hiding the stone away, I tried hard for "normal" and strode to a slightly less icy stretch of beach where I thought the raft would land. I kept telling myself Antarctica was full of scientists, and this batch could be from any ship —or research base—but I didn't believe my own hype.

I'd called Konstantin. Despite my ambivalence about magic's existence, I'd dragged out the miracle stone and followed instructions about using it. That I hadn't relegated it to the realm of the impossible told me how worried I was.

Shy of running—a fool's errand because if the raft's occupants meant me harm they'd catch me eventually—I'd shot my wad. No more options. Safest bet was to play dumb. I'd never done that particularly well, but there's a first time for everything.

The next few minutes lasted forever. The raft scraped ice, and the pilot sprang over the pontoons, dragging the anchor rope with him. Now that they were closer, my bet was they were all men. Tall with heavy bodies and wide shoulders. Their faces were hidden behind hoods, goggles, and balaclavas.

I fully expected the penguins, a curious lot if ever there was one, would stream out of the sea to examine the raft and its occupants, but none of them did. The few seals on the beach veered away too, hustling their bulk into the ocean.

Oh-oh. Animals sensed danger. Their hasty egress validated my fear.

Once the raft's pilot had buried the anchor with a few handy rocks, he straightened. I'd walked near enough to talk, but I wanted to hear what his voice sounded like before I said anything.

"What are you doing here?" he asked in strongly accented English. I ran the inflection through my mental databanks. Not Russian. Maybe Scandinavian, but with a very old-fashioned edge. Probably because I didn't answer right away, he fired off what I presumed was the same query in two other languages. German and maybe French or Italian.

I settled on truth woven with fiction. "My ship was boarded. I'm the only survivor."

"You do not seem glad for rescue." Another of the raft's passengers had joined us.

I shrugged. "Because I have no idea which side you're on. For all I know, you're part of the contingent that boarded our ship and killed everyone."

"What are we waiting for?" The third and fourth men strode near. "We must leave."

I made shooing motions. "Fine. Go."

"You will accompany us," the pilot said.

"We cannot leave you here," man number two chimed in.

"Where are you going?" I asked. "What is the name of your ship?"

"We are from...Arctwsko." The pilot hesitated before butchering the name of the Polish base, and my blood ran cold. I'd spent enough time at Arctowski to know all the scientists, and I'd never run into anyone who talked like this bunch did. Even if I couldn't see them well enough to identify them, I knew from hearing them they had to be lying.

"I'll be fine." I smiled. "I put out a distress call with my satellite transponder. Help is on the way."

The men glanced from one to the other. Something eerie passed between them, like when Konstantin and Katya talked mind-to-mind, yet not quite the same.

The pilot tried to grab my arm. I twisted away from him. "I'm not going anywhere with you. If you want to wait until the ship comes for me, that's fine, but I'm staying right here."

The pilot lunged for me again. I evaded him, but the other three men were positioning themselves around me, cutting off any possibility of escape. "Why are you here?" I asked.

"For you, why else?" The pilot's expression made my heart feel like someone had wrapped a fist around it and squeezed hard.

Still doing my best to play dumb, I said, "Huh? Makes no sense."

"You summoned aid." The pilot spread his arms. "We are here."

"Yes, in response to your...satellite summons," another man said from somewhere behind me.

"Then why didn't you say so from the beginning?" I was buying time, staving off the inevitable, but I'd be damned if I'd get into a Zodiac with this bunch. Not willingly.

"We assumed you would know," the second man said smoothly.

I started to point out a whole lot of inconsistencies. Instead, I smiled again and said, "Privacy, please. If I'm going to go with you, I need to relieve myself first."

Amid grumbling, the men who were behind me joined the other two. I waited until they were facing the water rather than me, and walked as fast as I could toward a jumble of ice blocks. Once I was behind them, I squatted to get most of my body beneath their line of sight.

Where could I go?

More importantly, who the hell were those men? Were they even people? Or were these some of the serpents wearing their human bodies? They seemed fluent in many languages—just like Konstantin.

I could crawl, but they'd see me soon enough. I could dig, but that wouldn't be fast enough. Determined to maximize whatever time I'd bought myself, I remained crouched behind the ice.

One of the men yelled at me to hurry about the same time as I heard dragons bugling from above. From its place in my pocket, the stone sent out waves of heat. I started to stand, but I was safer where I was. Konstantin and Katya might be here, but I was a long way from being home free.

I craned my neck upward and saw blasts of fire arcing from both dragons. A gust of displaced air right next to me turned into Johan. I was panting from fear when I managed. "They taught you to teleport?"

"No. Explanations can wait. We have to help."

"How?" My voice was a squeak.

"Those are sea-serpents. The longer they remain human, the weaker they will become. We were gone so long because we were gathering information. Our job is to keep them human—and on land—for as long as possible. They must be in the sea, or they cannot shift."

With my teeth clenched to keep them from chattering, I surged to my feet and ran after Johan, right toward the four things that only looked like men. I tried to tell myself it was better than cowering behind my icy shelter, but I didn't quite believe it.

CHAPTER 11

After leaving Erin on the beach, Konstantin flew higher than he normally would have with Katya winging along beside him. Johan didn't appear to have any fear of heights, which was a plus. The ships came into view quickly. Konstantin battled fury and disbelief while he hastily draped a shield around himself and his twin. Where before there'd been a handful of serpents, now both ships were crawling with them. Many had left the water and slithered across open deck space.

Decks running dark red with blood.

Shrill cries, like dragon bugling but with deeper discordant notes mixed in, rose in bursts.

In between the serpents, men and women crouched, their faces smeared red as they stuffed body parts from dead crew members into their mouths. At least it solved the question of whether serpents could still take human form.

The grisly scene also violated one of the covenants binding dragonkind. Humans were off the menu unless exceptional circumstances intervened, like a war where they were dead, anyway. Even then, they were to be avoided unless starvation threatened.

His dragon wanted to blast the serpents with fire, but he held it back. The killing urge was strong, and his bondmate chafed under his determination to keep it from making an enormous mistake. He couldn't allow it to gain the upper hand, though. If he did, it would be the start of a long, downhill slide that wouldn't end well.

He swallowed back fire and smoke with stern admonitions they'd leave this place before they'd declare war—a war they were certain to lose. This was one instance where they needed to remain invisible. Badly outnumbered, they'd do well to find out what they could. At this point, anything would be an improvement over his current level of knowledge, which was shrouded in myth and history.

He wanted to talk with Katya but couldn't risk any display of magic. Subtle as it was, even telepathy might alert one of the serpents to their presence. He circled higher still and watched as serpents glided up and over the ships' railings as they came and went.

He had no idea how many humans they'd killed, but the feast would strengthen them. Unfortunately. Angling his head, he focused his dragon's hearing. Far sharper than his own, it brought bits and pieces of conversation his way. The serpents spoke in the dragons' ancient language. He hadn't used it in centuries, but he still understood it well enough.

"Better than we expected," floated up to him.

"Brilliantly executed."

"Good choice."

"Never have left if we hadn't run out of food."

"Ha! Ran our world dry, don't you mean?"

"That's one interpretation."

"Nag. Nag. Nag. We may have helped it along, but it wasn't doing well."

An enormous serpent with scales in a drudgy gray black reared his head back and laid his upper body flat against a bulkhead. From there, he slithered to the next deck up. Once he was situated where everyone could see him, he bugled long and loud.

Konstantin understood he was demanding silence. Perhaps this was their leader? He waited, wanting to hear whatever the serpent had to say. Their position was risky, but he was willing to chance another few minutes. Any serpent who looked up wouldn't see them, not exactly, but they'd likely notice the blurry spot where Konstantin's ward didn't quite blend with the sky.

Katya's wings beat faster where she hovered slightly above him. She was nervous but determined to stay the course. This might be their best opportunity to find something out, maybe critical information that would help them oust the goddess-damned serpents once and for all.

Next to the serpent demanding silence, a wavery spot punched through the icy air. Konstantin's eye's widened. He knew exactly what it was even before still more serpents glided through the newly-formed portal. Exiting onto the ship, they didn't hesitate before diving into the dark, choppy water.

Water that was rapidly icing over. Were the serpents helping it freeze, or was the ocean so outraged by the unnatural incursion, it was taking matters into its own hands?

After the fifteenth serpent, Konstantin quit counting. How many didn't matter. What did was getting rid of them.

"I have opened a new gateway," the gray-and-black serpent announced. "Earth will be a fertile place for us to recover our lost powers."

A reddish serpent rose until a meter of scaled body swayed above the rocking deck. It looked up at the one who'd spoken. "You chose well, Surek. Few people are here. We can strengthen ourselves while remaining out of sight."

"You have been here before, correct?" Surek asked.

The red serpent bobbed its head. "By the time our presence becomes common knowledge, we will once again be strong enough to remain in human form without risking death."

Konstantin shot an excited glance upward. Katya nodded her understanding. Apparently, the serpents were vulnerable as humans, a problem dragonkind never had. Of course, coaxing them to don their human bodies posed its own set of difficulties, but one challenge at a time.

"What happens next?" another serpent, this one green, asked.

Surek focused spinning dark eyes—dragon's eyes—on

the red serpent, the one theoretically familiar with Earth. "What do you think, Klem?"

"Some of us, as many as possible, should masquerade as human. That way, if anyone stumbles across us, we will escape notice." His tongue flicked in and out before he said, "We cannot remain on these ships. Humans have organizations that track such things, and the vessels may have already been reported missing. Particularly in light of the other ship having been boarded and its occupants dispatched."

"If not here, then where shall we build a temporary haven while we regain our full strength?" Surek asked.

"Land is nearby. We can tunnel within it to create lairs that will escape notice. Once our magic is fully restored, we will teleport to other places on Earth and put the remainder of our plan into action."

Konstantin fanned his wings, waiting to see what the plan consisted of, but no one elucidated it. Probably because they'd discussed it twenty ways from Sunday before leaving whichever world they'd decimated.

"Check within the ships for clothing," Surek ordered. "Clean your faces of blood. Once you are attired as humans —and be sure to don a lot of clothing; humans are fragile and cannot withstand extreme cold—launch rafts. Between this ship and the other, I count six. Each raft will select a different spot to land. When you arrive, you will uncover options for underground excavation. We will communicate via telepathy, and the most promising location will be where we end up. Questions?"

No one raised any.

The group moved faster than Konstantin would have thought possible. Within only a few moments, two rafts bobbed in the icy waves. Engines roared to life, and the Zodiacs took off, cutting through water that had turned almost black as it thickened to icy sludge. Through the entire discussion, not one serpent had bothered to cast so much as a stray glance upward. Perhaps it boded well for being able to overpower them with a lesser force than theirs.

Lesser, but more than him and Katya. He wanted to know what her dragon had found. So far, there hadn't been time to delve into its search for others who were near enough to help.

She brushed a wingtip against his, signaling her intent they should leave. He'd almost forgotten about Johan perched on her back. The man had been quiet, seemingly understanding they needed to escape detection.

Erin's voice calling his name reverberated through his mind. It was the extra push he needed. She was defenseless and exposed where he'd left her. Before he realized how many sea-serpents they faced, and their intent to swarm over the headlands, he'd thought her safe enough.

She must have seen one of the rafts. Would she intuit something was amiss with its occupants? Maybe.

Wheeling, he hastened back the way they'd flown earlier. One of the rafts had already landed. At first, he couldn't see Erin, and his dragon's fury rendered the beast unmanageable. He couldn't have held back its fire no matter how hard he tried.

Flames shot from his mouth. Ash and smoke followed. So much for stealth.

Katya sputtered, clearly having similar control problems. A blast of magic sent Johan pinwheeling off her back surrounded by a protective sphere. It would deliver him to the beach below, freeing Katya to fight by his side.

With fire spewing from him like a volcano, he took stock. Four serpents in human form shouldn't be all that hard to dispatch. Not if they were as susceptible as they'd claimed to be. Their discussion suggested they were mortal as humans, which meant they could be killed.

"Do not let them return to the sea," Katya screeched into his mind.

It was solid advice. Once they were in the sea, they'd reach for their serpent bodies and vanish beneath the surface where he'd never be able to find them. Since the serpents knew he and Katya were up here, there was no more reason for caution. A focused beam of magic located Erin. She and Johan were right next to each other.

No longer worried about her, or at least not as worried, he kicked open the floodgates and encouraged his dragon to be as feral and bloodthirsty as it wanted. Fire rained from the skies. From Katya too. It burned the clothing off the serpents, and their human hides turned first red then black and blistered.

Three of the serpents were well and truly on fire, but Konstantin kept right on feeding more flames into the mix. When they incinerated in front of him, he'd believe they were dead. Unholy shrieks filled the air. Surely, they were calling the others with telepathy, but if Konstantin played this right, he'd be long gone—along with Katya, Johan, and Erin—before another bunch of serpents showed up.

Magic streamed from Katya, mixing with the flames, and all three serpents exploded, the stench of burning flesh and seared scales rotten and acrid.

"Where's the last one?" he shouted at his sister. He narrowed his eyes, but it was impossible to see through the smoke and ash slurry below.

"There!" She all but dove from the skies.

When he got lower, he saw Johan, Erin, and the last serpent. It had done its damnedest to escape and had nearly made it to the water's edge when Johan and Erin tackled it. As things sat, it writhed face down on the ice, reaching for the water.

Erin had one foot, Johan the other. They dragged the thing back onto the shore. The two of them had taken an enormous chance. If the serpent had been anywhere close to normal strength, it would have flattened them with magic. Murdered them and leapt into the sea. No more advantage to being airborne, so he slid heavily onto the beach and trumpeted. He needed Erin and Johan to move, but couldn't communicate with them telepathically. Nor was there time to shift.

They must have understood because they let go of the serpent and ran a few yards away, out of range of his fire. Katya landed next to him. Between the two of them, they doused the serpent with flames.

"Please," he cried before fire engulfed him. "Please. We were once the same as you."

"Tell someone who gives a damn," Konstantin shouted, reverting to the dragon's tongue, easily manageable in his beast form.

"Good enough," Katya yelled. "We need to leave. Now."

He heard a distant engine and wondered why the hell the serpents hadn't just teleported. Had they truly grown so weak transport magic was beyond them? No time to figure it out.

He opened his magical center. Power flared around him, creating a glowing nimbus. He gestured to Erin and Johan, and they ran to his side. The spell wasn't elegant, but it would do. His aim was to move them fast without leaving a trail. There had to be a serpent or two who could still teleport, and he did not want unexpected company in his home.

The distinctive feel of his power, electric with strength, surrounded all of them. His dragon added its own enchantment, falling headlong into a major contribution to his spell. His bondmate had done well today. It had slipped its leash once, but the lapse was understandable. Erin had been in danger. The dragon was beginning to view her as their mate and would protect her with every bit of power it commanded.

Never mind she wasn't interested in them.

He remembered her outburst where she'd accused him of all kinds of things, right before she'd tossed out that birthing a mixed race child might kill her. The walls of his great room shimmered into being around them. He switched from teleport to shift magic as soon as his talons scraped the marble floor.

"Are you sure none of them will follow us?" Erin asked. She unzipped the top of her suit and shook her hood back. Blonde hair curled wetly around her face, sticking out in spots, and she shielded her eyes from the brightness of his shift spell.

He shook his head. Responding would have to wait until he was done shifting.

"It seems unlikely," Johan murmured. "They did talk about building their own lairs, though. Would they dig this deep?"

"I don't believe so." Katya was almost human again, her talons changing back to long, shapely fingers.

"You did," Erin pointed out. "If you could burrow miles beneath the surface, and they're like you, my assumption is—"

"Something happened to their magic," Konstantin cut in. "Hold up a moment. Let's go to the kitchen and I'll tell you what we saw and heard." At her nod, he added, "This is the last time we leave anyone behind. It's too dangerous."

Questions fairly danced through her mind. He saw them reflected in her eyes. Before any more spilled out, he hurried up the stairs to the next level. A bit of magic uncovered more flasks of the mildly alcoholic beverage he and Katya took turns brewing. While he retrieved something to drink, his sister pulled sheets of kelp and a tray of dried seal meat from a cupboard.

Erin patted the front of her black suit. An alarmed look bloomed on her face. "The stone. What happened to it?"

He angled a glance her way. "I fashioned it for a specific purpose. Once it was no longer needed, it rejoined the air I created it with."

A mix of unsettled emotions blazed from her, but all she said was, "Glad I didn't lose it."

He dug in to the food Katya had set out. For a time, everyone ate in silence. Once he'd taken the worst of the edge off his hunger, he sketched out the information they'd acquired from their aerial perch.

Erin nodded solemnly, regarding him through narrowed eyes. "I wondered why the one we attacked didn't slip out of our grasp and crush us with magic."

"I did not expect it to." Johan reached across and patted Erin's arm. "But there was no time for an explanation of why I thought it was safe to jump on it. Once it reached the sea, it would have escaped."

"Mmph. And told the others," Erin muttered. "If it hadn't already."

"We did good work today." Konstantin regarded his sister. "What news did your dragon bring?"

Katya looked away, and he steeled himself for bad news. "No dragon shifters on Earth except us, but several live on nearby worlds. The problem will be convincing them this is a battle worth fighting. They decided Earth was a lost world long ago, not a promising place for dragons for all the reasons you and I know all too well."

"Did their reasons include the damage we have inflicted

on the planet?" Johan asked.

"Partially," Konstantin replied. "We were forced away from our last world because it imploded into its sun. We live forever. It means we're used to having to exchange one world for another, so the problems Earth faces are not a deterrent in and of themselves."

"When my dragon went looking for assistance, we didn't appreciate the full scope of the sea-serpent problem," Katya said. "Then, we figured there were only a few, but their leader, that Surek person, opened a portal to where they used to live. For all we know, it's still disgorging serpents."

"It does change things," Konstantin agreed.

"You have to say more than that." Erin knitted her brows together.

He cast about for soft words, but there weren't any. "Dragons live for battles. We were forged in fire, and it has shaped who we are. One of our original roles was to mediate and enforce the laws binding magic wielders."

Erin cleared her throat. "How many different kinds are there? Real ones, not the TV shows and books Johan loves."

"But they are connected," Johan protested. "Every type of character in science fiction and fantasy was crafted because the author knew something, had seen something, or someone relayed a tale too fantastic not to be true."

"Not all of us assume the fantastic has its roots in reality," Erin commented with a smile.

"Yes, yes. We have enough problems without sidetracking into philosophical discussion points."

"I suppose you're right," she replied.

Konstantin watched the exchange but didn't add to it. Erin was still struggling with whether magic was real, and her retreat to signposts from her familiar world was understandable.

"You didn't answer me." She looked him dead in the eyes. "How many kinds of magical creatures are there?"

The dogged expression on her face—determination to proceed no matter what the cost—made him respect her. "I can't give you an exact number." He reached for the nearer of two flasks and drank deeply. "But I can list general categories."

Holding up a hand, he ticked off a list, using his fingers as props. "Witches. Fae—White and Dark. Druids. Faeries. Other types of shifters, and they encompass everything from wolves to bears to birds to rodents. Sorcerers. Magicians."

Erin's eyes rounded in surprise. "That many."

"It's far from a comprehensive list," he told her. "I just hit the high points. Magic is part of the roots of all worlds. It was here long before humans became so numerous they figured they owned Earth."

"These other worlds," Johan cut in, "do they also include people like us? Those who are not magical?"

"Of course," Katya answered.

"How many of them are there, roughly?" Erin asked.

"That's your second numbers question," Konstantin observed.

"I like to know what I'm dealing with. Is that a problem?"

"No. Not at all, but..." He stopped talking. He'd been about to say she was missing the most important aspects of the puzzle, but she had to start somewhere. Perhaps numbers felt manageable, and the rest of it was so far afield, she couldn't even formulate questions.

"What is our next move?" Johan asked. "Surely, we are not going to sit down here while those atrocities gain a toehold."

"We can't take them on by ourselves," Konstantin said. "Especially, not after today. We caught them by surprise. It won't happen twice."

"Yes. They know we're here," Katya agreed. "We no longer have the element of surprise."

"Where are the closest of our kin?" he asked Katya.

"The Fleisher group of borderworlds."

"What are they?" Erin directed the question at Johan, but he shook his head.

"Not part of anything I've read," he answered her.

"It's a constellation of a dozen separate worlds, perhaps a day's journey from here. Most are inhabited, but if I remember correctly two don't have a breathable atmosphere," Konstantin replied.

"Can we come with you?" Johan leaned forward. Clearly, the adventure part of things appealed to him.

"I'm not thinking we'll have a choice," Erin muttered. "Konstantin said we all have to stick together from now on."

Konstantin still had his hand on the flask. He set it down. They'd reached a crux point, and he needed Erin and Johan to agree with how he wanted to proceed. He was certain of Johan, but Erin might balk.

"What is it?" she pressed. "I'm coming to know that

look you get when you're figuring out how to take something I'll recoil from and dress it up to make it more palatable."

He nodded. "Right you are. While Katya and I don't think twice about employing magic to travel from world to world or for other reasons, the places we go are not nearly as safe for individuals without magic."

"Can you include us in a long teleport spell?" She arched a brow.

"Yes, but you'd be vulnerable the entire time, and even more defenseless once we arrived at our destination. In this instance, there will be multiple destinations, which amplifies the risk factors."

"I'll take my chances." She smiled gamely.

"It's a bad idea, one which puts the rest of us at risk—" he began.

"Then I'll remain here," she said.

"Also not a good choice," Katya said.

"We need to hear them out, consider their advice," Johan spoke up.

"What? You're ganging up on me?" Erin pushed back from the table and got to her feet.

Before she could walk out of the room, Konstantin snagged her with a spell and snatched her up in his arms. Once he had a good grip on her, he carried her toward the steps, kicking and screaming at him to put her down.

Johan hurried toward them. "Is that really necessary?"

"I won't hurt her." Annoyed at having to explain himself, Konstantin opened his mouth to order Johan back to his chair, but Katya saved him from saying something he might end up regretting.

Sliding in next to Johan, she hooked an arm beneath his. "Come with me. We shall talk. Erin is safe with my brother."

Konstantin felt subtle magic woven in with her words. Johan turned toward her and murmured, "Of course. Where would you like us to sit?"

"Can't you see what he's doing?" Erin squawked. "Whatever he left out, we all need to hear it. Together. In the same room."

Firmly captured by Katya's magic, Johan didn't even turn around.

Konstantin added compulsion to the command. "You will hear me out. For that, we require privacy."

"I won't listen. Put me down, you fucking—fucking pirate."

He wanted to laugh, but it would be a mistake. He'd been called far worse over the long years of his life. Adding a touch of directional magic, he brought them out in his small library off the downstairs great room.

As soon as the book-and-scroll-filled walls formed around them, he did, indeed set her on her feet still hissing epithets at him. He took a few steps back and crossed his arms over his chest. "We will be here as long as it takes. Let me know when you're ready to talk with me."

She launched herself at him, but he held her at bay with magic. Sooner or later, she'd get past this outlandish display of emotion and settle down. The sea-serpents must have spooked her, but babying her was the wrong thing to do. She needed to tap into strength, not weakness.

And he was just the dragon to help her do that. Gods she was gorgeous when she was mad. Color was high in her face, and her chest heaved with anger. What he wouldn't give to see her naked, her skin rosy from passion rather than rage. Deep within, his dragon cheered him on, and his cock rose to attention.

If this had been a few hundred years before, he'd have simply taken her. Maids liked a forceful man, then, but times had changed. He'd have to make himself so irresistible, she threw herself into his arms.

But first, she had to stop ranting and stomping around. He paid out the subtle threads of a calming spell. It might be cheating, but he'd never been patient when he wanted something as badly as he wanted Erin.

"Put me down, you cretin. Put me down! Fucker! Bastard!" Wriggling and kicking did absolutely no good. It was like being chained to a boulder. If boulders had muscles that rippled against me, warm and tempting.

Consumed by disbelief that Konstantin had picked me up as if I were a misbehaving puppy, I bypassed how delicious it felt to be in his arms and substituted far worse words, but he ignored me.

When I stopped screeching—and to catch my breath—I stole a glance behind me. I had no idea where we were. A rounded room with floor-to-ceiling shelves curved around us. Books sporting cracked, peeling bindings, and scrolls that looked as if they might be made out of vellum, spilled from the shelves, creating stacks on the floor in spots.

If I weren't so put out at being dumped here as casually as if he'd taken out the trash, I would have wanted to examine the materials more closely. Always a sucker for old things, I recognized antiquities when I saw them.

Not expecting it to work, I launched myself at him again. No dice. He'd erected some kind of shielding. I couldn't scratch his eyes out—or get close enough to do anything. He just stood and watched me with a kind of long-suffering expression. No. I didn't get it exactly right. If he'd been human, I'd have nailed it, but his expressions had a layered aspect. As I'd spent more time around him, I'd gotten better at reading him.

He did feel aggravated, perhaps because I'd been ready to walk out of the room. And I would have if he hadn't stopped me. Beneath the irritation, though, sat a host of other less obvious emotions. He wanted something from me, wanted it badly enough to force his will onto me. My hands had curled into fists. I stretched out my fingers and rolled my shoulders back to release the tension sitting between them.

I wished he weren't so beautiful. It was hard to stay mad at the best looking man I'd ever seen. No exaggeration. Beyond his thick, shiny copper hair and magical eyes, he glowed with a kind of inner light that made him irresistible. Made me want to run my fingers over the defined muscles slabbing his chest and arms. Him being naked only made things worse, and I forced my eyes away from acres of rose-gold skin.

The direction of my thoughts made me shiver with longing, but I refused to ogle his cock.

What the fuck was wrong with me? I should be angry. Frightened. Outraged. Was this some weird variation of

Stockholm syndrome where I was bonding with my captor as a hedge against being stuck here?

I blew out a tight breath and flexed my fingers a few more times. My old life was dead. Dead. Never to be resurrected. Refocusing on his face, I said, "All right. Why am I here?"

"I already told you. We need to talk."

"What couldn't have been said in front of your sister and Johan?" I tilted my chin to project a defiance I was far from feeling.

He perched on the edge of a desk. Carved out of what might have been driftwood, it was the only piece of furniture beyond the shelves. "Do I have your word you won't bolt until we're done?"

I scanned the room. No windows. No doors. I lifted my lip in a sneer. "The odds are good, Dragon-boy. You put me in a spot I can't escape from."

He grimaced. Me mocking him was a bad idea, but I wasn't at my best when I felt cornered. I steeled myself for a rebuke, but instead he said, "That was the general idea." He dropped his hands, and something changed. Whatever had surrounded me dissipated.

I shook myself and hunted for the calm center I'd always laid claim to when in rough spots. I'd begun honing it as a child. After a gazillion foster homes, I'd perfected my go-to haven, one that shielded me from the worst life could throw at me.

"All right." He rested his hands on his thighs. At least, it's where I think they were since letting my gaze roam below his waist was a very bad idea.

"Some of what I have to say will be a repeat of what you've heard before. It's difficult for me to sort out what I've told Katya from what I've said to you and Johan. Had I realized the breadth of the sea-serpent problem, I would never have intervened in your initial self-rescue attempt. You would have finished climbing out of the upper cavern. Johan's broken leg would eventually have killed him."

"You don't know that," I broke in, defensiveness having gotten the better of me. "I'm an excellent doctor. If I'd managed to secure help, moved him to warmth and safety, he'd have recovered."

Konstantin eyed me from beneath well-formed brown brows. "Do you really believe help would have been available? At that point, your ship had been commandeered by the Russians who boarded it. You would have been more likely to run into them than anyone else, and they would have killed you. Finishing the business they'd begun earlier."

I closed my teeth over my lower lip and looked away. What he'd said was true enough, but it still stung. Never mind it was the same conclusion I'd drawn not all that long ago. As a physician, I'd come to view death as a worthy adversary, and I didn't like losing. Once I laid hands on someone, I developed a proprietary interest in their recovery, and I'd stabilized Johan so he could live. Not so some Russian could club him in the head. Or shoot him.

Konstantin narrowed his eyes and kept talking.

"Regardless, when I spirited you and Johan into my realm, I had no idea Earth was about to turn into a supernatural battleground."

"Neither did the sea-serpents," I muttered.

He lunged off the desk, hand raised as if to strike me, but I refused to cower. "What?" I demanded. "We're into honesty here, no matter how inconvenient it is. My take-home message is the serpents chose Earth because they assumed they'd be undisturbed."

"True enough." Konstantin didn't return to his seat, but he did drop his hand to his side. "Apologies. What you said angered me. The serpents may not have anticipated finding dragons here, but their plan certainly included a war. They presumed they'd regain full use of their magic and then begin slaughtering humans. Because they feed on their victims, each death would make them stronger until they could simply cast a magical net wide enough to wipe out whoever was left."

"Do you have any idea what weakened them?"

"No." He hesitated long enough to draw a breath and blow it out. "Never, never underestimate them. When Y Ddraigh Goch banished them, he did so for good reasons. The serpents are nothing like us. I'm not sure they ever were. But do not waste a moment feeling sorry for them. They don't deserve air to breathe."

"I wasn't feeling sorry for them. Far from it. Leaving serpents out of the equation, you're saying, if you hadn't intervened, Johan and I would be dead."

He nodded. "You would be, probably at the hands of the

Russians. The ones on the beach were intent on revenge for the man I killed in the upper cavern. It was why they detonated explosives."

I considered pointing out if he'd left us alone, the Russian relocating my dead crew members might still be alive, but then I remembered Johan's plan to blast him to smithereens. Johan had been hale and hearty then, though, not languishing with a broken femur. The more I sorted through differing timelines, the more confusing things grew. Rather like an infinite set of algorithms where each choice activated several paths but closed off other ones.

The Russian corpse-squad had tossed grenades into the chromium dig site after Konstantin killed their companion, but more had shown up. They'd certainly have polished off Johan once they figured out he was still alive. Except he wouldn't have been. The grenades would almost certainly had killed him before anyone else had a chance.

Even if I'd been successful hiding from them, it would have left me in an impossible spot. I had water, but no food and no warmth. Eventually, I'd have died too.

I folded my hands in front of me. "I accept your premise, but I'd come to the same conclusion even before our little talk."

He tilted his head to one side. "No more arguments."

"Not about that. But you didn't drag me here to make sure I agreed with your assessment of Johan's and my chances of remaining alive absent your intervention."

"No. I did not."

He pressed his mouth into a thin line, and a muscle

danced beneath one eye. "Part of our covenant as magic-wielders is we do not intervene in human affairs. It is forbidden, and I broke our laws. There's no one to censure me, but I understand what I've done.

"Please. Don't interrupt for the next portion of what I wish to impart. The last time it arose, you became upset."

I'm good at reading people. Not that he was human, but he appeared genuinely concerned. I nodded. "All right."

"When I intruded into your sphere, you and Johan became my responsibility. It was one thing when the biggest problem we faced was Katya and I thinking it would be lovely if there were more dragon shifters. We've moved beyond that. Far beyond."

He took another measured breath. "It isn't safe for you anywhere. If I return you to one of the research installations, you'll die at sea-serpent hands. If you travel with us to other worlds, there are many threats that could also mean your death."

Konstantin shut his eyes for a moment. When he opened them, he said, "I am asking you to embrace magic, to open your heart and mind to becoming a dragon shifter. Before you answer me, you must know nothing is certain. Legends suggest such a transformation is possible, but I've never seen one."

I had questions, but he'd asked me to remain quiet, so I did. The thing that amazed—and bothered—me was why I wasn't shrieking, "Oh hell, no," in his face.

He scanned me in obvious appraisal. Maybe he'd figured

out I wasn't about to run screaming from the room—if it had been a place that actually had an exit point.

"How are you doing so far?" he asked.

"All right. You haven't told me anything I hadn't already figured out. Except maybe the part about it not being safe to be human even if I'm with you."

"It's worse than not safe. Assuming we can talk other dragons into joining us, and I'm confident they won't turn us down, we will be engaged in a battle to save your world. Even if we win, Earth will be forever changed. If we lose, the serpents will claim it as theirs and bar any but their own kind from entry."

I searched his statements for weak places, logical flaws, but didn't find any. For one thing, I didn't understand magical creatures, but films and television and fiction had promulgated plenty of alien war scenarios. Usually, humans came out on top, but that was because humans were the authors and script writers and actors.

I stood straighter. He was walking around something he hadn't yet said. "You're going to offer me a choice."

"Very good. I am, indeed. Either do your damnedest to become like me, or I shall return you to the Polish base where you can take your chances with the humans."

My eyes widened. I hadn't expected that. "Would Johan go to Arctowski too?"

"Not if he accepts Katya's offer to transform himself."

"What about both of us having to make the same decision?"

He shrugged. "My reasons for insisting on that went away. In view of the serpents, my demand was misguided."

I inhaled, surprised how shaky I felt. "What if one or both of us can't become dragon shifters?"

He opened his mouth, closed it, and tried again. "I don't know. We'll address the topic if we need to."

Before I could stop myself, I'd taken a step toward him. I wanted his arms around me, but it was stupid. I wasn't a child in need of comfort. I was a woman faced with an impossible choice. If Konstantin was to be believed—and I had no reason to doubt him—it came down to certain death at Arctowski versus God only knew what as a dragon shifter.

"I don't understand how any of this would work." My voice sounded thin and broken to me. "Even if I turned into...something like you, wouldn't it take years to learn how to use magic?"

"Yes, but your dragon would help." A complex array of emotion washed over his face. Relief. Worry. Hope. Fear. And probably others I missed in between. When he opened his arms, I was ashamed how little I hesitated before I walked into them. I'd gotten by without comfort or approval most of my life. Why did I suddenly need them now?

He wrapped his arms around my shoulders and just held me. One hand cradled my head. The other splayed across my back. "I know how frightened you must be." His deep voice rumbled near where my ear pressed against his chest.

I started to protest but shut up fast. I was terrified, and I'd be a fool not to admit it. I tilted my head back so I could look at him. "If I decide to do this, how would it happen?"

Nooooooo, an inner voice screamed, followed by, *Go to Arctowski and take your chances.*

He furled his brows, regarding me. "You need to be of one mind, or the transformation, which is far from a sure thing, will not be possible."

I'd noticed he seemed to know what I was thinking before, but this time it was so obvious I couldn't shove it aside. "Can you read my thoughts?"

"Of course. It's one of the lesser magics."

He still held the back of my head, and his fingers trailed across my back. Where he touched me, sparks ignited. I should wriggle out of his grasp, but I craved the support he offered and couldn't force myself to step away.

"You never told me the steps in the process." Cranking the words out was hard. I was afraid once I knew, there'd be no going back.

"You must want this, body and soul, with every fiber of your being. It means severing your connections with the human world forever. Not just for a short time. Your life will change in ways that are impossible to predict. It's a lot to take in. A lot to accept. Until you're certain, I can't answer your question about the steps in the process."

I wrenched away from his embrace but remained so close the heat from him seared me. "But I need all the facts," I protested. "Every detail. How can I make such a momentous decision without knowing?"

"The only fact you require is that you will no longer be human if our call for a dragon to bond with you meets with

success. No going back, Erin. It's either a full commitment—
or none at all."

"But that's not fair. You're asking me to embrace
something I know nothing about." I cringed. I sounded like a
whiny, spoiled child.

He took a step back. Where before his face had been
open, raw with emotions, now it was carefully smoothed
over. I couldn't read anything at all.

"You know more than you think," he said. "Your home is
under attack. The serpents are strong enough to overpower
any weapon mankind has at its disposal. We require magic
to combat the serpents. You could help. Or you can throw
your life away."

The smooth veneer cracked, and he cupped the side of
my face with his hand. "I care about you, Erin, but I can't let
that intrude. Not now. You must want magic, want to be a
dragon shifter regardless of how I feel about you. Feelings
you might harbor toward me are also irrelevant."

I started to insist I felt nothing for him, but it was a lie. If
he was as proficient at reading me as he claimed, I'd be
better served keeping my mouth shut. Besides, he was
correct. Any decision I came to had to be between me and
magic.

Between me and the unknown and marshaling my fear
enough to move forward.

What the hell was I so frightened of?

Why was I letting it hornswoggle me? I'd always been a
master at managing my fear and my anger and my outrage.

Pushing them to places they wouldn't get in the way. What was different now?

"The difference," he cut in smoothly, proving he was indeed living inside my head, "is you must suspend your inherent disbelief in the existence of magic. If you can't move past it, there will be no way for you to become a magical being."

It made sense. And I was being a ninny. Wasting everyone's time when time was of the essence. Even now, I envisioned the sea-serpents digging in somewhere above us and leeching power from Earth to sustain their magic, build it up, and make it strong enough to wreak havoc.

We had a tiny slice of time while they were vulnerable as humans. If we waited too long, they'd be immortal in both forms—just like the dragons.

Faced with hard evidence, how could I maintain my residual suspicion magic wasn't real?

I placed a hand over the one he still had curved around my jaw. "All right. I will do whatever it takes to become like you." My inner voice, the one that had lodged a protest before, was silent.

I felt something like an electric shock travel from my feet to my head. It might have come from me, but I suspected Konstantin was assessing my words. Checking to see if they represented my true intent, or if I still harbored enough doubts to sabotage our efforts.

The tingling changed from insistent to pleasant. He murmured, "Not perfect, but it might be enough," just before he crushed his mouth on mine.

The kiss stunned me enough I didn't turn my head right away. He tasted sweet and smoky, and his touch ignited me as if I'd been a pile of dry tinder just waiting for him to toss a match atop the heap.

I wanted to mine for information, to know what magic he'd weave to find a dragon for me, but my desire to never let go of him surpassed everything. I opened my mouth to him and wrapped my arms around his back, reveling in the muscles beneath my fingers.

His cock, the appendage I'd been surreptitiously ogling since the moment I laid eyes on him, rose in a column and pressed into my belly. Desire spilled through me in a hot tide, thick and sweet as melted honey. For one of the first times in my life, I ceded control, trusting the man in my arms wouldn't lead us astray.

Had he been human, I'd never have come to that conclusion. Perhaps I was destined for magic after all. I sparred with his tongue, and my nipples sent sparks to my belly. I'd just reached between us, intent on wrapping a hand around his cock, when he pulled his mouth away.

"You're amazing, but we have spells to cast."

So lost in wanting him, I wasn't monitoring what came out of my mouth, and I said, "Even if this doesn't work, I still want to make love."

Konstantin shook his head. "No negative thoughts. None at all. This will work, and we will mate as dragons." Steam puffed from his mouth, bathing me in mist.

It reminded me how real this was and sobered me up fast. Easy to get sidetracked by sex—it was familiar. The ground we'd tread next was as alien as anything I'd ever encountered, but I'd chosen it.

Like all my choices, once I made a commitment, I'd see it through.

"Good woman." His smile melted my heart—and a few other places as well. Not that they needed more melting.

Konstantin dropped his hands onto my shoulders and began to chant. The room dissolved around us; we floated in a sea of grayish mist. His words surrounded me, kept me from falling into the endless void below. I reached for him, grabbed his waist, and hung on.

After a while, the words that had been so much gibberish, made sense. It wasn't English, far from it, but I understood he was requesting aid from Y Ddraigh Goch to find me a dragon of my own.

CHAPTER 13

Konstantin wasn't certain why he'd kissed Erin, but he hadn't been able to resist. Maybe it was the dragon pushing him. Or maybe it was the allure of having her so close. Once she capitulated, decided to give magic a chance, he'd been charmed by her courage.

After an initial hesitation, she dissolved into his arms, kissing him back as if he were her only hedge against drowning in an unfamiliar sea. Her nipples had formed stiff peaks where they pressed against his chest, and his cock shot to attention, hard and full and ready. The scent of her arousal was like nectar, stoking his hunger. A cinnamon-vanilla mix with musky undernotes.

He'd kissed her for longer than he should have because he couldn't make himself stop. She had the most amazing lips, firm, full, and sensual, and she gave as good as she got.

Teasing his tongue with hers and exchanging biting and sucking kisses for softer, deeper ones.

She pressed a hand between their bodies, her intent crystal clear, but once she touched him, he'd truly be lost. He broke away from the kiss and told her, "You're amazing, but we have spells to cast."

Regarding him from eyes that had darkened to midnight, she murmured, "Even if this doesn't work, I still want to make love."

He smiled and shook his head, steam billowing from his mouth. "No negative thoughts. None at all. This will work, and we will mate as dragons."

His cock, perilously close to losing control, shuddered at the thought of aerial lovemaking. To forestall anything that would get in the way of casting the magic to begin Erin's transformation, he dropped his hands onto her shoulders and began to chant.

He led them to a place between worlds, one that would make it easy to transition to the most promising location for Erin's first shift. Presuming his entreaties to his god were fruitful, Y Ddraigh Goch would point the way to where that might be.

She held onto him, fluid in his arms. He let himself hope. She hadn't told him no when he'd announced they'd mate as dragons, but she might be so overwhelmed by everything it hadn't registered. She wanted him, but there was so much she didn't know. Dragon matings were forever. She had to know that before they made love in either form.

He was free to have sex with humans, but sex with

another dragon shifter was permanent. It would bond them together forever. He'd been cowardly not to tell her, but he wasn't certain his spell would work. If it didn't, and she remained human, they could engage in all the sex they wanted.

If the world was a different place.

The urgency of dealing with the sea-serpents changed everything. If Erin couldn't transform herself, he'd have little choice but to return her to the human world, memories nicely erased so she wouldn't live out the rest of her life yearning after the dragon that got away. Human minds were fragile, and chasing after the bond that had eluded her would consume her mind. Perhaps not right away, but it would chip away at her sanity until nothing was left.

But bedding her as a human wasn't his desire. He longed for her with a singlemindedness that had eluded him through the long years of his existence. He didn't just want her to warm his bed. He wanted her by his side, sharing his life. For that, she had to be like him.

And, of course, she had to return his desire for a lifelong mate. She lusted after him, but whether it extended beyond the heat coursing through her remained to be seen. He was adept at reading minds, but intuiting intent required different skills. Ones more subtle than what he'd employed.

He continued chanting. Concern pricked him because of how long this was taking. If Y Ddraigh Goch approved of creating new dragon shifters from humans, he would have answered by now. That he hadn't meant he had to be considering the wisdom of such a move.

One thing Konstantin hadn't done was tell his god about the serpents. He'd assumed Y Ddraigh Goch already knew, but perhaps he didn't. Switching away from his spell, he laid out the threat facing Earth. Not that the god would give a speckled dragon's foot about the third planet from the sun in this solar system, but he would care about the serpents escaping from their enforced isolation.

If Konstantin remembered anything about him, he'd not only care. He'd be furious, and his rage would drive action. Message delivered, he returned to his spell, the one that should end with a dragon for Erin.

She glanced at him, questions in her eyes, but this wasn't a time for conversation or explanations. "All is well," he told her and hoped to hell it was true.

Were Katya and Johan doing the same thing? Was that at the root of Y Ddraigh Goch's reluctance? Concern that once he kicked this particular gate open, it would mean hundreds of new dragon shifters?

Time passed in the space between worlds, but it was meaningless since it held no link to real time anywhere else. Sooner or later, the god would answer him. Perhaps not with words. If Konstantin slid back to his lair beneath the polar ice cap, he'd understand well enough.

Would he try again? Maybe. It was important enough to argue the point.

Within him, his dragon grew restive. It wasn't patient, but then no dragon was. An edgy lot, they far preferred action to waiting around. He tightened his control over it.

And waited.

Finally, after hours or maybe days, the air developed a different feel. Erin had been drowsing, eyes shut, leaning against him as they floated in the ether between worlds. The change was understated at first, but it gathered momentum fast.

Erin's eyes flew open. "What's happening?"

He gripped her shoulders. "I'm not certain, but we will have an outcome soon."

"Yes, but which one?"

"If I knew, I'd tell you."

He focused his attention inward hoping for clues from his dragon, but the beast had retreated after he rejected its bid for freedom. Air pounded against him in waves, not unlike the sea. Dragon scents of smoke and sunbaked clay surrounded them.

He kept up his chant. He'd done it this long despite a throat long past the point of pain. A few bugles would clear things up, but they weren't part of his casting. The air sheltering them peeled back in layers not unlike a theater curtain, revealing an oblong gateway that glittered with silver and gold tones.

"Hold tight to me," he instructed and lifted Erin into his arms before jumping through the portal.

Something was about to happen, and it wasn't them being swept back to his starting point. If refusal was Y Ddraigh Goch's intent, the god wouldn't have bothered with such an elaborate gateway.

The cushy spot between worlds yielded to a black, airless void. He tucked Erin's head into his shoulder and murmured, "Don't panic. This part never lasts long."

Confident words, but even his superior lung capacity, courtesy of his dragon, was stretched thin by the time air molecules reappeared. He panted, sucking them in. The blackness shattered around him, replaced by a surreal landscape. He was used to eerie worlds, ones inhabited by prehistoric creatures no one had laid eyes on in millennia, but this place held a macabre beauty that stole his attention.

Erin writhed in his arms. "Put me down. What the hell is this place?"

He set her on her feet, and she turned in a full circle. Fascinated, he did the same. A violet sky was streaked with silver. Twin somethings, maybe moons, cast so much light they might have been suns after all. Trees grew all around them. Huge, ancient trees with gnarled silver bark and limbs like an arcane ballet of twisting arms and legs.

Silver and orange leaves hung from the branches and rustled, although the air was perfectly still. Space between the trees allowed him to see for a long way. Rolling land extended on all sides, butting up against less-gentle foothills perhaps a kilometer distant. The dirt beneath his feet held a coppery cast, and it was chilly.

"What is this place?" Erin repeated.

"A borderworld, yet one I've never been to." The sound of rushing water beckoned. He could swear it hadn't been there a few moments before, but he said, "Come on."

Sure enough, a few zigs and zags between trees brought them to a creek burbling out of an enormous rock. Bending, he cupped his hands and drank. The water laved his abraded throat, raw from hours of chanting.

Erin crouched beside him. "How do you know it's safe?" she demanded.

He turned toward her, water dripping down his chin. "I'm immortal."

She rolled her eyes. "Oh yeah. I'd forgotten that part, mostly because it seems impossible."

"Why?" He drank more, slaking his thirst.

"Doesn't matter."

"Are you thirsty?"

"Yeah, but not enough to take a chance on an unknown water source."

He slid up the bank and sat on a large flat rock, patting the place next to him. "I believe we are here because Y Ddraigh Goch has looked favorably on my request to transform you." He hesitated, hunting for words.

"Whatever it is, just say it. You've got that *make it agreeable* look again."

"Maybe because there's no way I can describe the process. You want to understand what will happen next, and I don't know. Not exactly. I was born to my dual nature, so I have no direct experience with what will happen to you."

"You can speculate," she pressed.

"I could, but it might be very far off base." Steam puffed from his mouth as his dragon attempted to soothe her.

She batted it aside. Her forehead furrowed into worried lines, but she looked determined, shoulders straight, chin tilted upward.

He ached to help her, to ease whatever would come next, but this was a path she'd have to follow on her own.

"Earlier, your chanting…" she began, and then shook her head and tried again. "I couldn't understand what you were saying at first, but after a while, the words made sense. Almost as if they'd turned into English, except they hadn't."

Surprise jostled him. Her transformation had already begun, but not in a way he could have predicted. If he'd known, his faith would have been stronger, and he wouldn't have worried quite so much.

"It might be good news," he murmured.

"So you know what it means?" she asked.

"Maybe." In case he was wrong, he didn't want to raise false hope. "It could signify that your dragon has already begun the process of joining with you. Dragons speak all languages. If it melded its consciousness with yours, my mantra would have become understandable."

Erin turned her hands palms up. "I don't feel any different."

He inhaled sharply, nostrils flaring. Should he ask his dragon to encourage the other one waiting in the wings to bond with Erin? Was there even such a dragon hanging about?

He wished he knew more.

Perhaps because he'd been thinking about his beast, it raced to the fore, pressing for a shift with unusual insistence given there was nothing to kill nearby. Fire shot from his mouth, followed by ash and smoke.

The summons was so urgent, he told Erin, "I'm going to

shift. My dragon is wise. It must know something, and it's demanding its form be primary."

"What should I do?"

With the last of his human mouth, he said, "Remove your clothes so they don't end up in shreds."

His dragon bugled laughter; Konstantin had to admit it was funny for him to tell a woman he desperately desired to get naked when lovemaking wasn't imminent.

The dragon formed quickly. Wings. Talons. Forelegs. Hind legs. Scales. Through it all, he watched as Erin peeled away layers of clothing. Her body was stunning with rounded breasts tipped by pink nipples. They stood in peaks but probably from fear and cold, rather than lust. Her shoulders were broad and well-formed, her stomach flat between flared hips. She was facing him, so he couldn't see her ass, but he visualized it as high and full. A triangle of golden curls sat between her long legs. His dragon cock hardened, curving next to his scaled belly.

He told his beast to stand down. Erin still didn't know any of the rules surrounding dragon-shifter matings. Hell, she wasn't a dragon shifter. Not yet, anyway. She'd folded her arms beneath her breasts and rocked from foot to foot. He'd bet anything she had to be cold. This borderworld, lush and elegant as it was, didn't hold much warmth.

Konstantin settled near enough for some of the heat radiating from his hide to help.

"Tell her to welcome me!" blasted into his mind.

Erin huddled against his scaled front, oblivious to the dragon's words, which meant she hadn't heard it. He lumbered back a pace or two and bent to draw in the dirt with a talon.

Welcome your bondmate.

"How?" she stared up at him.

"Can you hear me?" he tried telepathy. She didn't respond, so he scraped a hind foot over his first message and wrote:

TALK OUT LOUD. ASK HER TO BECOME ONE WITH YOU.

Erin nodded and stood tall, opening her arms to the sides. "Konstantin says you are close. I want to become like him, a dragon shifter. I have a lot to learn, but I am willing."

Konstantin waited. Her entreaty had sounded genuine to him, but nothing happened. He projected his mind voice to the dragon. *"I wish to meet you. Show yourself and bond with her."*

"No. What she said isn't good enough. She views this as a chore. Something necessary, but not wanted."

He wrested the upper hand from his dragon and forced a shift. He needed his vocal chords, not writing in the dirt. Shifting fast took a toll, and he was panting by the time he stood next to her.

"Am I doing something wrong?" she asked.

He nodded, working to catch his breath. "The dragon is here, but she senses your ambivalence. Remember when I told you that you had to want this with every fiber of your being? No doubts? No looking back?"

"Yes, I remember, but how can I do that?" She sounded forlorn. "I'm foreswearing everything that ever meant everything to me. It's not easy."

"Nothing worthwhile ever is." He did a quick and dirty sorting within himself and opted for honesty. "I've been selfish. I want you to become like me because I want you as my mate. I pushed that reason to the top of my agenda, but it has no place there. Every dragon is needed to fight sea-serpents. That is what should be primary. I care about Earth, but nothing like you do. My motivation is to annihilate the serpents."

"I understand. You and Katya were planning to leave Earth, anyway."

"Yes, we were. Back to my soul-baring, we can cavort in bed all we want with you humans, but you can never stand by my side through eternity unless you're a dragon shifter and we're mated. A forever proposition."

Her eyes widened. Through teeth that were starting to chatter, she said, "Mate, as in be married? When you said it before, I assumed you just meant make love."

"Yes. Mate as in married."

Erin surged forward and he held her. She needed warmth and comfort and reassurance. "I—I'm honored, I think, but we barely know one another," she murmured.

"That, my dear, is a purely human convention. Magical beings know when their mates appear. You're mine."

"I'd love to swallow that one whole, but I need to think about it."

He stroked her hair, grateful she wasn't shivering as hard. "Of course, you do. Besides, that's not why we're here."

"No, it isn't," she agreed and stepped out of his arms. "I don't suppose mating with you is sufficient reason for the dragon either, is it? I have to want her for herself, not for what she'll buy for me."

He nodded. "Exactly. This is one of many reasons I'm so taken with you. You're quick-witted and insightful."

She offered a lopsided smile. "Idle flattery, but keep it coming. Let me try again. Not because of the prospect of becoming your mate but because magic is starting to grow on me. The more I see of it, the more I want to be able to do it myself."

"Good reason." He gripped her hand. "You must be sure about me. If you mate with me, we shall be bound inextricably."

She drew back, freeing her hand. "No divorce?"

He shook his head. "No. We mate for life, which turns out to be forever."

"Which is why I need time to think about it. Making a mistake would be awful—for both of us."

Konstantin nailed her with his gaze. "It's precisely why your dragon is holding back. That bond is permanent as well, and she needs you to be certain of your choice."

Erin turned away and knelt, hands clasped in supplication. When she spoke, her voice was clear and strong. "I agree I wasn't fully on board a little while ago. I've done the best I can to clear my doubts. It will take time for us to get to know one another, and I'm hoping you'll teach me how to be a good bondmate to you. I'm a decent doctor, but I studied years to become one. It will take a long time before I'm a partner you can be proud of, but I'm not a quitter. I'll do whatever it takes to make this work. I want to become a dragon shifter. Please. Bond with me."

Konstantin waited. She'd meant every word, and if they weren't enough, he had no idea what would be. He should have told her how important it was not to allow the dragon to gain the upper hand, but it could wait until after she was bonded. If the dragon believed it could run the show, it might be more willing to establish a bond.

As he'd already told Erin, precisely like mating, dragon shifter bonds were eternal.

He cleared his mind and prayed to Y Ddraigh Goch, asking the god to encourage the dragon to take a chance on Erin. The permanency of the arrangement made dragons skittish.

The air turned a brilliant red around where Erin knelt, glowing hotly. At first, she smiled and reached both arms upward, but then she began to scream. Horrible, tortured cries rang from her.

He sprang forward, intent on placing his body between her and whatever was causing her to shriek as if her body were being stretched across a rack. Before he took two steps, his dragon forced a shift, fire shooting from his mouth in a cascade of heat and smoke and ash.

"Remain where you stand." Y Ddraigh Goch's deep voice was unmistakable. *"You wanted this. You prayed to me for it, and now you must allow it to run its course."*

Another gut-wrenching groan burbled from Erin. Blood shot from her mouth, staining her chin and dripping down her naked chest. She clawed at her hair, tearing out clumps of it. Her body twisted at unnatural angles, the snap of bones painfully clear as the dragon attempted to launch its much larger form, borrowing from Erin's along the way.

"*Will she survive?*" Konstantin asked, aghast at the spectacle unwinding in front of him.

"*I do not know,*" the god replied.

"*Has any human come through this transformation?*"

Y Ddraigh Goch didn't reply.

His dragon rampaged, wanting freedom from his will. Maybe it could see the other dragon and aimed to take it on in combat. But his god had ordered him not to intervene. Heart breaking within his scaled chest, Konstantin offered what support he could, which wasn't a whole hell of a lot from several meters away.

If he'd known...

If I'd known, then what? he asked himself bitterly, but no answers came beyond harsh knowledge he'd been a fool to break one of dragonkind's cardinal rules: Never intervene in human affairs.

He had, and the shattered heap of bones barely clinging to life was the result. If she died, forfeited on the altar of his hubris, it would be a grim lesson. One that would mark him for the rest of his days.

CHAPTER 14

At first, I was certain my last gambit worked. I felt dragon energy closing from all sides. Different from Konstantin's or Katya's, yet now that I knew what it felt like, it was definitely another dragon. I opened myself as much as I could, heart, mind, and soul, and thought only of the dragon.

I'd been blown away, flustered and pleased and scared to death by Konstantin's assertion about wanting me for his wife. Or mate. Or however dragons described such things. On the one hand, it was heady and alluring. On the other, it was one more nail in the "I'll never be human again" coffin.

But I wouldn't, or I wouldn't be here on my knees in the freezing cold subjugating myself and doing my damnedest to be worthy of the dragon I had yet to lay eyes on. What color would she be? How big? Were all of them old? How about the ones born bonded? Did they grow up right along with their human sides?

I swept all of it aside. If this was successful, I'd have several lifetimes to find answers for all my questions. Something about that last mind-clearing seemed to do the trick. The dragon energy I'd felt pulsing closer and closer, ripe with the smells of hearth fires and sunbaked herbs, dropped around me like a shroud.

I couldn't breathe, but I told myself I was imagining it.

Until whatever swathed me pressed closer and closer. No longer soft and yielding, it was as hard as sheets of steel. And it kept right on tightening, choking the life out of me.

I screamed while I still had breath as a cry for help, but the next yowls were spontaneous. I hurt. Everywhere. My body was being torn into a million pieces, tied to four horses and drawn and quartered. Keelhauled off an ancient schooner. The latter was accurate since breathing was such a battle my vision, what was left of it, grayed at the edges, hazing over.

From a long way off, I heard the distinctive sound of bones snapping, and then I realized they were mine. Pain is a funny thing. The mind can only experience so much of it. Ramping up the sensations doesn't make you hurt any more. By now, I'd heard both thigh bones snap, a few ribs, and maybe two of my neck vertebrae.

Agony shot through me again and again. All the times I'd casually asked patients to rate their pain on a scale of one to ten were a fucking, bloody ass joke. Mine was at a million, and it just kept on rolling. Red-hot pokers jabbed me from all sides. I tasted blood. Had I spit it up from damaged lungs? Or had I bitten through my cheek or my lip?

Did it even matter?

"Kill me," I moaned. I'd moved past shrieking. It took energy I no longer had. "Just kill me and get it over with. I'm dead, anyway."

"*You selfish bitch,*" reverberated through my head. "*I did not go to all this trouble to have you give up and die on me. Fight through this. I'm waiting at the other end.*"

Great. I was hallucinating.

"Go away. Let me die," I mumbled.

"*Be very sure, human, before you send me away.*"

I blinked through a mosaic of red. Must be petechial hemorrhages in my retinas. Useless knowledge, but stubborn as hell. It wouldn't go away. My inner doctor voice kept right on cataloguing every malfunction even as my body edged toward death.

It was not why I'd gone to medical school.

Something formed across my visual field. Random neurons firing from my dying brain. I squeezed my eyes shut, but the thing grew clearer. Dragonesque. Brilliant red, shining from an unidentifiable light source.

"*I am here.*" Fire flowed from the dragon's mouth like a lazy lava flow. "*Reach for me. I cannot do this for you.*"

The last of the bonds tethering me to my body dissolved. The pain, constant, grinding, gnashing, scraping may have ebbed the tiniest bit. Understanding whipped me across my abraded face and kept right on flogging my broken body. I was right about the Grim Reaper, sickle and all, standing by. This was a fight to the death, but I had a choice.

My dragon was here. She was waiting. Not nicely or patiently, but she hadn't left.

Not yet.

The only way I'd survive was if I dropped every barrier, including the ones I'd erected against pain, and invited her into my body so I could become her. The process or transition or whatever it was had progressed to the point where if I couldn't complete it, I would die.

No, I am dying, I corrected myself. No one lost as much blood as I had or broke as many bones and survived. How that would bode for what was left of Erin Ryan remained to be seen.

But I couldn't worry about her.

I had one task, and it was to complete my transformation, turn into the red dragon. I couldn't do it by rational means. I threw everything wide open, ignoring pain spikes that threatened to rob me of consciousness.

"I want this," I cried. "Make it happen."

Being bathed in fire couldn't have felt worse. Every undamaged neuron screeched in protest. A few more bones shattered, but dragon energy moved from around me to inside. What was left of my shattered body swelled, took on new form. The pain, so intense it was unbearable, ended abruptly, leaving me opening and closing my mouth like a landed fish.

Except it wasn't my mouth. Not anymore. Rows of teeth

clanged together. I peeled my eyes open to a very different vista than what I'd seen before. For one thing, I was at least two feet taller, perhaps as much as three. My vision held a layered aspect, nothing like the view through my human eyes. A quick glance revealed red scales. When I twisted my head atop its long, sinuous neck, I spied wings neatly folded across my back.

When I opened my mouth, fire spewed forth, and I hastily averted my head to avoid hitting a wonderful old tree.

Konstantin lumbered into view, or maybe he'd been right next to me all along. Fire streamed from his mouth too, and he angled his head until his cheek brushed mine, the scales clanking and catching. *"Damn it, Erin. You're all right. I was frightened for you and guilty because all this was my fault."*

Within me, I became aware of a second consciousness—the dragon's. She wasn't pleased. Three bugles, rife with rebuke shot from my mouth. I wanted to talk, but I had no idea how to manage it. I tried thinking, *"My dragon says you should have had more faith in her."*

And waited.

"Not quite," Konstantin said. *"I know you're trying to talk, but it didn't come through. First, hold me in your thoughts. Next, think your words slowly. Try it."*

I followed his instructions and repeated the same sentence.

This time, he nodded. *"She is absolutely correct."*

I took a few tentative steps, first to one side and then to the other. I unfurled my wings. Running my gaze over them,

I did a few hasty physics equations and decided they'd be inadequate to move my current bulk off the ground.

My dragon didn't care for my line of reasoning. I felt a heavy urge to fly, but I wasn't ready. Not ten minutes ago, I'd been certain I was dead.

"You must learn to trust me." My dragon's voice, now that I could listen to her without a mist of pain altering everything, was deep and rich, a pleasant contralto.

"What if we fall out of the sky?" I countered.

"Pfft." More fire blasted skyward. *"It wasn't looking promising a little bit ago, but you're a dragon shifter now. I am your dragon. We are bonded. It cannot be undone. Do not make me sorry I took a chance on you."*

"Do you have a name?" I asked.

"Yes, but you couldn't pronounce it, and it isn't important. We are going to fly. This is what we were born for, and you will love it. Our dragon body is ungainly on land, but ideally suited for flight."

"I was listening in," Konstantin said. *"Apologies to both of you for taking that liberty. Flying is an excellent idea, but not for very long this first time."*

A critical roar rang from me. Apparently my dragon didn't like it when Konstantin told it what to do.

Still riddled with ambivalence, I considered flying. Even if I'd suddenly joined the ranks of the immortal, it would still hurt like hell to hit the ground from a hundred feet up. My pain quotient was overfull for today.

"This is one time when you can allow your dragon to take the

lead," Konstantin told me. *"You may as well. She won't back down on this. Flight is your birthright."*

Smoke puffed from my open jaws. I didn't even realize I'd been holding my new alter ego back until I withdrew my mental control over us both. Much like an observer in the back seat of a car, I watched while we trudged to a clearer spot. Konstantin took to the skies first, black wings beating the air to gain altitude.

Next it was my turn. Damn, but it was hard not to batten down the hatches again. To exert what felt like fragile restraint over the two of us. I reminded myself how much I'd always loved flying. My dragon must have been privy to all my thoughts, which was odd since I had no idea what she was thinking. Regardless, once she soaked in that I enjoyed the sensation of flight, our wings shot out to the sides, flapped a few times, and we took off.

Unlike my expectation we'd lumber down the corridor between old gnarled trees like a plane that hadn't bothered to check weight and balance fighting a stiff crosswind, we soared smoothly into the air with nary a hiccup.

The dragon swooped and banked and flew figure-eights. After the first few minutes, I stopped being afraid we'd succumb to gravity and end up squashed like bugs, and started enjoying the sensation of air flowing beneath my— our?—wings.

"*Well?*" The question came from my dragon.

"*This is wonderful. I love it, but I'm tired.*"

"*That's because we're hungry,*" she told me.

Konstantin had been flying next to us, mirroring our aerial ballet. *"Food will be just the thing,"* he agreed.

My dragon trumpeted and swooped so low one of our wings clipped an overgrown clump of bushes. We landed abruptly next to a lake that showed up out of nowhere. Next thing I knew, we'd lumbered into it until the water came halfway up our chest.

"Listen through my ears," she told me.

I quieted the riot in my head and focused my hearing. Swooshing sounds came from beneath the dark water. Before I could comment, the dragon dipped slightly and came up with a fat, wriggling fish in one taloned foreleg. She popped it into our mouth and taste exploded on our tongue. Scales and salty blood and delicate tender meat.

We ate three more before Konstantin bugled from the bank.

My dragon was busy chewing and swallowing, so I experimented with re-establishing control over our shared body. It wasn't too hard, so I turned and bugled back. He'd located something rather like a beaver or marmot or other mid-sized rodent, and it hung half in and half out of his mouth.

"Long enough for your first time," he told me.

"It is not," my dragon lodged a protest and did its damnedest to turn our body back around.

Damn. She was really strong, but I had a feeling if I let her win I'd regret it, so I pushed through the water, intent on reaching the shore. The muddy bottom sucked at my huge hind feet, but I plodded along. After the first half dozen steps, it grew easier.

Almost as if the dragon didn't want to engage in a pitched battle over something that wasn't very important.

I joined Konstantin on the bank. Whatever he'd eaten was gone. I followed his telepathy instructions, held him in my mind, and asked, *"How do I shift back? Will it hurt as much? And what about my body? Will it be as trashed as it was when I left it behind?"*

I should have been terrified. The specter of enduring even a fraction of the pain it had cost me to join with the dragon was daunting enough to make me want to stay a dragon. Forever.

Except I didn't want to. Not really.

I had a hell of a lot to learn, and it would be easier to absorb lessons in my human form. Assuming I still had one that wasn't a candidate for a level one trauma center.

"I can teach you everything you need to know." My dragon's words held a crafty undernote, but they were alluring, as if she'd seeded them with magic.

"I appreciate the offer, but I've spent my life as human. You'll still be within me when I am, right?"

I was banking things would work similarly to how they did with Konstantin and Katya.

"Yes," the dragon grumbled, *"but it's not the same. Our dragon form is superior in every way. You should prefer it."*

I considered pointing out Konstantin didn't, but it didn't seem very tactful.

Light flashed and flickered around Konstantin as he traded wings and scales for a chest and back and arms and legs. He made it look easy, but he'd started out bonded to his dragon.

Obviously, my process was different.

He stood before me and bowed his head respectfully. "I wish to thank your dragon side from the depths of my soul. Your shift was long and hard, and I feared you would die, yet she stuck with you."

Steam puffed from my mouth, courtesy of my dragon, and billowed around Konstantin. I supposed it was her way of accepting his compliment.

He nodded. "To answer your questions, it should not hurt as much to shift back, and I am hoping your body will have repaired itself."

"What if it hasn't?" My question must have come out garbled because he hesitated before answering.

"I will employ magic to heal what I can. Once you are stable, we will return to my home, where Katya will add to my efforts. She has healing ability."

"I'm ready. I guess." A familiar tightening sensation clutched at my gut. I was scared, but I had every right to be. Something about the dragon's form muted my terror, but didn't obliterate it.

The shining nimbus around Konstantin had faded, and he stood facing me. "Hold your human form in your mind, the way it was before your shift. Imagine sliding out of the dragon and into it."

I stared at him, still getting used to the layered vision that was apparently part and parcel of being a dragon. His instructions had been simple, yet it couldn't be that easy. Changing into the dragon had been absolute hell.

"Erin." His tone was sharp. "You cannot hesitate, or you'll end up stuck in the limbo-land that was almost your undoing. Believe you can shift. Visualize it, and let it happen."

I nodded while bits of residual ash flew from my mouth. The dragon wasn't fighting me. I sensed I was back in the driver's seat of our operation. Maybe I was more motivated this time because I wanted my familiar form with an almost physical ache. Not that I wasn't enamored by my dragon and flying, but I needed time to put everything into perspective.

I took a deep breath, blew out smoke, and forced a visual of how I saw myself. Tall. Too thin. Messy. No makeup. On a good day, I remembered to brush my hair. One of the best things about being a surgeon was I lived in scrubs. No need for fancy clothes, a good thing since I didn't own many.

Once I had a solid representation of me, I dove headlong into it. Something like a light beam flickered around me, but the sensation was mild compared with before. Stretching rather than ripping. Bending rather than breaking. I ended up in a heap of tangled limbs sprawled across the cold ground in the center of a glowing, golden ball.

I'd been toasty warm as a dragon, but I started to shiver almost immediately. Konstantin knelt next to me. I felt his intense gaze raking my body from head to toe, but there was nothing sexual in his appraisal. He was searching for injured places.

I should be doing the same, but I felt stunned, as if someone had clubbed me and I was groggy.

"I don't see any damage," he said. "Can you sit?"

I started to protest that many things weren't immediately apparent to a visual inspection, but kept the words within my throat. I didn't hurt anywhere. My limbs weren't bent at unnatural angles. When I told my body to roll off my belly and into a cross-legged sit, it obeyed me.

I wrapped my arms around my legs, shivering in earnest now. "How is this possible? When I left my body behind, it wasn't far from being clinically dead."

"Magic healed it while you were within the dragon."

It was an explanation, but not one that made sense to me. "All those books and scrolls. Do they have information that will help me make sense of all this?"

He nodded. "Yes, but me teaching you will be faster."

I started to tell him he didn't have to do that, but it wasn't true. I got gingerly to my feet, still incredulous I wasn't mortally injured. "Where did I leave my clothes?" Something occurred to me. "You don't seem cold. Why am I?"

He smiled, and it lit his face from within, making him a delight for my eyes. "I'm using magic to warm myself."

"Mmph. I have a lot to learn."

"Indeed, you do. Shall we practice using magic to locate your garments?"

I had about as much energy as a starving rat, but rather than whining, I said, "Sure."

"Most magic begins with visualizing what you want.

Hold a mental picture of your clothing and tell me what happens."

I thought about how I'd stacked my discarded garments. "Okay. I see them, but nothing changed."

"Try harder."

I was so cold, it was tough to do anything but curl into a ball to conserve what little body heat I had left. "I don't have much *harder* left to try with."

He moved behind me and wrapped his arms around my shoulders. Something like a glittery shock jolted through me, mildly uncomfortable, but the feeling I'd had where I was about to pitch face forward into the dirt departed fast.

"What did you do?"

"Infused some of my magic into you." He stepped away and faced me, his expression stern. Nothing soft or compassionate was left when he repeated, "Try harder."

I ground my teeth and made a grab for the visual I'd created of my garments. Prickly heat stabbed me, but a boot flew through the air. I had to feint to one side so it wouldn't hit me in the head. The second boot followed, and then the rest of my discarded clothing items. As if drawn by a magnet, they reformed into a stack where I'd been standing.

As I stood over them dressing as fast as I could, Konstantin started to laugh. "What the fuck is so funny?" I managed through chattering teeth.

"Nothing," he chortled, followed by, "Everything. I've never taught anyone how to use their power before. It will be a learning curve for us both. I'm not laughing at you."

"The hell you're not," I muttered and squatted in the dirt to get my socks and boots on.

He waited until I was back on my feet and asked. "Ready to go home?"

"Not until you tell me what was so funny." I folded my arms beneath my breasts, grateful for my insulated suit and all the layers beneath.

"After I mixed my magic with yours, it made it easier for me to see what you were doing. I knew straight away you'd used way too much air in your drawing spell, but I wanted to see what would happen. Everyone's use of power is different. All dragons have an affinity for fire, but your second element seems to be air."

I stared at him. He may as well be speaking Swahili. He tried to wrap his arms around me, but I evaded his grip.

"You don't teach anyone by laughing at their first attempts." I tried for dignity, but it wasn't easy because I remembered patronizing bastard surgeons mocking me early in my training.

They'd made me a better doctor, for all their denigrating comments.

"I'm sorry," he said. "This is as new for me as it is for you."

"Never mind." I flapped both hands, feeling like an ungrateful twit because I'd lodged any complaints at all. "Walk me through how you'll get us out of here."

"Are you sure you're not too tired?"

The solicitousness in his tone almost undid me, but this wasn't a time to play the helpless female card and fall into his arms. Not that he wouldn't have taken care of me, but I was used to taking care of myself.

No reason to stop now.

"Nope. I really want to know."

Konstantin nodded. "All right. Teleport spells require equal amounts of fire and air with a small amount of earth mixed in. The earth element acts as a lodestone and will draw us toward our destination..."

CHAPTER 15

Konstantin had assumed Erin would shed her clothing and they'd fall into one another's arms as soon as they returned to his lair beneath Earth's southern pole. Nothing could have been further from the truth. Not only was Erin still fully dressed—minus her outer suit—she'd insisted they take up residence in the library, and she'd been peppering him with questions for hours, taking notes with a quill pen and an ink mixture he'd come up with that was more or less indelible.

Periodically, she'd stop to practice something they'd been talking about. When her efforts blew up in her face, she tried again until she got it right.

Magic hung in the air. Power imbued with her particular scent. Wildflowers and herbs and hot clay. He'd sniffed the air again and again, hoping for the cinnamon-vanilla mix that had filled his nostrils when she'd been pressed against his body, lust streaming from her in thick waves.

But it hadn't been there. He'd begun their library session with his cock at half mast, hopeful for encouragement. It had subsided long since. Magic had a dampening effect on lust. Unless he was a dragon. Then it fanned the flames to an inferno.

He stole a glance at Erin with her head bent over yet one more scroll. A thick curl was threaded around one hand as she pushed hair out of her eyes. It was as if she'd traded her interest in him for a crash course in magic. A feral, possessive part of him—the dragon nature—lodged protest after protest.

If he listened to his dragon, he should push the scrolls to one side and strip off her clothes. Study could wait; dragons came by magic intuitively. They had no use for books. If they didn't know something, they asked another dragon. Preferably an older one.

He tried to explain to the dragon that he respected Erin's efforts to embrace something that was foreign to her. He'd be stupid to sabotage her hard work. She'd told her dragon she'd do whatever it took to build her skillset.

Clearly, she was a woman of her word.

Making love with him could wait. Sooner or later, she'd need a respite from elements and minerals and spells. When it happened, he'd be there.

A welter of open books and scrolls scattered around where she'd set herself up in a corner of the room. One part of the transformation that had been handy was she was able to read the various arcane languages in his source materials. She'd been delighted with that particular newfound talent.

Katya and Johan were nowhere to be found. He wasn't worried about them. Not yet, but if they didn't return in a day or so, he'd go looking for them. Probably with Erin in tow. She was as determined as anyone he'd ever seen about absorbing as much magical knowledge as she could.

He brought food down twice. And drink. Despite the refreshments, she was fading. Sometimes her eyes fluttered shut before she forced them open. Finally, after she'd taken a five-minute catnap, he scooted next to her on the floor and splayed a hand over the scroll in front of her. One end was held down with a thick, imposing tome with runes running up and down its ancient leather binding. She had her foot over the other side and was deep into a diagram. As he leaned closer, he saw it had to do with transmutation of matter. Handy for teleporting both with and without your body.

He smiled. He hadn't thought about astral projection in years.

Erin pushed at his hand. He didn't move it.

"What?" She finally focused on him. An ink smear ran down one cheek, but her blue eyes glowed with fierce intelligence.

"You don't have to learn everything at once."

"Maybe not." She shrugged. "But I love stretching my mind. There's an entire universe I had no idea even existed, and it's endless. Besides"—her brow creased into vertical lines above her nose—"those serpents aren't going to move any slower because I'm a neophyte. I have to immerse myself, so I have a prayer of being more than deadweight next time there's a battle."

His heart swelled with tenderness. "I'm proud of you, but it's time for a break. Get up. Stretch your legs. Maybe we could take a dip in the lake. And you need to practice your transitions. We could do it down here, but outside is easier."

She winced. "Um, yeah. The one to dragon was so rocky, I'm almost afraid to try it again."

"Speaking of dragons, what's yours been doing?"

"Reading over my shoulder. Or under it, or through it. Regardless. She's right here." Erin tapped her breastbone. "I feel her inside me. It should be weird, but it feels right somehow, like it's precisely where she's supposed to be."

Relief swept through him, but he did his best to hide it. It wouldn't do to let her dragon know he'd been worried about it running roughshod over her. Dragons could be petulant and headstrong and very into doing things their way. When you were born bonded, your dragon was forced to watch over you as you grew. They developed a fondness for the child who would grow into their mate, and it had a modulating effect on their high-handedness.

He flowed to his feet and offered her a hand. "Come on. I think better after I get a bit of distance from something."

She took his hand and let him help her. "Research bears out that observation." She scanned the room, noting the empty dishes. "I don't even remember eating. Thanks for taking care of us."

"You needn't thank me."

Her head snapped up. "Cripes. Where's Johan? And your sister?"

"I'm not sure, but it's not time to worry yet. Not quite."

"Were they here when we got back? I was in such a godawful hurry to dig in and start learning, I didn't give them a thought." She made a face. "Doesn't make me much of a friend, does it?"

"You're fine. Your plate is pretty full." He aimed for support but didn't want to underplay his concern about Katya's extended absence. It wasn't like her. Wherever she was, Johan was almost certainly with her.

"A dip in the lake would be refreshing." She raked her unruly hair back from her face. "Do you have any biodegradable soap?"

"I'm not sure what that is, so no."

He wrapped them in magic and moved them to the shore of the nearest of the string of lakes. She wanted to know exactly what he was doing, so he outlined the steps as he put them into action.

"Teleport spells will be slightly different for you," he continued, "because your magic isn't the same as mine."

"How can you know? I'm still at the barest beginnings of figuring out which pigeonhole I fit into per the lore I'm reading."

"Because I understand magic, and I sense what you have to work with." He furled his brows. "Are you going into the water fully clothed?"

She laughed, sounding lighter than she had in a long

time. "I guess not. I got so wrapped up in figuring things out, I feel like I have one foot in fairyland."

Her words made him laugh. "Nope. Try both feet."

She sat and levered one boot off, followed by the other. Her trousers followed, and then the layers beneath and her stockings. Both pairs. Slowly, her body came into view. Long red scars, fading to pink, ran the length of both legs and along her arms. More markings traveled across her ribs and back.

Erin trailed a fingertip over one of the deeper ones on her right leg. "All those injuries were real. And they did, miraculously, heal."

"Did you think you'd imagined them?" He waited for her at the water's edge but turned away so his erection wouldn't be so obvious. It was a spontaneous reaction to her beauty and his desire for her. He hoped she'd welcome it—and him—but he wasn't certain.

She'd been more distant since they returned. Perhaps she'd considered what he said about dragon matings being permanent and wasn't quite ready to tie herself to him forever. Fire burned its way up his chest and out his mouth. His dragon didn't care for his interpretation.

Erin was their mate. Any self-respecting dragon would jump in with sparks and fire and ensure she didn't get away.

Her energy drew near as she walked to the shoreline. "I'm not sure what I thought," she replied in answer to his question. "Part of me knew I was near death. Another part kept coming up with excuses like hallucinations." She waltzed past him, hips swinging jauntily.

He'd been right about her ass. High and round and perfect, it begged to be grabbed. His cock grew harder still, and his fingers itched to settle on her breasts or her ass or anywhere on her enticing body.

"Coming?" she called over one shoulder. "This was your idea." The water had reached her waist, and she dove beneath its surface.

He plunged forward until the lake was deep enough for swimming and joined her stroking through the still waters. Because they were so far beneath Earth's surface, the lake rarely sported so much as a ripple. No wind down here, and the proximity to the Earth's crust kept the temperature reasonably warm.

She twisted in the water, splashed him, and said, "Bet you can't catch me."

"You're on!"

Erin led him a merry chase, above and below the surface as she ducked and wove and evaded his efforts to grab her. He surfaced to laugh. She must have been a fish in an earlier life.

And then he remembered the dragons' connection to sea-serpents. Long ago, all of them had been exceptionally nimble beneath the waves. She stroked past and tapped his arm, but he'd been cataloging her moves. When she feinted right, he was ready for her and blocked her, catching her handily.

With a hand on each shoulder, he pulled her against him. Her eyes were still the same ocean-blue, but they'd developed the whirling deep-green centers characteristic of dragons. She looked at him, long and hard, her expression turning wistful.

"Such a beautiful man." She closed her arms around his back and hung on, winding her legs around his waist.

Her breasts were crushed against his chest, and he lowered his hands until they gripped her perfect ass. Their faces were right next to each other. When she tilted hers in clear invitation, he kissed her.

As if nothing had intervened between their last kiss and now, passion took off like a team of galloping horses. The vanilla-cinnamon scent he'd longed for was there in spades, thick enough to eat. Possessiveness filled Konstantin until all he longed for was to brand the woman in his arms—make her his.

Their tongues thrashed against each other. Steam puffed from her nostrils, surrounding them. He rejoiced. It had to be a sign her dragon wouldn't stand in the way. Dragons had their own social structure, their own ideas about who should be mated to whom.

He might know in his bones Erin was slated to be his, but her dragon was under absolutely no obligation to agree with his assessment.

Erin caught his lower lip between her teeth and nipped him. He bit back, fingers digging into the alluring globes of her ass. He yearned for her. Ached for her. His cock was poised at her entrance, so near he felt the heat of her sing to him through the water.

All he had to do was thrust upward, and she'd be around

him with all her glorious heat and snugness and rippling muscles. He could almost feel her tightening around him, imagine the pulsing of climax when it took her. It made his balls roar for release. He had to have her. Had to make her his.

She ripped her mouth away and ran her tongue over to his ear, plunging it inside. He gasped and lunged upward, intent on fulfilling the mate bond. She glided out of his reach, aided by the water's buoyancy. Her eyes were liquid with need, and her breath came fast, but she'd unwound her legs from his waist.

"But I—" rasped from him before he got hold of himself. Telling her how aroused he was wouldn't make a difference. She already knew.

"I know. Come on." She swam for shore, switching to walking when the water grew shallow.

He followed her to where she'd left her clothes, unclear if she was going to accept him or not. He had no idea what he'd do if she refused his offer. He'd laid himself bare before her. No woman had ever turned him down, but the stakes had never been this high.

He'd never asked a woman to be his mate. Even before the other dragons had left, when he could have asked any of several females—most of whom would probably have said yes—he'd held back. None of them were right for him. Erin was.

She turned and molded her body against his. She curved a hand around his achingly erect cock. He groaned, ashamed of how much he longed for her. Wet hair dragged over his skin as she moved lower until she knelt before him and took him into her mouth.

Heat from her burst around him as she ran her lips the length of his shaft, nipping and biting as she went. A swirl of her tongue around the head, and she took him deep into her again. She milked him with one hand and cradled his balls with the other, pressing against a place at the base of them that almost made the top of his head blow off.

He grasped her head between his hands and thrust into her mouth. It wasn't the coupling he longed for, but it was unique and spicy and sensual rolled into one. She made little moaning noises as she laved him with her tongue. It damn near killed him to pull out of her mouth, but he wanted to taste her too.

He drew them down onto her pile of clothing, smoothing the garments into protection from the dirt. After a quick, hot kiss, he drew his mouth downward along her neck to her collarbones, tonguing the hollow between them.

Her breasts with their distended nipples were close, so close. He fastened his mouth over one and sucked enthusiastically. She arched her back, trying to get closer to his kisses. He twirled the other nipple between a thumb and forefinger, pinching hard. Trading back and forth, he lashed his tongue from nipple to nipple.

She shrieked and writhed beneath him. He felt her dual nature. Felt her dragon urging him on. It wanted his cock, but Erin's unspoken message had been clear. They could play at sex and not be forever bound. It was less than he wanted, but he'd take her any way he could get her.

She made a grab for his cock but couldn't reach it. Next, she shoved a hand between her legs. He raised his mouth from a nipple, loving how it glistened wetly from his saliva. "Uh-uh. You're mine, woman. Pleasure flows from me."

He batted her hand out of the way and slid his between her legs. The wet heat of her drew him inside the lush secrets of her body. He plumbed her with his fingers before moving his head between her legs. Before he latched his mouth around her clit, she jackknifed her body so she could suckle him. Exploring her, pleasuring her, had taken the edge off his immediate need to come. The minute she plunged her mouth over him, warm and urgent, his arousal shot back to center stage.

He closed his mouth over her clit and slid his tongue around both sides and across the top. Like the miniature penis it was, it grew and quivered beneath his touch. Working her between his mouth and his hand, he felt the tension grow as her climax first blossomed and then crested. Her rhythmic contractions were ever so hard to resist. He yearned to let go, come in her willing mouth, but he'd make her come one more time first.

By holding back, he could maintain the fine edge of lust and need that raced through him like a fine, old whiskey. He sucked harder and pumped his fingers in and out of her, tickling the special places nerves clustered thickly.

She rocked against him, gasping and moaning. The hotter she got, the harder she sucked him. But it worked both ways. The hotter he got, the more creative his touches and licks and bites. He felt her next orgasm seed itself from the remains of the one that had just blasted through her.

Shameless, he fed magic into her spiraling passion, driving her higher and higher until her lust shattered against him. The climax he'd been holding back bubbled from his balls, sheeting from him in jet after jet of thick, white heat. She kept right on sucking until he was done, lapping his semen.

Once he was certain he'd wrung the last bit of pleasure from her climax, he twisted until they faced each other and crashed his mouth over hers. She tasted of him, bitter and salt and fire, and it aroused him all over again. Threading his hands through her hair, he lifted his face from hers.

"Erin. Darling. I love you."

She smiled. Soft, lazy, alluring. "I think I love you too, but we have to be certain. Until we are, we can pretend we're kids."

"I don't understand." He cupped the side of her face.

"No. You probably wouldn't. Humans don't usually start right out having sex. We do things like, well like what you and I just did. Eventually, they lead to the real thing."

"I don't understand. Why play at it?"

"It's a good question with a whole lot of complicated answers wrapped up in religion and social conventions. None of them matter. I'm 90 percent certain, but I need more time with you."

His heart cracked open and melted. "You're my mate, Erin Ryan. Mine. I'll wait through the ages for you if I have to."

She laughed and leaned into his touch. "I forgot how long we live. You won't have to wait that long. Let's get through our first fight and a few other nitpicky things first."

It was his turn to chuckle. "How do you know we'll have any fights?"

"We already have. All couples do. Beyond that, you might decide I'm a total dud in the magic department. I'm not sealing the deal to give both of us an escape hatch."

"I don't want one. I want you."

She closed her eyes. When she opened them, she said, "I'm happy. I shouldn't be. There's so much facing us, I should be scared to my bones and back in the study absorbing as much as my brain can hold."

"I can take us inside."

She nodded. "Guess I need to get dressed. It's not warm enough to be naked, unless I'm in your arms. Then it's fine."

Since he never wanted to let go of her, he said, "I'd love to offer my body as a heat source, but how about if I teach you how to use magic to warm yourself?"

Her eyes crinkled at the corners as she smiled. "That would be wonderful. Want to start now?"

He nodded. "Soon." What he really wanted was to hold her just like he was doing and never let go, but it wasn't practical. *Two more minutes,* he told himself. *And then we'll rejoin the real world.*

It might have been more than two minutes. They drowsed in one another's arms, sleepy and sated from sex.

"Kon. I need you," shook him awake fast.

"I heard that." Erin sounded fuzzy and worried. "Was it Katya?"

"Yes." He scrambled to his feet and drew Erin to hers. Magic jumped to his call as he set seeking spells in motion.

"Tell me what you're doing," Erin said. "I can't help if you don't include me."

Konstantin raked a hand through his tangled hair, torn between the urgent note in his sister's sending and Erin's request to help. "We don't have much time," he told her, "but I can build my spells out loud and explain what I've done later."

"That would be wonderful." She closed her teeth over her lower lip. "I don't want to be a bother, but there's so much I don't know."

He opened the tip of one finger with an incisor and sprinkled blood in the air. It floated, awaiting his command. Before he set it in motion, he said, "Katya shares my blood. A seeking spell that's blood-based is one of the strongest of all. Once I activate it, all we'll need to do is follow."

"Got it." She hastily pulled on her discarded clothing as he pumped energy into his casting. By the time she was dressed, the army of blood drops rose straight into the air.

He changed up the rhythm and cadence of his magic, summoning a teleport spell. He'd catch up with his blood on the surface.

Erin moved close, within the circle of his magic. She felt right there, like she'd been born to be a part of him and his power. Igniting his spell, he sent them winging upward, away from the cozy protection that hid them from the rest of the world.

The protection his dragon hated, and that had nearly been the death of Katya's bond with her beast. "Be careful," he warned Erin. "I'll do my best, but we may end up in the middle of a passel of sea-serpents."

"What happens if we do?"

He laughed one short, fire-tinged bark. "We turn into dragons, force them into their human bodies, and kill them. And then, we find my sister and Johan."

CHAPTER 16

$\mathcal{I}$'d never wanted anything quite so intensely as I wanted Konstantin's cock inside me, but I was scared too. What if we grew to hate each other? The specter of being together forever was daunting. He seemed to be sure, but I wasn't. We were so different, different enough even some of the things I said confused him.

Not so different any more, my implacable inner voice declared.

"Not different at all," my dragon weighed in, adding, *"He is ours."*

I pushed a mental wince aside. Maybe being a dragon shifter changed everything. Of course it did, except I hadn't been one long enough to fully appreciate the extent of the alterations in myself. So far, my linguistic skills had taken a quantum leap forward. And I was stronger. A whole lot stronger.

Other than that, I was a total klutz in the magic department. Konstantin had been incredibly supportive of my ineptitude. Would he be this supportive if we were five years into it, and I was still making stupid mistakes?

Worry for Katya and Johan filled me. Actually, I was far more worried about Johan. Katya had resources to take care of herself. For one thing, she had a dragon. For another, she was immortal. Had Johan made the jump to dragon shifter? Had there been some problem? Was it why Katya had reached out to Konstantin?

I rolled my eyes. Lots of questions. Zero answers. When Konstantin wielded power, he made it look effortless. I hadn't exactly followed anything he'd done beyond his quick and dirty explanation about creating a seeking spell from his blood. Something about it acting as a magnet and leading us to Katya.

It wasn't all that simple, though. He'd mixed fire and air and a bit of water with stuff I couldn't identify. I'd still been working to sort it out when his next spell surrounded us both. Something about his magic felt right, as if I belonged within its purview. Was that part of the mate bond he'd talked about?

I needed him and his library. And a few years to absorb everything inside it. Except I wouldn't have any time at all. Not with the serpents growing in strength. My indoctrination was bound to be a baptism by fire, literally. My hands curled into fists as I hoped to hell I was up to the task.

"We're nearly at the surface," Konstantin informed me. "Ready yourself."

I wasn't sure what I could do, but I vowed I wouldn't be a liability. What he'd said earlier about killing serpents shot out of left field. Could I kill anything? I wasn't sure. I was trained to save lives, not end them. It was the same way I'd felt when Johan had thrust a gun into my hands—and expected me to use it.

Konstantin pushed me gently behind him as his transport spell frittered to nothing. Part of me was outraged. He had no right to play a knight errant. Or maybe he did. He sensed things I wasn't aware of. That would change as I grew more adept with magic, but it was still too new for me to do much more than flounder about.

An icy blast of wind told me we'd reached the shoreline. I poked my head around his shoulder and squinted against ice crystals blowing in a gale-force blast. They battered me and made me grateful for my staunch outer clothes. Maybe someday, I'd learn to keep my body warm, but today wasn't the day for that.

Konstantin angled his head from side to side. I assumed he was hunting for his blood couriers, although I didn't see how they could possibly survive the wind. I longed for goggles but hadn't been wearing any the day I'd been kidnapped and removed from the *Darya*. It felt like I'd lived through several lifetimes since then, but it hadn't been all that long. Not in real time.

The sea was iced over as far out as I could see, and I didn't understand why. It was high summer in Antarctica.

Still cold, but the sea ice should be minimal. The entire bay was frozen solid, so much so, I would have chanced walking on its surface.

An unfamiliar sensation rippled through me, centered beneath my breastbone. Smoke and ash filled my lungs; I opened my mouth to let them escape. Clearly, my dragon wanted us to be in its form, not mine. Had it noticed something too subtle for me to detect?

Likely, since most of my attention was caught up in staying on my feet. Konstantin provided a windscreen, but only from one direction. A sharp crack drove through my skull like an icepick, followed by one more. The ice pack was breaking up, but how was it even possible?

The rampaging sensation within me increased a hundredfold. Fire shot from my mouth, and I twisted my head to the side to avoid blasting Konstantin. He turned to me. Grim determination changed his Adonis good looks, turning his features harsh and sinister.

"Give your dragon her head. Do it now. No questions."

"But I have to undress." My words were ripped away by the wind. The prospect of another shift into my dragon form scared the crap out of me. I'd barely survived the last one, but I wasn't being rational. How could I be? The part of my brain that drove primitive emotions was buried deep and had almost no connection to my ability to reason.

"No time. Let your dragon take over and shift. Thank all the gods you're bonded."

I didn't have to do anything. Before I could release the hold I thought I had on my beast, my clothing ripped and the stretching, breaking, tearing sensation sent hot knives of agony all through me. Not nearly as bad as last time, though. Not as intense, nor did they last very long.

I remembered to visualize my red monster. It helped a lot. Soon after, I was flying, wings beating the air to take us higher. The same layered vision took over. It enhanced my depth orientation and allowed me to judge distances in a vertical plane.

Konstantin's black dragon soared next to us.

The sharp crack that had been the beginning of my dragon taking matters into her own hands repeated. After several more intense snapping sounds, sea-serpent heads poked through the ice.

"What a bunch of lazy bastards," Konstantin said, fire streaming from his open mouth.

"I don't understand." Christ! Getting words out was a struggle. My dragon was riding high on being in control. It was a hell of a wakeup call. Konstantin had sketched out a little bit about how critical it was for me to keep the upper hand. The ease with which my beast had wrested control away from me told me how much work I had to do.

"Apparently, they decided digging out a lair was too much trouble. So they formed an ice sheet and used it to hide beneath."

More of my crash course came home to roost. *"You said we'd kill them, but they're immortal in their serpent bodies."*

At least twenty serpents had made short work of the ice. Where I could see through its cracked and broken surface, coils writhed. Maybe more of the fuckers, or just parts of the ones whose heads were above water. The air immediately above them hazed over with red.

"What is that?"

"Poison," he replied. *"It can't hurt us."*

The missing column of blood drops zipped in front of us, or maybe these were something else. Red globules dipped and swayed in front of Konstantin's dragon. He opened his mouth, and his long, forked red tongue flicked out and touched two of the globes.

My dragon puffed something with a yellowish tint toward the two blobs. I wanted to ask what we were doing. I felt like an actor in a play, but one who hadn't been offered a script. Hating my observer role, yet helpless to alter it, I watched while the two translucent balls fell out of the sky and made a beeline for two of the serpents. The layer of poison didn't even slow them down.

My mouth opened, and my dragon bugled, but it wasn't like anything I'd heard before. The sound was hypnotic, consisting of three repeating notes. While it got going, Konstantin's dragon added its own bugled message to the mix. The six tones blended with one another in an elaborate pattern that ebbed and flowed.

If my dragon hadn't been on top of keeping us airborne, I'd have followed those notes right into the shattered ice below. What the hell was this? A dragonesque version of the Pied Piper of Hamblin?

The targeted serpents slithered onto the ice, and thence to the beach. I felt magic grow around them, break into shards, and reform. Even if I didn't totally understand what was happening, they did. They were fighting for their lives.

My dragon kept up a flow of the ochre-colored smoke, mixed in with fire. We flew lower. I wasn't comfortable and tried my damnedest to use our wings. No dice. The dragon wasn't about to do anything except what she wanted. I worried my weakness would set a crappy precedent, but there wasn't a damn thing I could do about it.

One of the serpents broke apart, leaving a human body. Fury surrounded it, turning the air even redder, and he shook his fist at the skies. Konstantin blasted the newly-formed man with fire, stoking it until it formed a volcanic cone. Screams blanketed the still air but didn't last long. Flames burned merrily, and the stench of charred meat filled my nostrils.

The second serpent shifted too.

"Your turn," Konstantin flew next to me.

"I don't know how." It was weaker than fuck, but I needed information. *"Is it special fire that burns extra hot?"*

"Your dragon knows. Trust her."

I did. Fire simmered in my scaled chest, growing hotter and hotter until it spewed from my mouth, bathing the man beneath with liquid flames. Unlike his companion, this one was cowering. Compassion raked me as a pyre engulfed him. My dragon laughed uproariously, turning whatever I was feeling to anger.

"Save your pity," my beast said. *"He deserved a far worse death than what we gave him."*

I'd been focused on the two serpents lured by

Konstantin's spell and the musical notes that had fallen silent as soon as the first one reached land. When I scoured the waters beneath us, the rest of the sea-serpents had vanished. Acres of broken ice spread below, but nothing swam beneath it. Nowhere close, anyway.

"Bloody cowards," Konstantin shouted.

They might be our enemy, but I didn't blame them. Only the truly stupid hung around to be slaughtered. A sharp jab in the vicinity of my ribs told me my dragon sidekick didn't agree. For dragons, it was a black-and-white world, no shades of gray allowed. If even a single serpent returned, she'd kill it without a backward thought.

Questions brimmed over.

What kind of spell had forced the serpents onto land and then into shifting?

Could we replicate it until all of them were dead, or would we run out of magic?

Where did the blood drops come in?

Were they even the same blood, or some newly minted ones?

How about the music? What role had it played?

I wanted my mouth. I wanted my clothes. The ones lying on the ground in an unsalvageable heap.

Konstantin circled back to where we'd begun, skidding to a halt near a rocky bluff. Before I made a decision to follow him, my dragon had already set us down a foot or so away. A now-familiar surge of brilliance told me Konstantin would soon be human.

I wasn't at all sure I'd even be able to shift. Not if my

dragon didn't want me to. The sensation of being a bit player at the mercy of someone much stronger than myself gave me the creeps. It took me back to a childhood spent scared to my bones and skulking under beds and inside cupboards to avoid my father's wrath.

I would not go back to being that terrified little girl.

Not now. Not ever.

Taking a moment to make sure I recalled every aspect of the last time I'd left my dragon's body behind, I recreated the steps and pushed hard. Nothing happened. I could see my human form. There I stood right in front of me, but when I tried to fall into it, the dragon scales didn't so much as flutter.

"You. Will. Not. Rule. Me." I shouted as loud as I could muster in telepathy and pushed everything I had into shifting.

At first, I ran up against the same blank wall, but I kept right on pushing. I knew at a bone-deep, instinctual level if I lost this fight, I'd be lost forever. And I'd be damned if I'd turn into one of those dragon shifters Konstantin told me about. Ones who had to be banished because their dragon developed delusions of grandeur, and their human side was too weak to make a difference.

I was not weak. Goddammit.

Not weak at all.

I'd survived my father. And foster care. And social isolation because I was so petrified of caring about anyone. No way was a bullying dragon going to be my downfall.

All of a sudden, the barrier holding me back crumpled, and I crashed into my body, ending up belly down on frozen ground. Perhaps my dragon had taken exception to me labeling it a bully. I'd have to remember that tidbit. Panting and gasping, I felt Konstantin's hands on my waist as he lifted me and held me against him.

"Good work," he said, as if I'd just trotted in from a normal day at the clinic.

It felt perverse, but I started to laugh. Once mirth got hold of me, it wouldn't let go and I chuckled, chortled, and snorted while he held me.

"It's a wonder you can laugh about it," he said, once I'd settled down. "Your dragon made a bid for dominance. A determined one. I was afraid she'd succeed, but you subjugated her attempt. Congratulations."

"Is that what happened?" I'd begun to shiver, despite having his arms around me.

He nodded. "You and I talked about it, but nothing quite prepares you for the first time a dragon decides to test your endurance."

I closed my teeth over my lower lip, but it was numb from cold. "Will she try again?"

"Of course. Would you expect any less of her? Eventually, the attempts will be more for show and to remind you of the extent of her power, though."

"We still have to find Katya and Johan. And those serpents aren't gone for good, either."

"True on both fronts. We did teach them a lesson today, though. We are stronger than they are. And merciless." He focused his dark gaze on me. "Why did you hesitate?"

"Killing the second one?"

"Yes. Why?"

I shrugged, but it got lost in shivers. "He was begging for mercy."

Konstantin gripped the sides of my face. "Would you have offered clemency had I not flown next to you, urging you to action?"

"No. Uh, yes. Probably? In truth, I don't know." I shook myself from head to toe. "I put in close to forty years as a human. I'm a healer. I save lives. Killing isn't second nature for me. If someone begs for their life, the proper course is to condemn them to a long stint in prison or something."

"Dragons have no prisons. Nor do we offer mercy." He narrowed his eyes. "I understand why your dragon kicked up such a fuss about you shifting. She's trying to make you strong, force you to decide what's important to you."

"She knows everything in my mind, huh?" At his nod, I went on. "It's not fair since I have no fucking idea what she thinks or how she operates."

"This is a different way of life for you," he agreed. "No time to go inside for clothes. Visualize heat flowing up from the Earth's molten core. For this spell, use all fire. Nothing mixed with it. Once it's there, imagine it drawing heat upward until it surrounds you, warms you."

"What happens after it's there?"

"Modulate the flow so it doesn't drain all your power." He stepped away. "Better get cracking before you freeze."

I tried, but nothing happened. The frozen blocks my feet had turned into moved well beyond hurting until I couldn't feel them at all. If I didn't know the tissues were dying, it would have been a relief. Images of blackened toes so devoid of blood they could be clipped off with a scissor flashed through my mind.

I tried again. And again. Finally, Konstantin ginned up a flaming spear of his fire. Seeing how it pierced the dirt and feeling the force behind it, helped.

I was lightheaded from sucking frozen air into my lungs when a blast of heat caught me in the calves. Before I could harness it, it retreated.

"Nooooo," I shrieked and repeated what I'd done. This time, though, I was ready. When the warmth shot upward, I captured it and coaxed it around me. It was sloppy, but functional.

"Cut the flow of your magic to the bare minimum needed to maintain warmth," Konstantin instructed.

"Not until I'm warmer." Pain was starting in my semi-frozen feet and fingers. Agony that built before it subsided. To divert myself, I asked, "What did you do to force the serpents back to human?"

"Not I, but we. I redirected some of the blood trackers from earlier. You'll recall we share blood with the serpents. Using water and fire, I marked the tracking devices with runes specific to sea-serpents."

"Was that what you were doing with your tongue."

"Yes. Once created, they acted as homing pigeons. Your dragon added a very ancient element to my spell. So old, I'd forgotten about it until she started puffing ochre mist. Its other name is dream-smoke, and it lulls victims so they're less likely to fight back. Coupled with the music, those serpents didn't have a chance."

I'd stopped shivering, and I experimented with withdrawing some of the magic I'd used to warm myself. There'd be a point at which no more heat danced beneath my feet. It was up to me to find it.

"I'm guessing the serpents have to be close for what we did to work."

"Not that close," Konstantin said, "but the farther away they are, the more magic it takes to trap them. Magic isn't a bottomless commodity. You will find you require sleep and food to replenish your ability. Your dragon has far more magical stamina."

I made a face. "Not sure I trust her anymore."

"You do. And she respects you for standing up to her."

I didn't want to go there. The specter of living the rest of my life cohabiting with a creature who delighted in testing my mettle wasn't particularly appealing. I'd earned my chops by surviving medical school and a surgical residency, rife with hostile men who didn't believe women belonged in the operating room.

And now I had to start all over again from ground zero.

Steam puffed through my mouth. I rolled my eyes and muttered, "Now you want to make nice?" More steam sputtered from between my teeth, the dragon version of an olive branch.

I shook myself. I was acting like an entitled brat. No one owed me anything, least of all my bondmate. "Have you heard anything else from Katya?"

"No, and it worries me. I've tried to reach her, but she's not answering."

"I'm ready. Let's go find her."

He kissed me once, more of a "thank you, glad you're okay" kiss than anything deeper. "I wanted to make certain you'd recovered enough."

His concern touched me. In my other life, I'd maintained a detachment that precluded anyone getting close enough to care. "Thanks. Rustle up those blood balls, and we'll charge after them."

"Blood-infused seeking vectors." He corrected my verbiage. Like obedient minions, they materialized out of nowhere. One moment, the air in front of us was empty; the next, about two dozen balls bobbed, looking anxious to be of service.

"Do you know where we're going?" I asked.

"Probably a borderworld. If she were anywhere nearer, she'd have responded to my telepathy."

"Which means she must have moved."

He considered it. "You're right. Since she was able to reach me before, and I can't tap her now, it does suggest she and Johan are in a different spot."

I gnawed on my lip, feeling the bite of my teeth this time. "Are you worried about her?"

"Not especially, but Johan is vulnerable. If she could have left him to go for help, she would have."

"Could they have stumbled into another sea-serpent nest?" I was grasping at straws, revealing my ignorance of the magical world, but I didn't care.

"Possible, but unlikely. Other monstrosities exist, though. Lots of them. She and Johan could have run up against something far worse. Something dragon magic isn't a match for."

"But we can't be killed." I made a small face at my use of the inclusive pronoun. I was scarcely part of the *we* of dragonkind. Not yet.

"No, but we can be captured, tortured, imprisoned, cast into fire that burns us again and again. Sometimes immortality becomes a curse, and we wish for death."

His words cast a pall over me, and my nicely warm body shivered anyway, not from cold but from imagining a host of horrors. Konstantin's magic built around me as he moved his hands in an intricate pattern.

I intended to ask him to talk me through the steps of his working, but let it go so I wouldn't disturb his concentration. There should be time during our teleport. I'd ask him then. I inhaled the familiar scent of his power, sunbaked clay, hearth fire, and herbs. It soothed and inflamed me by turns. His arms were around me, yet I couldn't remember him putting them there.

Grateful for his strength and ability, I leaned against him, threading my arms beneath his. We floated in the place between worlds, the same arena where we'd waited for my fate to unfold. For the first time maybe ever, I placed my trust in someone besides myself. It felt good and right and scary as hell, but I'd made my choice when I accepted the transition to dragon shifter.

Somehow, I'd thought it would make me invulnerable, even more of a force unto myself, needing no one.

"We all need someone, darling." Konstantin's deep voice rumbled near my ear.

"Leave a woman some privacy." I kicked back my head and met his beautiful golden eyes.

He tossed his head back and laughed. After a while, I joined him. When our mirth had run its course, I said, "Between you—who've taken up residence in my head—and the dragon, privacy is a thing of the past, huh?"

He answered my question with one of his own. "Is that such a bad thing?"

"No." I tilted my chin at a defiant angle. "Privacy is definitely overrated."

"There's my girl."

In another life, in another time, I'd have corrected him harshly for calling me a girl, but being his girl was the best gift of all. I'd wait until Katya and Johan were safe, and then I'd tell him. I waited, expecting a comment that he already knew, but he was wise enough to remain silent. Maybe he'd even act surprised when the moment came, and I told him I wanted to be his mate.

"Talk me through the teleport spell."

"I thought you'd never ask." His eyes gleamed with deep intelligence. "You know how I marked the vectors with sea-serpent runes?" When I nodded, he went on. "Because Katya is my sister, my twin, all I needed to do was instruct the vectors to look for an exact match..."

YOU'VE REACHED the end of the first book in the Ice Dragon Trilogy. While it's fresh in your mind, please leave a review for *Feral Ice*. It doesn't have to be fancy, a couple of sentences about why you enjoyed it would be so appreciated.

The next book, *Cursed Ice*, is Katya and Johan's story. It begins where this story left off. Once we extricate them from the mess they're in, everyone will return to Earth and take on the sea-serpents in *Primal Ice*, closing volume of this trilogy. Smarter than they look, and not nearly as lazy as Konstantin pegged them, the serpents haven't been idle.

Read on for a sample of *Cursed Ice*.

ABOUT THE AUTHOR

Ann Gimpel is a USA Today bestselling author. A lifelong aficionado of the unusual, she began writing speculative fiction a few years ago. Since then her short fiction has appeared in many webzines and anthologies. Her longer books run the gamut from urban fantasy to paranormal romance. Once upon a time, she nurtured clients. Now she nurtures dark, gritty fantasy stories that push hard against reality. When she's not writing, she's in the backcountry getting down and dirty with her camera. She's published over 70 books to date, with several more planned for 2019 and beyond. A husband, grown children, grandchildren, and wolf hybrids round out her family.

Keep up with her at www.anngimpel.com or http://anngimpel.blogspot.com

If you enjoyed what you read, get in line for special offers and pre-release special reads. Newsletter Signup!

My name is Johan Petris. I'm not entirely certain how it happened, but I've fallen off a cliff. Not a physical one, but one separating what I always believed was real from where I am now. I'm a metallurgical engineer, for chrissakes, and a Dutchman to boot. We're a bit of a dour lot. Hell, we barely encourage our children to engage in flights of fancy.

I admit to a closet fascination with science fiction and fantasy, but it wasn't anything I'd ever have admitted to anyone. Not out loud. My work fellows would have had a tough time taking me seriously if they thought I entertained myself with tales of alien visitation.

Or werewolves. Or vampires.

I'll spare you the details of how I ended up kilometers underground in a dragon shifter lair. That's a tale for another day. Let it suffice to say I'm here, along with Erin

Ryan, a doctor and biochemist. We're deep in discussions with our dragon shifter hosts to determine what comes next. Not surprisingly, radical differences in our belief systems have turned our chat into a contest of wills.

I feel for Erin, but I admire her spirit. She's having a much rougher time than me absorbing the idea of magic being anything other than an abstract construct. Too nervous to remain seated, she's pacing around the room asking questions. Blonde hair is billowing around her tall, spare body, and her blue eyes hold a worried cast.

I'm not sure why accepting magic is real hasn't been harder for me, but people are different that way. I have half an ear on Konstantin, one of the dragon shifters, describing several iterations of magic wielders. Only half, though. The rest of my mind is busy—reeling might be more accurate—with information about other worlds. Lots of them.

Apparently, we're headed toward a constellation of borderworlds to secure assistance from other magic wielders. Sea-serpents, a distant relative of the dragons, have invaded Earth. We're the only ones who know about them, so presumably, we have to act as the first line of defense—

A brilliant flash I've come to associate with dragon shifter magic made me squinch my eyes tight. When I opened them, Konstantin had crossed the kitchen and grabbed Erin. She was writhing in his grasp trying to get away.

I wasn't anxious to confront him. Richly muscled, he probably stood six feet six with shiny dark hair cascading around his shoulders. But I couldn't just sit there and let him manhandle Erin, either. She'd been my shipmate on an Antarctic research expedition. It's how we ended up in the Southern Ocean.

The dragons' cozy kitchen stretched around us. Carved out of earth, its walls sported rich veins of gold, silver, and other precious metals. Longer than it was wide, most of its contents were tucked behind magical panels. We'd been sitting around a large table, one that could easily seat twenty, before Erin jumped up and began pacing.

I hustled to where she and Konstantin stood and asked, "Is that really necessary?"

"I won't hurt her," Konstantin growled.

I'm certain he meant to dissuade me, but I didn't back down.

While I was considering what to say next, Katya, Konstantin's twin, and another dragon shifter materialized next to me and hooked an arm beneath mine. "Come with me. We shall talk. Erin is safe with my brother."

Katya is stunning. About the same height as Erin, she has masses of copper-colored curls. Most of the time, she's naked, which is a huge distraction. I admit I'm weak, but I'm a man, and we tend to be diverted by bare breasts and acres of leg. Both she and her brother have golden eyes with deep green centers. In dragon form—she's golden, and he's black —their eyes spin, casting a hypnotic net.

I felt power spilling from her, but I was helpless to do anything except acquiesce. It was a damned uncomfortable spot to be in. I value my free will, and it's been in short supply lately. My mouth opened, seemingly of its own accord, and I murmured, "Of course. Where would you like us to sit?"

"Can't you see what Konstantin's doing?" Erin squawked. "Whatever he left out, we all need to hear it. Together. In the same room."

I heard Erin, but her voice was coming from a long way away. Her complaint seemed petty, unimportant. Katya's warmth, pressing the length of my side, was paramount.

Somehow, we ended up one flight up sitting on one of the pallets scattered through a number of sleeping areas. She seized a length of fuzzy fabric and wound it around herself, almost as if she divined how much trouble her nudity created.

Whatever she'd done to get me to follow her upstairs dissipated. Worry for Erin filled me. "Where has Konstantin taken Erin? And for what purpose?" I asked without preamble. I tried for a stern enough tone Katya wouldn't blow me off.

Or muffle me with magic again.

She nodded. "It's understandable you'd be concerned, but my brother would never harm her."

I folded my legs beneath me and said, "Konstantin said the same thing. That he would not hurt her, but you did not answer either of my questions."

"No. I did not."

"Why? I still know nothing about his intentions."

Katya curved her fingers and raked them through her thick, unruly hair. The motion stretched the fabric tight across her breasts. I forced my gaze upward with firm instructions to keep my eyes on her face, not on the outline of her nipples.

After a pause, one that dragged out so long I was crafting what to say next to encourage her to talk, she said, "We're in a precarious predicament. Nor do we have time to waste."

I opened my mouth, but she shook her head. "Hear me out. We cannot leave you here in our home while we travel to various borderworlds seeking allies. If something unexpected happened, and we were unable to return, you and Erin would be stuck down here. There is no way to reach the surface without magic."

She spread her hands in front of her. "My twin is correct. It's far too dangerous to stumble around the universe with two humans in tow. For you and for us. We might end up fighting for your survival instead of lobbying for the help we so desperately need. Absent aid, Earth will be lost to the serpents."

"How can you know?" I asked, startled by the adamant tone of her statement.

"Because they're like us. It means I understand how they think, how they operate." She cast a sidelong glance my way.

"All right. You ruled out several options. What is left?"

She traded looking askance at me for raking me with an astute gaze that probably missed very little. "Only two options. We leave you on the surface—where you would be vulnerable to both the sea-serpents and the elements if we were gone overlong."

"Or?"

"Or we make a bid for each of you to become a dragon shifter." Her golden eyes never left my face.

"What? But neither of you are even certain such a thing is possible." I felt as if a mule had backed up and kicked me in the guts with both its rear hooves.

"No. We're not," she agreed. "Konstantin intuited Erin would be a harder sell than you. Fear lives in that one, although she covers it well. It's why he took her to a more private location. He will lay out her options, and then she will choose."

"What happens if she says no to becoming a dragon shifter?" It was an easier question to ask than one about me because it was a step removed from my own fate. But I bet the answer would be the same.

I ground my teeth in irritation at my cowardice. I didn't usually avoid tackling difficult situations, but this one was so bizarre I didn't have a place to slot it.

"Konstantin will probably deliver her to that Polish research base the two of you have mentioned."

Understanding flooded me, right along with guilty relief. Erin would never opt to be a dragon shifter. Not in this world or any other. "We are here until she decides, right? Because both of us have to make the same choice."

"No. We're here for two reasons. To move us out of the way and for you to think about what you want to do."

I frowned, remembering an earlier conversation, one of the first we'd had with the dragon shifter twins. "But Erin and I are ruled by a single fate, correct?"

Katya shook her head. "No longer true." She offered me a

soft smile. "For a transformation to have a ghost of a chance of success, you must want it with everything in you. The same is true of Erin. Neither of you can ride on the other's coattails."

I turned the information over, considering it. "If I demur, you will see I end up at Arctowski, the Polish base?"

"Yes. It will be a death sentence. The nearest humans will be the first targeted by the sea-serpents."

"Mmph. So I would be better served having you leave me in Europe?"

"You would, indeed." She paused long enough to take a measured breath. "I would erase your memories. While I would be as careful as possible, you would lose some that are bound up with your time with us."

"I understand. Some of my memories of Erin would be at risk."

Katya nodded solemnly. "Would that be a problem?"

Her tone was studiedly neutral, so I couldn't read what might lay behind it. Part of me hoped she might be a tiny bit jealous, but I was being ridiculous. "Not a problem so much as it pokes my control freak buttons," I mumbled.

"What exactly are they?"

I chuckled. "Humans are an odd lot. We nurture the illusion we are masters of our own ships." I took a breath and blew it out, my amusement fading. "Every time you or your brother uses magic to force an outcome, I resent the hell out of it. I am used to living in a world where people make requests, and I am free to accept or decline."

She knitted her coppery brows together. "Does that

mean you never have to do things that bother you? Or that you disagree with?"

"Of course not." I stopped before blindly blundering forward. Perhaps the freedom I'd cherished wasn't anything beyond a carefully constructed illusion.

"So you're not truly free?" she pressed.

"I guess not, but..." My voice faltered. How could I explain the nexus between manners and social expectations and outcomes?

"Never mind. It's not important. You know your choices. What is your decision?"

"Just like that?" Time shrank around me until I felt physical pressure compressing my chest like a steel band.

"Yes. Just like that. I'm happy to answer questions, but when we leave this room, it will either be to travel to the place between worlds where we shall petition Y Ddraigh Goch for a dragon of your own. Or to a spot on earth of your choosing. Which shall it be?"

She'd said she welcomed questions, and they bombarded me from all sides. "What if I try and cannot, uh, transform into something like you?"

"Then we retreat to Plan B and I deliver you somewhere on Earth."

"Minus my memories."

Katya nodded. "Of course." She tilted her head to one side, and I couldn't look away. No one had a right to be as beautiful as she was. Her skin glowed golden, almost begging me to reach out and stroke my fingertips over its surface.

She dropped a hand on top of my thigh. The heat from her traveled through my thick, polar outerwear and prickled the skin beneath. "I'm not being cruel. Humans are a fragile lot. Your minds can only absorb so much. Holding memories of a failed attempt to bond with a dragon would eventually drive you mad. You would replay it again and again. You would blame yourself. You would want to try again, but once shut, that gate will never reopen."

"So either way, I would lose my memories? If I fail at a transformation, or if I do not try at all?"

Katya nodded.

"I understand." It was the prudent response, although privately I wasn't certain she knew what she was talking about. How could she? From what she and her brother had said, they'd spent almost zero time with humans. Perhaps she was underestimating me. I rolled my mental eyes. Over-confidence had nearly been my undoing more than once.

It was how I'd ended up chucked in the chromium dig site with my femur broken. Erin set it, but Katya had healed me with magic. At the time, I'd had no idea how I'd recovered so fast, but I hadn't questioned my fortune, either.

"Questions?" Katya pressed.

I wrenched my mind back to the ones uppermost in my mind. "This transformation. If it works, won't it take really a long time for me to learn to control my magic?"

"Your dragon would help with that. The main problem will be maintaining control over the dragon." Breath rattled through her teeth. "They're an independent bunch. When they're not in your mind—or in their dragon form wherever you happen to live—they're free to travel where they will."

"But we have only one body?" I clarified. "Either the man or the dragon."

"Yes and no." She tossed an errant clump of hair back over a shoulder. "The dragons have their own world. I suspect they're corporeal in their own place."

"Why would you not know that?"

"It's a good question." Katya's nostrils flared. "Even though we're bonded, the relationship is lopsided. My dragon knows everything about me, but the only things I know about it are what it wants me to know."

"You've never traveled to the dragons' world?"

"No. None of us have. It's barred to everyone but dragons."

My forehead scrunched into a mass of lines. Obviously, we didn't have hours and hours for me to quiz Katya. What could I ask that would cut through several layers of my ambivalence?

If Erin had asked me if I wanted to be a dragon shifter even a few hours before, I'd have answered with a hearty affirmation. But now that the choice actually lay before me, I was of so many minds it was disconcerting.

"What are the advantages of this...lopsided relationship?" I focused on Katya wanting to pick up on her nonverbal cues as well as her words. For once, I wasn't half-aroused by her curves.

Probably because I was focused on the most critical decision of my life.

She met my straightforward gaze unflinchingly. "It's a hard question to answer. Since I was born with a dual nature, my dragon has been part of me forever." She closed her teeth over her lower lip. "It's like having a beloved companion. One who knows all of you, the good and the bad, and holds your feet to the fire when you've done something wrong.

"My dragon has been my closest friend—and my worst enemy. I hated her when she abandoned me after I refused to leave Earth. In retrospect, if I'd listened to her, Kon and I would be better off."

It seemed she had more to say, so I waited.

"When my dragon left, first I was angry, but then I was desolate. I missed her terribly. It was as if someone had cut off my right hand. Not the greatest metaphor, but I felt a critical part of me was missing."

"Did you ask her to come back?"

Katya's golden eyes skittered away. "Not for a very long time."

"What stopped you?"

She still didn't look at me. "Pride. The dragon left me. I figured she could find her own way back. Truth was I thought she owed me an apology." Bitter laughter bubbled. "Doesn't work that way."

"How did she find her way back to you?" I was curious to hear what had finally turned the tide.

"Kon's dragon did something. I have no idea what, but she returned as abruptly as she'd left. And we took off running as if we'd never been apart." Katya stole a glance my way. "It's good to have her back. I'm whole again."

I pinched the bridge of my nose between a thumb and forefinger. Nothing Katya had said made me want a dragon of my own. I was fiercely independent, and the thought of another being telling me what to do—or even weighing in with an opinion—made my skin crawl.

But the specter of being dropped off in the Netherlands —if I chose to go home—didn't hold much appeal, either. Right now, I had knowledge of a serious threat to all life on Earth. Once Katya got done with me, I wouldn't remember any of it.

Fat, dumb, and happy, I'd molder on the sidelines, fiddling while Rome burned. Maybe not quite that bad, but I had an uncomfortable premonition about the serpents. "Once the sea-serpents develop momentum," I asked Katya, "roughly how long will it take them to establish control of Earth?"

"Not long at all. Men have nothing at their disposal that will make the slightest dent in a magical war. They'll fall by the wayside in less than a single generation. Perhaps less. Depends how many serpents their leader, Surek, imports from wherever they came from."

Her response didn't surprise me, but nor did it make my choice any simpler. If I had her return me to my human kin —and that could happen even if I made a bid for a dragon and failed—I'd find out about the threat to Earth along with everyone else. We'd mount what defense we could, and fail.

Not how I'd envisioned myself ending up. Taking the coward's way out.

I was in a position where I could make a difference. If I pulled my head out of my rump and acted like a man.

I stumbled to me feet and stood as tall as I could, vertebrae cracking as I pushed my shoulders back. "I wish to become a dragon shifter."

Katya rolled to her feet and regarded me. Magic prickled where she jabbed me with it, no doubt testing my words. My resolve.

"Not quite good enough," she said. At least she had the grace to sound disappointed, but she didn't mitigate her words.

"What do you mean?" I sputtered. "Of course I harbor doubts. I would be a right fool not to have them, but—"

She made a chopping motion. "You must want this with every fiber of your being, or you're wasting both of our time. The dragon will sense your hesitation"—she blew out a tight breath—"if we even got that far. Our first stop is Y Ddraigh Goch. If the dragon god is not convinced of your purity of heart, he'll send us packing."

I turned my hands palms up. "I will offer the best within me."

Her harsh expression softened, but not by much. "I'm sure you will. For now, take a walk outside. Perhaps down by the lake. I will confer with my dragon, and I want to visit the surface to keep an eye on the serpents. In roughly one turn of the glass, I shall return, and we will see which direction opens before us."

Before I could protest I was as certain as I was likely to get, the air around her turned glistening and liquid, and she was gone.

I blinked stupidly at the place she'd stood before turning and trudging up another set of risers to the large stone door that led outside. Taking a walk was a good idea. It was easier to problem solve when I was on the move. Somehow, she'd known that about me.

As the heavy door swung shut behind me, I thought about Erin. Should I try to find her? I shook my head. I couldn't help her any more than she could help me. Determined to find a way to mute my concerns, I set off through an unusual underground paradise carved deep beneath Antarctica's ice cap. It was warm down here. I'd mapped the string of subterranean lakes from my lab on the *Darya*, the research vessel I'd been dragged away from by Russians intent on stealing what they could of Antarctica's mineral wealth.

I may have mapped these lakes, but I'd had no idea they'd be so beautiful.

Not much point looking back, though. That life was lost to me.

Besides, thinking about Erin or the *Darya* were diversionary tactics. What I had to do was dig deep and figure out if I could open my metaphorical arms to a dragon and mean it.

Unsure what the result would be, I set off at a trot for the nearest lake half a kilometer distant. I was a proud man. Maybe too proud, verging on arrogance. And independent as hell. Peeling back the layers of a persona I'd cultivated for my entire adult life wouldn't be easy.

The prospect scared the holy crap out of me, but the other alternative—the one where I forfeited my memories and returned to the world I'd left behind—held very little appeal.

Maybe I was making this too hard, but I had to carve out a spot for my dragon. One where it would feel cherished. A short bark of laughter startled me until I realized it had come from me. I wasn't used to sharing anything with anyone.

How in the hell would I share my innermost everything with an arrogant, critical dragon?

A snort followed the laughter. Might not be as impossible as all that. When you chopped the fluff away, dragons were a lot like me.

Short-tempered. Opinionated. Sure of themselves.

I reached the lake shore and dropped onto a flattish rock. As I stared at the mirror-bright surface, a plan took shape. The longer I gazed at the lake, the surer I was I could pull it off.

"Serious alterations in the status quo," I mumbled.

But what else was new? My previous circumstances had vanished when Russians forced me off the *Darya*. I'd be an idiot to long for the impossible. My past was deader than dead. The sooner the reality of that sank in, the better for everyone.

Especially me.

www.ingramcontent.com/pod-product-compliance
Lightning Source LLC
Chambersburg PA
CBHW071135180726
48291CB00007B/2188